Not What They Expected

Sutton Series Book 2

Chantal DeYoe

Living Out Our Christian Faith Publishing LLC

Book Cover Art by Christopher DeYoe

Book Cover Design by Lynn Andreozzi

First Edition 2025

Contents

Preface

To My Readers of
Right Where They Belong: Sutton Series Book 1
(tiny spoiler if you haven't read it!)

In Book 1 you met Marcus and Corinne. In Book 2, you're getting to know Thomas and Elizabeth.

What???

I know, I know. You were hoping for a sequel. Have patience! Marcus and Corinne are around. They're just not in Sutton yet.

That's right. We've gone back in time! When this book opens, Marcus is still in law school and has suffered through his second divorce. Corinne is in college, getting ready to date that unnamed fellow who so helpfully thought he could dictate her life once they married.

I hope you don't mind. And I hope you won't worry; Marcus and Corinne will be back. They may still be getting educated during Thomas and Elizabeth's story, but many of their friends from Book 1—your favorite characters—are waiting for you in the pages ahead, along with some new and dreadfully lovable ones.

And can I let you in on a little secret? I think you're going to delight in Thomas and Elizabeth just as much as you did Marcus and Corinne.

Maybe even more.

Happy Reading,

Chantal

Part One

Living Out Our Christian Faith Publishing LLC

1

When Elizabeth Shepard graduated from college and returned home, it was on purpose, but it wasn't without drama. Both her best friend and her boyfriend thought she was crazy to leave the city and take a teaching position in a small town near home.

"How can you possibly want to leave Cincinnati to go live in Podunk, USA?" her best friend asked.

"Don't be rude," Elizabeth admonished.

"Whatever. It doesn't make sense. You belong here, Elizabeth."

The statement left Elizabeth with the unhappy realization that if the friend she'd spent four years with knew her so little as to think she belonged in the city, then she didn't know her at all.

The boyfriend caused more than just an unhappy realization. He was taking a job at an engineering firm in the city and wanted

Elizabeth to find a nice post in a suburban school. So she'd be nearby.

For her part, Elizabeth was tired of explaining that she wanted to live close to her parents. Her aging parents, as she continually reminded him.

"Exactly how long do you plan to live up north?" he asked. Elizabeth always had to stifle a smile when he spoke that way of her home. She'd never thought of it as north.

"I don't know. As long as I need to."

"Long distance isn't easy, you know. And what if we decide to get married? At some point you're going to have to cut the apron strings, Lizzy."

What if we don't decide to get married? Elizabeth wondered.

As she made the three-hour drive home at the end of her last day of internship in the city, she pondered his statement over and over again. It had been the final nail in the coffin of their relationship, at least in her opinion, but she couldn't decide if it was because of his callous attitude toward her family situation—or the fact that he called her Lizzy.

It was still light out when Elizabeth arrived at her parents' farmhouse. They both came out onto the porch to greet her with open arms.

"Elizabeth! Welcome home!" Her mother wrapped her in a warm embrace.

"Oh, my dear, how good it is to see you!" her father said as he pulled her into his arms and kissed her on the cheek.

All this, even though they'd seen her just two weeks before. Elizabeth was so weary and so emotional that she couldn't stop the tears from brimming over.

"Oh, honey, come on in," her mother said. "Have you eaten?" Elizabeth shook her head. "Well, then, that's where we'll start." She ushered her into the house, and her father got her overnight bag from the car.

While Elizabeth washed up, her mother warmed a plate of food. Then they all sat down at the table together, and Elizabeth caught them up on the latest in the boyfriend saga.

"If he'd been willing to compromise, maybe things would be different," she told them. She took a bite of meatloaf and chewed thoughtfully. "It's like he didn't care about what's important to me."

Her parents made eye contact over her head as she finished her food. They had met the boyfriend on one occasion. Just one.

"Last night while I was packing my car, he followed me back and forth from the apartment—not helping—just trying to argue me into staying." She rolled her eyes. "Like that's going to work. He wasn't like that when we first met."

"On his best behavior?" her mother asked gently.

Elizabeth looked up at her. "Maybe. I honestly don't know."

"Well, it's good you realized you're headed in different directions," her father said. Elizabeth raised an eyebrow, and he chuckled. "No pun intended. I mean in what you each want out of life."

Elizabeth leaned back in her chair. "I wasted two years with him."

"Not necessarily," her mother said. "Nothing we go through is a waste, if we allow God to use it for our good. Plus, you didn't always know that the two of you would want such different things."

Elizabeth didn't reply. The truth, which her parents didn't know, was that she had always intended to come home. At least, ever since Thanksgiving her freshman year when she made her first trip back and saw her parents through the lens of having been away for three months.

Elizabeth's father, Bob Shepard, was seventy-seven years old, and her mom, Laurel, was sixty-five. The age of all her classmates' grandparents. This had never bothered her; her parents were just her parents. She loved them, and they loved her. But that Thanksgiving, she saw their age for the first time, and so she began traveling home at least one weekend a month, a habit she continued all throughout college.

So no, Elizabeth couldn't claim innocence in that regard; she had always known what she wanted. And Chad had always been very open about his career plans as well. It made sense for him to stay in the city; that's where the big jobs were. If he hadn't taken her seriously when she talked about home and teaching near there, and if Elizabeth hadn't bothered to consider the ramifications of their differing goals earlier in their relationship, then they were both to blame for wasting each other's time.

2

T homas Schaefer didn't usually clean up after work. Instead, he went straight over to his folks' house and to the carport out back where he was working on a car. It was a late 90s Honda Accord, and as soon as he had it purring and beautiful, he was going to sell it.

Then he'd buy another one and do the same thing. And then another. And another. Eventually, he'd work his way up to his dream car, and that one he'd keep.

He was tightening a bolt under the hood when the grating voice of his sister's best friend, Dee Dee, rang out. "Tommy!" His hand stilled and he closed his eyes for a moment, then continued right on with his task.

She sidled up next to him and pressed against his side. "Whatcha doin'?" It was always the same question. Thomas didn't answer.

Dee Dee trailed her hand up his arm and across his shoulder. Before she could wrap her fingers in his wavy blonde hair, he shrugged her off. "Stop it, Dee Dee."

"Mmm." She pouted her lips and dropped her hand, but she didn't move away. There was a part of Thomas that wanted to tell her to get lost, but it was buried deep under another, kinder part that felt it would be rude to do so.

Plus, it wouldn't have done any good. Dee Dee had been after him since high school, and Thomas was at a complete loss how to convince her he wasn't interested. Not for the first time, he wished he had his own shop, complete with a locking door.

"How much longer you gonna be?" she asked.

"I dunno."

"Well JB, Karen, and I wanna go see a movie tonight."

"Have fun."

Dee Dee snorted. "Don't be stupid. You're coming with us."

Thomas shook his head. "No thanks."

"Why not?"

Because I don't want to foot the bill for everyone, he thought. *Or even go.* Out loud he said, "Not interested."

"You don't even know what we're going to see!"

And so it went until JB and Karen showed up to join the battle. "C'mon, Tommy. You know you want to." That was JB. He and Thomas worked together at Thomas's father's automotive shop. They'd been friends since elementary school. JB and Karen, Thomas's sister, had been dating since high school.

It wasn't surprising that Dee Dee had laid claim to Thomas. They were always thrown together by virtue of the friend group. Sometimes Thomas lay awake at night, thinking he needed new friends. But then he felt guilty. Besides, where would he find some of those?

He came out of his reverie to hear JB saying, "Dude, are you listening?"

"I'm listening," Thomas replied. "We'll go to the track tomorrow, like we planned. I'm not going to the movies tonight."

"But—"

"Don't bother," Karen said, contempt dripping from her voice. "He'll never change his mind once he's made it up."

What's wrong with that? Thomas thought. *I know what I want.*

Then he heard Karen mutter under her breath. "You're just like Dad."

His head shot up. "I am not!" Karen glared at him, not backing down.

Thomas pulled a grease rag from his back pocket and wiped his hands. He dropped the wrench in his toolbox and slammed the hood of the car. "I'm going home." His friends said nothing as he got in his truck and drove away.

At home, Thomas unlaced his work boots and left them by the door. He threw a frozen pizza in the oven and then got in the shower. The sweat he could wash away, but the residue from his friends' constant badgering stuck to him like the grease that was permanently etched into his fingerprints and lodged under his nails.

He stood under the stream until the buzzer sounded, then quickly dried off and donned a pair of boxer shorts. Pulling the pizza from the oven, he threw half of it onto a plate and left the other half on the counter. He grabbed a pop from the fridge and then padded barefoot into his living room, where he sat down on the couch and propped his feet up on the coffee table. After a brief prayer of thanks for the food, he dug in.

Thomas's home was an above-garage apartment just a few blocks from his parents' house. It belonged to an older couple from church. It was small, with a single bedroom and a tiny kitchen that wasn't really separate from the living area. It had been used as guest lodging in the past, but the husband and wife had been happy enough to rent it to Thomas when he'd asked them about it a couple of years earlier.

Even though it wasn't far from his parents' home, at least it was separate and afforded Thomas some respite from the otherwise constant presence of his family in his everyday life. Not only did JB work at his father's garage, so did his mother and his sister. Between work, church on Sundays, and his mother's required Sunday dinners, he had little chance to ever have a break from them all.

3

Saturday morning JB, Karen, and Dee Dee pulled up in JB's old beater to pick up Thomas and head to the track. Thomas opened the front passenger side door where Karen sat smirking at him.

"Move it, Karen," Thomas said.

She rolled her eyes and got out of the car to sit in the back next to Dee Dee. Dee Dee was still bleary-eyed from who-knows-what the night before.

"All right, peeps, pony up. We're gonna need fuel," JB said.

"I spent all my money on beer last night." Dee Dee belched and then flopped her head against the window and fell asleep.

"Tommy, can I borrow? I'm broke too," Karen said.

Thomas looked from her to JB, who raised his eyebrows and held out his hand, waggling his fingers as he did so. Thomas sighed and pulled one of the twenties out of his wallet that he'd put there to use at the track.

"Thank you." JB snatched the bill from his hand.

Next time, I should drive myself, Thomas thought. *It'd be cheaper.*

The racetrack was humming with activity by the time they parked in one of the grass lots mid-morning. Drivers and pit crews were hard at work, making sure their cars were ready to race. Dedicated fans who spent the entire weekend at the track filled the camping areas, hailing friends and newcomers alike.

"Let's get some breakfast," Karen said. "I'm starved."

"I'm up for that," JB said, looking expectantly at Thomas.

"I'm going to the pits," Thomas said.

"Ugh, I can't stand the thought of food," Dee Dee muttered. "I'm going with Tommy."

"Oh, man!" JB complained. "C'mon, Karen." He grabbed her by the hand and stomped off.

The first half hour wasn't so bad. Dee Dee was still sleepy and hung over, or so Thomas assumed. Either way, she was quiet. But eventually she perked up and moved closer to Thomas as he watched a crew make a feverish last-minute adjustment before a run.

"What are they doing, Tommy?"

"Getting ready to race." He knew it was pointless to offer anything more.

"Mmm." Dee Dee looked around. "I wonder where JB and Karen are."

Thomas didn't answer. He knew what was coming next.

"We should go find them." She wrapped her arm around his and looked up at him through mascara-smudged eyes. "Besides, I'm ready for breakfast now."

"They're probably still at the food trucks. Shouldn't be too hard to find them." He disengaged his arm. "You go on. I'll catch up later."

Dee Dee scowled and looked as if she were all set to argue. Thomas offered her a small smile. "I'm glad you're feeling better."

It was enough. Without another word she disappeared into the crowd to find their friends. He'd thrown her a bone, and she'd taken it. Thomas sighed. He knew he'd pay the price later, but he'd deal with that when the time came. For now, he turned his attention to the cars. With Dee Dee gone he could really engage. These teams loved to talk about their machines, and Thomas loved learning about them.

4

Elizabeth had fallen asleep as soon as her head hit the pillow Friday night. When she awoke early the next morning, it wasn't to the sound of sirens or fighting neighbors. It was to the sound of birds. Almost before the sky was even beginning to lighten, they were happy for the new day and not shy about letting the whole world know. Elizabeth smiled and closed her eyes, soaking in the peaceful sound.

Before long she heard stirring in her parents' room next door. Dad would be out at the barn by the time the sun peeked over the horizon, and Mom would have a hearty country breakfast on the table by the time he came in.

Elizabeth threw back the covers. She slipped on a pair of jeans, socks, and a t-shirt. She stepped out the door and down the stairs to take a quick turn in the bathroom. Then she gathered up her rubber boots from the mudroom and carried them out to the back steps where she sat down and waited.

A couple of cats joined her, expecting to be fed but content for the moment to be petted. The dog trotted up from where she'd been patrolling the perimeter all night long, keeping away deer and predators alike. Elizabeth had time to give her a good scratch behind the ears before the screen door squeaked and her father stepped outside.

"Morning," he said.

"Morning, Daddy," Elizabeth answered. She pulled on her boots, and they walked side by side out to the barn. The cows were at the gate, waiting. The chickens were still on the roost, but they were calling softly as they waited for enough light to begin their day.

While her father milked, Elizabeth fed the steer. Then she cleaned out the water buckets, opened the chicken gate, and filled their grain feeder. It wasn't the time of year for hay yet, so she reacquainted herself with the baby heifer who'd been born that spring.

Once the milking was done, Elizabeth and her father worked together to feed the pigs. There were only two of them, but they were big and feisty and you had to be careful. Plus her father had never gotten beyond wanting to protect Elizabeth from them.

When they finished, they leaned on the gate and watched the pigs fight over their food. "Good to have you home," he said, "even if it is just for one night."

Elizabeth inhaled deeply the scent of farm life, pigs and all. "It's always good to be home."

After the breakfast dishes were washed, dried, and put away, moving day began. Her folks had helped her locate a small house to rent in Sutton where she'd begin teaching in just over a week. Between several weekend trips home over the summer and numerous phone calls, they'd worked together to secure basic furniture and whatever appliances she needed. A small crew from her parents' church were on hand to help with moving the large items. Elizabeth and her mother packed up her parents' car with everything that Elizabeth had been storing at home for four years.

It struck her that this, rather than going away to college, was her real moving out. A lump rose in her throat at the thought, but she quickly swallowed it and comforted herself with the knowledge that she'd chosen her location well. Sutton was a mere thirty minutes from her parents' farm.

Some of the church ladies had packed up coolers of food to feed everyone at midday, and Elizabeth was grateful to them all. Their church family had always been willing to offer hands-on help to anyone who needed it. She had leaned on them a number of times over the past four years, just to check in on her folks every so often when she couldn't be there herself.

The crew was so efficient that Elizabeth was easily able to function in her new house that very night. She wandered from room to room, touching the curtains, the furniture, and the remaining boxes. *This is my home*, she thought, and she liked it.

It didn't, however, stop her from heading right back out of town the next morning to be with her parents for worship. It was her first weekend back, after all, and she wanted to see everyone at her home church. There would be plenty of time to figure out what she wanted to do for worship long-term.

It was a good reunion and a good service, but Elizabeth didn't linger. She still had much to do to settle in and get ready to teach, and she had just one week to do it in.

5

The alarm clock rang as usual on Sunday morning, but Thomas didn't get right up. Instead, he threw his arm over his head and lay there. He was weary. Not of worship, but of his life. Or maybe just the people in his life. It's not that he wanted away from them. At least, he didn't think so. He just could have done with a little less of them.

Then Thomas felt guilty. His dad's shop was a family business after all. Everybody had a role to play. And there was nothing wrong with his mom wanting them all together for dinner once a week.

But Sunday mornings were hard. His folks expected him and his sister to sit with them, even though they were both adults and Thomas didn't live at home anymore. If they didn't, both he and his sister paid the price. Stern disapproval from their father and wounded silence from their mother.

Karen coped by skipping as much as possible, but that wasn't an option for Thomas. His faith was important to him. Had been ever since that church camp he went to the summer after seventh grade. Sending him there was one good thing his parents had done in raising him. There he responded to Jesus for the very first time and found something he'd been missing in his life.

Last week, the new pastor over at the Baptist church had been in the shop to get some work done on his car. As Thomas processed his credit card, the man asked him, "Are you a believer, Thomas?"

Thomas looked up in surprise at the direct question but answered without hesitation. "Yes, sir."

"That's mighty fine news. Makes us brothers, you know." He winked at Thomas. "Mind if I post a flyer?" He motioned toward the bulletin board in the waiting area. It was covered with business cards, for sale notices, help wanted ads, and pictures of missing pets. "We've got a new sermon series starting, and I want to let people know about it."

"Sure, go ahead."

Thomas had studied the flyer, and it came to mind now as he lay in bed. It's not like he'd be skipping, like Karen did. He'd still be in worship, just somewhere else. He decided the silent wrath of his parents would be worth it for a little break from the family.

Decision made, he threw back the covers, headed for the shower, and got ready for church.

It was okay, the service. The Baptist minister was no Pastor Stephen, but his teaching was solid. Thomas recognized many of the people there; he knew most folks in town through his work at the shop. They were friendly and welcoming, and one long-time customer was bold enough to say, "I thought you and your family were over at Grace Community."

"Yes, sir," Thomas agreed. When the old man raised his eyebrows expectantly, Thomas made this excuse, "I'm just checking out the new sermon series your pastor posted on the board at the shop."

"Ah." The old man chuckled and clapped him on the shoulder. "We'll see how long that lasts."

His words didn't do much to put Thomas at ease about his decision, but once Thomas focused his attention on worship, he was able to push them from his mind, relax, and enjoy the break from his family.

Until he stepped in the door of his parents' house for Sunday dinner, that is. The kitchen was off to the left of the entryway, and the smell of fried chicken greeted him as it always did. In front of him was the table, not yet set. The combined dining/living room and open doorway to the kitchen made it easy to see how things stood with a single glance.

On this day, the air was thick with displeasure. Karen didn't help matters when she walked by him and whispered, "Even I was in church this morning."

She flopped down on the couch and made it worse by saying loud enough for everyone to hear, "What's a matter, Tommy? Too much beer yesterday?"

Thomas shook his head in frustration. *She knows I don't drink,* he thought. *Why does she do that?*

Knowing didn't prevent his father from questioning, though. "Were you drinking yesterday?" he asked, lowering his newspaper to his lap.

"No, sir." Thomas stopped and leaned against the back of an armchair.

"Then where were you this morning?"

"Went over to the Baptist church." Karen snorted and their father's eyes bored into Thomas's. Thomas continued. "I decided to check out that new sermon series the pastor put up on the board." He shrugged. "It was pretty good." He held his father's gaze until his father returned to his newspaper. Then Thomas turned and went into the kitchen.

"Hi, Mom," he said and gave her a one-armed hug. A hug she didn't return but didn't refuse. She also didn't return the greeting. Instead, she beat the masher hard against the pan of potatoes. Thomas took the utensil from her hand and finished the task. His mother huffed but grabbed the jug of milk and added some to the mixture.

Once they were the right consistency, Thomas scooped them into the serving bowl his mother had set out. She stood and watched him and finally said, "What's so special about the Baptist church?" Of course she had heard every word.

"Nothing. Just wanted something different, I guess."

"So we're not good enough for you anymore, is that it?" She yanked open the oven door to check on the dinner rolls and then slammed it shut again.

Thomas's weariness returned. "No, Mom. That's not it."

"Doreen!" This was Thomas's father, calling from the living room. "How long 'til dinner?"

"It'd be ready sooner if Karen would get her butt in here and help!" She pulled plates and bowls and glasses from the cupboards.

"I'll do it, Mom," Thomas said.

"Karen, get in the kitchen and help your mother," Thomas's father said. "Thomas, you come on out of there."

It was the same every Sunday. His mother stressed, his father waiting to be served. Karen doing as little as possible, and Thomas counting the minutes until he could get away.

6

E lizabeth was up before the sun again on Monday. Out on the farm, that was a time of restful but expectant quiet when the nocturnal creatures were winding down. Besides the awakening birds, the only other sound might be the dog making one last round to ensure the safety of her people and her place.

The city never slept, or so it seemed to Elizabeth, and while her roommates at college could be lulled by the rhythm of rubber on asphalt from the nearby freeway, Elizabeth had never grown indifferent to the sound of sirens at all hours.

Here in Sutton, the pre-dawn twilight held yet other evidence of life. The *thwap* of a newspaper hitting its mark. The click of a neighbor's door as they let the dog out. Vehicle noise from someone returning from a late-night shift—or leaving for an early one.

By the time the birds were in full voice, Elizabeth was dressed, fed, and had the coffee table spread with her books and papers. She had lesson plans to prepare. Lots of them.

One unique aspect of teaching in a small town was the number of preps she'd have. In the city, during her student-teaching semester, she'd had six classes of sophomores. The same material, six times over. By the end of each day she was so sick of it that she wanted to scream.

Some of her fellow education majors were mortified when she reported that she'd be teaching all the freshmen, all the sophomores, and all the juniors at her new placement. It would be a lot, having three sets of lesson plans to prepare for each day, but Elizabeth was up for the challenge. It might be busy, but she'd rather be busy and working hard than bored to tears by doing the same thing over and over again.

By lunchtime Elizabeth had a rough outline, including required elements and selections for literature. She would spend the rest of her week nailing down the details. Her goal was to have daily lesson plans laid out for the first quarter so she could have a successful start to the year. As a new teacher, she wanted to be prepared. Plus the clock was ticking; students would be in the classroom next Monday.

With that in mind, Elizabeth figured she'd better get her other business finished up this week too. She spent the afternoon taking care of things related to being a new resident in town—like moving utilities to her name, setting up banking, and getting a library card.

The other thing she needed to do was get an oil change on her car. The light had come on during her drive home Friday, and she wanted to make sure everything was in good working order for the start of the school year. Elizabeth hoped to deal with as little stuff like that as possible once school started so she could focus her attention on the classroom.

So it was that her last stop of the day before heading home to make supper was at Schaefer's Automotive Repair.

When the bell jangled on the shop door late Monday afternoon, Thomas wiped his hands on a rag and headed to the counter. His bay was closest to the front and his customer service far better than JB's.

Just inside the door, Thomas stopped. The woman was perusing the chaos of flyers on the bulletin board and was turned away from him, but that didn't stop him from recognizing her. Long brown hair, pulled back in a simple ponytail. Long shapely legs encased in rugged blue jeans, even on a hot summer day. *Elizabeth Shepard.* Thomas's pulse quickened.

She turned when she heard the door, and her eyes immediately widened in recognition. "Thomas!" she said and walked to the counter. "Oh my gosh. I haven't seen you in forever!" She reached out a hand, which he shook without even realizing it.

"Hello, Elizabeth," he heard himself saying. "What brings you here?"

Elizabeth's eyes sparkled. "To the shop, or to town?"

Thomas ducked his head. "Both, I guess."

"Well," she said. "I just moved to Sutton."

Thomas's head shot up in surprise.

She nodded. "I'm going to be teaching up at the high school."

Elizabeth Shepard living in Sutton? Right here in my town? It took a moment before he realized he was staring at her. She grinned when he shook himself out of his reverie. Embarrassed, he found his voice and said, "Congratulations. I figured you were gone forever once you left for college." Then he ducked his head again. *Why did I say that?*

"Oh, no," Elizabeth said, apparently not thinking anything of it. "I didn't like the city. Plus I want to be close to Mom and Dad. They're getting older, you know…" Her voice trailed off.

Thomas thought this over. "I think they're doing all right."

"Do you?" She studied his face as if to discern the truth of his words. He could see the concern, and the hope, in her eyes.

He nodded, and she continued. "That's good to hear. I worry about them." They were both silent for a moment, and then Elizabeth said, "Anyway, I'm here at the shop because I need an oil change on my car."

Thomas pulled out the appointment book. "This week?"

"If possible. School starts next Monday and I'm trying to get all this stuff done before then."

He penciled her in for Wednesday and made sure that his name was assigned to the task. "If you can drop it off by nine, that'd be good," he told her. "Welcome home." Then he was embarrassed again, because Sutton wasn't really her home. But again she didn't seem to notice.

"Thanks, Thomas." She flashed him a smile. "It's good to be back."

Thomas stared after her as she walked out the door, got in her car, and drove away. An ember had reignited in his heart. He smiled a private, satisfied smile as he put away the appointment book.

Then the shop door opened, and JB appeared. "Thomas?" he said in a sing-song voice. "Since when are you Thomas?"

Thomas closed his eyes briefly. "Since forever."

"Mmm, whatever," JB said. "Who was that?"

"Elizabeth."

JB sucked in his breath. "That girl you were so in love with during school?" Thomas nodded. "Holy crap!" JB said. "She's hot!"

Thomas couldn't help but grin. JB wasn't wrong. Elizabeth was hot. And amazing and friendly. And way out of his league. Thomas sighed. She always had been, and he'd always known it. But it had never stopped him from being in love with her.

JB was staring at him. "No wonder Dee Dee can't get you in bed. You've still got it bad for that girl."

"Shut up." Thomas grabbed his shop rag and snapped it at JB, who ducked away and disappeared through the door, laughing as he went.

Thomas scowled after him. "That's not the reason," he muttered. *At least, not all of it.*

His friend's ribbing might be annoying, but it couldn't ruin Thomas's good mood from having seen Elizabeth again. In fact, it was fortunate that all he had left to do was clean up his bay before clocking out. If he'd had another vehicle to work on, he probably would have put windshield wiper fluid in for the oil and caused all kinds of problems.

7

Elizabeth had a somewhat different response to the reunion. Her thought was, *So Thomas is still in Sutton. Huh.* She had fond memories of him as the first boy who'd had an obvious crush on her. As a pre-teen, it was highly gratifying. As time went on, however, and the crush continued but didn't advance, it kind of lost its effect. While still appreciative of his admiration, Elizabeth had preferred to focus her energies on boys who were more motivated to ask her out on dates.

Besides, she only saw Thomas a few times a year. She was twelve the summer he first began accompanying his father on farm calls. Jack Schaefer knew how important it was for farmers to have their equipment operational and years before had begun offering repair service right to the field, or wherever they needed it. Thomas inherited his father's skill with machines and at age thirteen was already an asset to him in his work.

Anyway, Elizabeth's father was glad enough to have someone else handle the heavy lifting when it came to maintaining his equipment, and so Thomas and his father might be out two or three times a summer. Elizabeth made sure always to be on hand to soak up the admiration of the shy, quiet boy.

Once they were both in high school, they ran into each other at ball games on occasion. Their schools were rivals in the same league. Elizabeth was always friendly and said hello when she saw him there, but he never did more than say, "Hello, Elizabeth," and duck his head shyly.

Elizabeth chuckled at the memory and then sighed over the passing away of those simpler times. Dating in high school wasn't nearly as complicated as it had been in college.

It was an excited Elizabeth who marched herself off to school that next Monday morning—and a much older and wiser Elizabeth who dragged herself back home again that afternoon. She had just two questions: one, why had she bothered spending so much time lesson planning? And two, why in the heck didn't schools have air conditioning in the twenty-first century?

She dropped her bag inside the door, punched on the small window AC unit, and flopped down on the couch. She kicked off her shoes and dropped off to sleep.

When she awoke a half hour later, the room was cooler and she felt better. She had done plenty of outdoor work in her teens, and while it could be deadly hot out in the sun, she was used to that. The heat build-up in her classroom was an entirely different story. Maybe it was because she hadn't expected it, or maybe it was because there was no moving air if you weren't in the direct line of a fan. Either way, it was suffocating. Tomorrow she'd make sure to dress accordingly.

She lay still a moment longer, soaking in the nice, cool air. As the sleep receded from her brain, her broken lesson plans reclaimed her attention, and she sighed. The English classroom was challenging. There were so many unique topics to cover.

It's not like that in other classrooms! she thought. *In math, you study one thing, out of one book, for a whole year.* In English, they wanted you to teach writing and literature and spelling and vocabulary and grammar.

She sat upright and thought some more. Even history and government and science—they pretty much went straight through a single textbook. She stretched her arms overhead and yawned. *Surely that's easier,* she thought. *Isn't it?*

Suspicious that her assessment was just the lingering result of an exhausting first day in the classroom, Elizabeth pushed the thought from her mind. She needed to worry about her own classroom—not everybody else's.

Elizabeth had laid out units on each topic for each grade level for the entire first nine weeks of school. But even on this first day, unique as it was meeting the students and handing out books and creating seating charts, Elizabeth realized one very important thing: how fast each class period went. With all the literature she had to teach and all the writing skills her students needed to demonstrate by year's end, she couldn't see how it was going to work.

She finally tore herself away from the couch and headed to the kitchen. The house wasn't large, but with no moving air, the

AC hadn't touched that room. She added a fan to her shopping list, fixed a cold supper, and ate quickly at her small round table. As she did so, she thought.

She'd personally never had any issues with spelling or vocabulary. In her own school years, those had been easy grades and required zero study. But she knew not all students were the same and that most of them needed encouragement to improve their skills.

As she munched on an apple, she thought back to all the times she'd sat at the table in her parents' kitchen with a pencil in her hand, usually while her mother was cooking. At first, she'd written out the alphabet over and over again. Then all of her family's names. And eventually simple letters to her grandparents.

In fact, Elizabeth had grown to love writing right there at that very table, in the warmth of the family kitchen, with the support of a mom who was always willing to help her spell a word or sort out her thoughts. *If only there were a way to recreate that setting for my students,* she thought.

Elizabeth wrinkled her nose as she contemplated the idea. It could never be exactly the same, from her family table to a classroom of twenty-five, but maybe she could find a way to incorporate some elements of it. *Definitely worth thinking about,* she thought. But for right now, she had to get ready for tomorrow, and the next day, and the day after that.

Elizabeth sighed and gathered up the remains from her meal, depositing her trash in the can and wiping away the crumbs. Then she vacated to the living room, hauled out her bag, and spread its contents on the coffee table once again. She spent the next several hours endeavoring to make sense of the chaos.

Late that night she had what she believed to be a more realistic plan for the first nine-week period. A framework with plenty of flexibility built in. Planning in such great detail, as she had at first, hadn't actually been helpful.

When Elizabeth arrived extra-early on Tuesday morning, she was surprised to see another teacher hanging out in the hall outside her room. "Morning!" the woman said. "You're Elizabeth, right?"

"That I am."

"Tracy Edelman. We met at in-service."

While the woman looked vaguely familiar, the name was not; Elizabeth had met a lot of people at in-service. Plus, the woman had spoken quickly and run her words together such that Elizabeth wasn't sure if she was speaking with Tray, Trace, or Tracy—and some last name that accounted for the remainder of the sounds which had issued forth.

"Ah, yes," Elizabeth said. "And I should call you...?"

The woman rolled her eyes. "Tracy, of course. I see you've got that new teacher look of desperation in your eye."

Elizabeth groaned. "Is it that obvious?"

Tracy scoffed. "Showing up at seven a.m. is a dead giveaway."

Elizabeth furrowed her brow as she reached for the door. "Then why are you here at seven a.m.?"

"Waiting for you."

Elizabeth was so startled that her hand froze on the knob. "Why?"

Tracy smiled, her eyes turning warm for a moment. "This is my third year of teaching, but I remember what it was like my first. I thought it would be good if you had a friend on hand to help you through it."

Never had Elizabeth felt more grateful to anyone in her life. "Thank you. I'd love that."

"Excellent." Tracy clapped her hands together. "Let's get your very large bag dropped off and then we'll go down to the teacher's lounge."

"Oh, no. I've got prep to do."

"It'll wait. You need your first lesson in death-by-teacher-lounge coffee, and I need to make introductions." Elizabeth allowed herself to be dragged away to the teacher lounge, even though she was pretty sure it was a mistake.

As it turns out, it wasn't. There she met Gavin, the physical education teacher. He was built like a barrel—and addicted to doughnuts. Paul taught in the social sciences and was much quieter and thoughtful than either of the other two.

"I see you survived your first day," Gavin said and laughed. He and Paul were the only ones there, but the doughnut box was already down by five. "If you get any tough guys in your classes, you just let me know. I'll come over and set 'em straight." He puffed out his chest and strutted around the table. They all laughed, even though they knew that such a thing could never happen.

As Elizabeth downed her first cup of teacher-lounge coffee, the talk turned to faith. Somebody said something about praying for the ability to survive the school year, and from there Paul asked the question, "Do you go to church, Elizabeth?"

Tracy crumpled the paper from her doughnut noisily and made a toss toward the trash can. She missed, groaned, and then scooted back her chair to go pick it up.

"I do," Elizabeth said, "but I haven't visited any here in town yet. I've been going to my home church with my folks so far."

"Well, we all go to Grace Community," Paul said, and gestured around the table. "You should join us."

"Thanks! I'll check it out."

Elizabeth did in fact survive her first week as a full-time high school English teacher. She did so by virtue of her work ethic, energy, and strong will—and with the help of her new friends.

On Saturday she headed home to see her parents and participate in whatever tasks the late August Saturday had in store. That turned out to be canning tomatoes and green beans with her mother. As they worked together hour after hour, she told her mom all the stories from her week. Some they laughed over, others they were shocked by. Finally the conversation came around to the teachers that Elizabeth had met.

"They've already helped me so much, Mom. If for no other reason than to make me laugh."

"I'm so glad to hear it," her mom said.

Elizabeth hesitated a moment and then said, "They invited me to church too."

"They did? That's wonderful!"

"Do you think so?" Elizabeth asked.

"Of course! God has surrounded you with brothers and sisters in Christ right there in your new job. It's absolutely wonderful!"

"That's true," Elizabeth said. "But I'll miss going to church with you guys."

"Oh, honey, you've got to live your own life. We love seeing you and worshiping with you, but we don't expect it to be all the time." Her mother scrutinized Elizabeth's face. "You know that, right?"

"Yeah, I do." But deep down inside herself Elizabeth wondered how long that would last. How long before her parents would need her help with things like getting to church?

8

In the nearly two weeks since Thomas had been reunited with Elizabeth at the shop, he'd spent two more Saturdays at the racetrack, ten more evenings working on his car, and way more hours in Dee Dee's company than he cared to think about.

Oh, and zero time with Elizabeth. As careful as he'd been to put her appointment on his own schedule, it hadn't given him another chance to see her. She'd dropped her car off before the shop opened, and when she picked it up later that day, he was out on a farm call. Most of the time his father took those, but he was buried deep in a transmission replacement and didn't want to step away.

It was part of the job, and Thomas knew that, but he was disappointed to have missed the opportunity to see her again. Instead he contented himself with daydreaming about her. Wondering where she lived, what she did with her free time, how he could run into her again. The thought never crossed his mind to pick up the phone and call.

Thomas had been thirteen years old when he met Elizabeth for the first time. In fact, it was right after he came home from that church camp. At supper on Sunday evening his father had said, "Thomas, you'll come with me on my farm calls tomorrow."

He was beyond thrilled. He'd been hanging around the shop forever, as much as he dared, and helping whenever he could manage to slip in beside his father. And now to get to actually work with him, on purpose, and on the big machines!

Then at the very first call that very first morning, Thomas met Elizabeth. Between church camp, working with his dad on farm equipment, and finding the girl of his dreams, it was the best week of young Thomas's life.

Ten years later, it still was.

Thomas went to the Baptist church again on Sunday and braced himself for yet another round of parental disapproval. When he walked in the door, however, things were...different. Sort of. His father was still installed in his armchair behind the newspaper. Karen was still slinking around trying to avoid kitchen duty. But his mother—she was humming.

At first Thomas thought it had to have been the radio. But when he peeked his head around the corner and into the kitchen, he discovered that the sound was coming straight from his mother's mouth. He stood frozen to the spot, wondering what on earth had put her in such a good mood.

She turned from the stove and saw him. "Hello, honey," she said and came right over to give him a hug. "How are you today?"

Thomas hugged her automatically and dropped a kiss at her temple. "Hi, Mom. I'm fine."

"I'm so glad to hear it!" She turned back to the stove and to her humming. Thomas frowned, not quite certain he trusted the unusually good mood she was in.

And with good reason. At the dinner table, right in the middle of the endless stream of chatter his mother kept up, she dropped in this gem. "We got to meet the new English teacher at church this morning. What was her name?" She directed the question toward Karen, who just rolled her eyes.

"Who cares?" she muttered under her breath.

But Thomas's hands froze halfway to his mouth, his fried chicken all but forgotten. He glanced up and across the table, not meaning to catch his sister's eye. When he did, she smiled real slow and then decided to answer her mother's question. "Elizabeth, wasn't it, Mother? Elizabeth Shepard?"

"Oh, that's right," their mom said and waved her hand. "Jack, isn't she from the Shepards up north where you do farm calls?"

Jack just grunted and shoveled more mashed potatoes into his mouth.

Thomas recovered just enough to raise the piece of chicken and take a bite so he didn't have to speak. Instead, he looked toward his mother and raised his eyebrows in acknowledgement. It was all she needed to continue.

"Nice girl. I think you know her, don't you, Thomas?" Thomas nodded but kept on eating. His mother kept on chattering.

He had never spoken of his feelings for Elizabeth to anyone, and yet somehow they all knew. His family, his friends. JB had given him endless grief about it in school. Thankfully Dee Dee's jealousy had faded in the years since Elizabeth had been gone. But now here was his mother, bringing it all out into the open.

Oh, he knew what she was doing, and why she was so happy. She figured Elizabeth Shepard at Grace Community Church was a surefire way to get her son back into their pew on Sunday mornings.

Well, she's not wrong, Thomas thought. *If I can see Elizabeth at church every single week, it'll be worth giving up the break from my family.*

Besides, he really did miss his church.

Decision made, Thomas didn't waste a moment. That evening he placed a call to Roger Beck to confirm that Sunday School would be starting that next week. He'd missed that over the summer too.

When the day arrived, he was there early and poked his head in the door. Both Roger and his wife Nancy were already inside. "Too soon to come in?" he asked.

Both heads came up in unison. "Not at all!" Roger said. "Good to see you, Thomas." They shook hands.

Nancy gave him a hug. "We've missed you these past few weeks."

Thomas liked that they'd noticed his absence. "Yeah." He wondered about telling them where he'd been and decided that if anybody would understand, it would be these two. "I went to visit the Baptist church."

"Oh, Pastor Dale," Roger said. "How'd you like his messages?"

"They were okay. Not as good as Pastor Stephen's."

"We are blessed for sure," Nancy said. "And very glad you didn't like it over there too much." She winked at him.

Thomas grinned and ducked his head. Roger handed him some books, and Thomas distributed them around the table. Before he finished, other class members began trickling in. As he rounded the last corner and placed the last book, Elizabeth walked in the door.

Thomas's legs went wobbly, and he promptly sat down in the nearest chair. He hadn't considered the possibility that she might join the Sunday School class. All he'd been hoping for was a chance to see her at church, maybe say hello. But if she was going to be in Sunday School...

"All right, everybody. Let's settle in," Roger called out.

Having just come into the room, Elizabeth took a seat near the door on the opposite side of the table from Thomas. When she looked up and saw him, she smiled and raised a hand in greeting. Thomas returned the gesture.

"Welcome back, everyone," Roger said. "We've got some new faces, so why don't we go around and introduce ourselves?"

Besides Elizabeth, there were two other new people in the class, both of them teachers. Grace Community seemed to be a magnet for them. Everyone else in the room, Thomas already knew.

"Nancy and I did a lot of thinking and praying over the summer about what we wanted to study with all of you this fall. What we finally felt led to is what we're calling *Living Out Our Faith in a Hostile World*."

Several people around the table murmured in surprise. Roger chuckled. "We might as well start right there. What about this topic surprises you?"

The sound in the room shifted from murmur to scuffle as people got busy studying their hands or their books, hoping someone else would answer and they wouldn't have to.

Roger just waited. His wife, Nancy, was seated beside him, and anytime she could catch someone's eye, she smiled reassuringly.

Thomas didn't think it was so surprising. On the contrary, he was quite familiar with the concept. But he didn't say so.

Across the table, Elizabeth scrunched up her face and stifled a yawn. Thomas couldn't tell if she was bored or tired. He didn't have time to wonder, though, because someone finally spoke up to answer Roger's question. It was Becky Fleming, one of the teachers in the room.

"I guess it's the word *hostile* that surprises me. Hostile in what way? I think people are pretty friendly."

"Okay, good. What else?" Roger said. Now that someone had broken the ice, several people shared their thoughts.

"Becky, you know how it is in the classroom, right? We can't start a conversation about faith, even when it's relevant. I guess I'd call that hostile."

Several people nodded assent.

"Yeah, and you can get in trouble for it just like you can for sexual harassment." A titter went around the table, and the speaker defended himself. "Well, it's true!"

Roger came to his rescue. "You're right; it is true. And this reality, the fact that we as Christians are being shut down from talking about our faith, is one of things we want to discuss in this study. Why it's happening and what God's Word tells us about how we should respond."

Thomas was thoughtful as he gathered up his belongings at the end of class. He wasn't sure if the study would apply to him or not; the hostility he experienced in life wasn't because of his faith. But it didn't matter; he was going to be in the class either way.

Elizabeth was deep in conversation with Roger and Nancy. Most of the other people were already gone. Thomas made his way slowly around the far side of the table, not wanting to interrupt them but at the same time hoping he might get a chance to say hello to Elizabeth.

And he did. They approached the door at the same time, and he held it open for her. "After you," he said.

"Thanks," she said and exited the room.

Thomas fell into step beside her. "Sounds like a good study," he ventured to say.

"It does," she agreed. "And Roger and Nancy seem to be good teachers." She looked up at him. "Have you been in their class before?"

"Oh yeah."

"That's cool." Elizabeth then launched into talking about her conversation with them after class. She was quite animated, and while Thomas heard the words, mostly he was savoring the reality of being in her presence, short-lived though it was. It wasn't a long walk to the sanctuary, and once inside, Elizabeth's fellow teachers hailed her to come sit with them in the section just inside the education wing door.

"See you, Thomas," she said by way of farewell, and slid in among her friends.

"Yeah, see you," he replied and made his way to a farther section of the curved sanctuary where he joined his family for worship. His mother was beaming.

9

"**H**ey, Tracy," Elizabeth said as she scooted into the pew. "Hey yourself."

"Missed you in Sunday School. It sounds like it's going to be good."

Tracy frowned. "Yeah, I don't go. I need my beauty sleep."

"Oh," Elizabeth said, but had no time to wonder at it, because Tracy spoke again.

"Who was that?"

"Who?"

Tracy raised an eyebrow at her friend. "That guy? The one you walked into the sanctuary with?"

"Oh, Thomas?"

"Oh, Thomas?" Tracy mimicked. "Do we already have a boyfriend?"

"What?" Elizabeth almost squeaked. "No! We've known each other forever."

"Mm hmm." Tracy looked across the sanctuary and caught Thomas looking at Elizabeth. "Well, it won't be long."

Elizabeth huffed. "I doubt it."

Tracy leaned in. "I could talk to him for you, if you want. You know, help things along."

This annoyed Elizabeth. "Talk to him for yourself if you're so interested."

"No, thanks." Tracy sniffed. "He's got grease under his nails."

Elizabeth rounded on her friend. "What's wrong with that? I've got dirt under mine." She raised her hand, nails out, to prove her point.

Tracy just smirked and looked away. "Whatever." It was her final word on the subject and as it turned out, Elizabeth's too because the music had begun and worship was underway.

It wasn't until she got home, changed clothes, and was eating lunch that Elizabeth had time to think more about the events of the morning. First of all, Sunday School had fascinated her and not just because of the topic. It was the way Roger and Nancy led the class. They encouraged people to think and gave them time to do so. She was almost embarrassed to admit she had spent as much time thinking about that—and how she could implement such a methodology in her classroom—as she had about the topic.

Mixed in with those thoughts was her dismay over the exchange with Tracy. It had come out of nowhere—and fast. She couldn't believe how rude her friend was. Elizabeth had nothing but respect for hard work and couldn't have cared less about grease under somebody's nails.

But Thomas Schaefer as a love interest? Never once had he asked her out when they were in high school, even though she was certain he still nursed a crush. If he couldn't bring himself to do it then, why would now be any different?

Although, their interaction was already different than it had been in school. They'd conversed more in the couple of times they'd seen each other than they had in all the years they were growing up.

"Hmm," Elizabeth mused as she scraped the remains of her lunch into the trash. Then she frowned as odor wafted up from the receptacle. Even after four years of living away from the farm, it still bothered her to throw away food. One dog and handful of chickens could eat up nearly every bit of food waste a household could produce. *A farm household*, she reminded herself, *which I am not*.

She carried out the trash and washed up the dishes. All the while a sense of dissatisfaction grew within her. *This is stupid! What do food scraps have to do with anything?* she wondered irritably. Then a huge yawn overtook her and she finally realized what her problem was: she was exhausted. School work was keeping her up at night.

Somehow Elizabeth had been unprepared for the hours and hours required outside of the classroom just to keep up with grading papers. It had only been a couple of weeks and already she felt like she was drowning. She had not expected to need her Sundays just to stay afloat. Sunday had always been a day off from the regular work of the week, but she just couldn't see how to accomplish it.

Once the kitchen was passable, she stopped in the living room, spied her overflowing bag—and groaned.

Just a little nap, she thought. *That'll make everything better.* She turned her back on the bag, dragged herself off to the bedroom, and flopped down on her bed.

When Elizabeth woke up a couple of hours later, she did feel better. After a few delicious moments of yawning and stretching to clear the muddle from her brain, she got up and headed to the bathroom. As she washed her hands and splashed water on her face, her thoughts returned to the interaction with Tracy. They were new friends and didn't know each other very well yet, so Elizabeth couldn't be certain of the other woman's intent.

It hardly mattered, though. Teasing's goal was never to make someone feel good. This Elizabeth knew from experience. All throughout her school years, anytime somebody new learned about her older parents, they thought it their duty to poke fun. Elizabeth thought it her duty not to let them.

In the early years she had suffered a few arguments and more than a few tears, but with the help of her parents had learned to use words and humor to defuse the uncomfortable situations. It developed into a skill that ultimately gained her the respect of her classmates.

This particular interaction though, the one with Tracy, was nagging at her. For one thing she reacted instead of responding. She didn't do a good job of handling it at all. She could probably chalk it up to exhaustion, but it felt like more than that. She just couldn't put her finger on it. *What was it?* she wondered.

Elizabeth went into the living room to face her overflowing school bag. It didn't seem quite as daunting as it had earlier, but the pile of papers was still several hours long. She made herself comfortable on the couch and dug in.

About a third of the way through the stack, she came upon a brutally honest essay by one of her female freshman students. It was this paragraph, right at the end, that took her breath away:

> *I know the assignment was to write about something I learned this summer. I figure that means something good, but what good is there to learn from losing a friend? Especially over something so stupid. I don't know. Part of me keeps hoping we can be friends again, but that's probably dumb because she was horrible to me. Every time I see her, every time I even think about her, my insides get all twisty and I feel like I'm going to throw up. It's not the good kind of twisty you get when you see a guy you like. This is different, and it doesn't feel good at all. So I guess what I learned is, it really hurts to lose a friend that way. What I want to know is, does that ever go away?*

Elizabeth dropped the paper into her lap. That's exactly how her insides felt when Tracy mentioned the word *boyfriend*!

Is that what's bothering me? she wondered. *The thought of a boyfriend?*

Elizabeth got up and wandered through the kitchen. Off to the left it opened into a small hallway which led to the bathroom, the laundry room, her bedroom—and just to complete the circuit—the living room again. In her bedroom was a set of French doors which opened onto a small deck at the back of her house. She pulled them open and stepped outside. It was cooler than out front. A line of old growth trees on the left side of the property shaded the yard from the brutal heat of the western sun.

She leaned against a post and frowned at nothing. It didn't make sense. Elizabeth loved going out, always had. Boyfriend or not, group or one on one, it didn't matter. She just enjoyed socializing and attending events of all kinds. That's what she and her friends had done in college. It's what she and Chad—

Elizabeth's insides twisted up. She gasped and pushed away from the post. *Is this about Chad?*

All summer long as Elizabeth had worked at her internship with high-risk youth in the inner city, Chad had harangued her to change her mind and stay in Cincinnati in the fall. At the time it had just been annoying. Exhausting, even. But she hadn't thought there'd been any lasting damage.

Sure, she'd come home a little weepy over it, but not for long. A good night's sleep had washed away any nostalgia for what was lost. Chad and Elizabeth apart was the right path for both of them. But being gun-shy about dating at all? That just wasn't her! Anger against him welled up inside of her. Why couldn't he have just accepted their break-up and moved on?

Elizabeth stepped inside the house and back to the kitchen to snag a pop from the fridge. Then she went back to her stack of papers, grabbed the red pen, and after a good bit of pondering, wrote this at the bottom of the girl's essay:

> *Losing someone you care about is never easy. It adds a layer of sorrow that never fully goes away but rather gets woven into the fabric of who we are. I think the goal is to embrace it alongside our good memories and in that way, not let it overwhelm us. A very honest essay. Good work.*

Elizabeth set the paper aside and moved on to the next, but in the back of her mind she couldn't help but wonder how to take her own advice.

10

When Thomas first started working on cars in his free time, he'd still lived at home, but that hadn't made it any easier to convince his dad to give him space to work. Seeking the use of the carport—the old carport that his parents hadn't used in years—had brought a huge wave of criticism down on his head.

"Whatchu wanna bring an old junker here for?" his dad asked.

"I want to fix it up and sell it."

"Planning to go into business for yourself?" his father sneered.

"No, I just want to do this on the side."

A grunt was his only reply.

But Thomas had been so eager to begin his first restoration project that he hadn't given up. He'd returned again and again to make his pitch, bearing the abuse and figuring out the answers to his father's every objection.

It had finally paid off—after months of asking. His dad was out of excuses and probably tired of hearing him on the subject. Either way, Thomas had gotten permission and been working on cars out there ever since.

The difficulty was winter. There was simply no way to heat the space under a carport, and when snow piled up in January and February, it made access impossible anyway.

Thomas wanted a new solution.

Problem was, the best one he could think of still involved his dad. The shop had three working bays that faced out toward the street, but there was another one in the back of the building that faced off to the side. Nobody ever went in there; it was filled with junk. Thomas felt sure that with a little bit of elbow grease, he could clean it out and turn it into a perfect workspace. He didn't see how his dad could have any quarrel with that. No reasonable one, anyway.

Once he decided the question had to be asked, he didn't want to wait, but he did need to make sure the timing was right. His father's good moods were rare, and Thomas had to wait for one if he had any hope of succeeding. That he had learned from the carport.

A few days later as Thomas, JB, and his father each worked in their respective bays, JB stopped working, cocked his head to the side, and said, "The hell is that?" It was whistling, a sound never before heard beneath the roof of Schaefer Automotive, and it was coming from Jack's bay.

JB's jaw dropped. He turned to Thomas, his eyes wide in disbelief. Thomas just shrugged and did everything in his power not to grin at the look on his friend's face. That, and the fact that his opportunity had just arrived.

JB was always out the door promptly at five. Thomas was often close behind, but today he hung back. He cleaned up his space, clocked out, and then went back out to the shop to lean against the tool bench.

Truth was, he had always loved watching his father work under the hood, more than his father liked to be watched. But it was fascinating to see him coax life out of a dead engine. He gave such care to each individual component as he ensured it was in perfect working condition.

Sometimes Thomas felt jealous of those car parts.

Pushing that thought aside, he watched and waited, choosing not to speak until his father did. He could tell his father knew he was there, but it was several minutes before the older man broke silence.

"What do you need, son?" he asked.

"Want to talk to you about cleaning out the fourth bay and moving into there from the carport." There was no sense in beating about the bush. Such things just annoyed his father.

His father said nothing and kept on working.

Thomas continued. "The weather's going to be turning cold—"

"Yep. Like it does every year."

Thomas nodded. "I'd like to start working through the winter."

Silence. Again.

Thomas waited for a moment and then tried a different approach. "I'll clean it out myself, organize it, whatever you want done with everything."

"What I want 'with everything'," his father said, straightening up from his work, "is for it all to stay right where it is." He slammed the hood shut and turned to face Thomas. "You begged me for that carport."

"I know."

"Well, then." He turned away and grabbed a broom.

"I'm ready to upgrade," Thomas said.

His father snorted and pushed his broom with short, vicious strokes. "Yeah, and this upgrade has costs. You prepared for that?"

Thomas blinked. He wasn't. He hadn't even thought about it.

When he didn't respond, his father spoke again. "I didn't think so. Lights, heat. I'm sure you expect to use my equipment. And I've seen how your friends flock around you while you're working." He shook his head. "I won't be having that here."

Thomas inhaled. "That's part of the reason I want to upgrade."

The broom stopped. "What do you mean?"

"I can't make them quit. I figure the only way is to have a shop where I can lock the door."

It was a moment before the broom started up again, a little more gently this time. "Well, I still don't want my stuff moved."

"What is all that?" Thomas blurted out before he thought.

"It's none of your business, is what it is. You stay out of there." The broom picked up its pace.

Stung, Thomas replied, "Yes, sir." Like he had a choice. The bay was locked. Always had been. The only way Thomas knew it was full was through the lone, grimy window in the door.

The conversation was over. Forever. Thomas knew he wouldn't get his father to budge. The carport had been vacant and it was a battle to get permission. Arguing for this space, with its costs and all the stuff that somehow was important, was more like a suicide mission.

Thomas pushed off the tool bench and without another word, left the shop.

All that evening he stared at his TV screen without really seeing it. He was thinking about the costs his father had mentioned. Utilities, equipment, anywhere he went he was going to have expenses. Rent, even. Thomas laced his fingers behind his head and leaned back into the couch cushion. He couldn't afford all that. He already lived paycheck to paycheck.

The truth was, he didn't know what he could afford. His philosophy was, if he had money in his pocket, he could spend it. He paid his rent, put gas in his truck, and bought food. After that, it was car parts and whatever his friends could mooch off him.

Something needs to change, he thought. *But what? And how?* And who could he even talk to about such a thing? Thomas had no idea.

11

Within just a few weeks of starting her job, Elizabeth realized she had a second problem with her lesson plans: they were all alike. Sure, she had three different grade levels, but she had scheduled all three of them the same: all the grammar at the same time, all the literature at the same time, and all the writing at the same time.

The result was that Elizabeth was bored, just as she had been during her student teaching experience. She didn't quite understand how she could be bored and overworked at the same time, but she was. Her methodology dumped about 150 like assignments into her lap at once, and all that similar grading was making Elizabeth feel like she was losing her mind.

She decided she needed to stagger the units to keep her interest—and her sanity. On Sunday, after succumbing to the nap that was threatening to become a weekly occurrence, she got out her lesson planning book and did some rearranging. It wouldn't reduce her grading burden, but it would mix it up a little.

After that, she jumped in her car and headed to her folks' house for supper. She arrived early enough to help her mom with the prep. When her dad came in from chores, he settled himself at the table, and the three of them chatted.

"How's your new church?" he wanted to know.

"It's good! I really like the Sunday School class. We're talking about how to live out our faith in a hostile world."

"That does sound like a good study!" her mom said. Then, "Are you getting enough sleep?"

Elizabeth bobbed her head. "Well, I took a nap after lunch today, so…"

"So did I!" her dad said and laughed out loud. "But then again, I am an old man."

"You are not!" Elizabeth exclaimed and went over to give him a hug.

"Oh, yes I am. But I am also right where God wants me to be." He winked at his daughter, and she returned to the counter and her task. It was a little game they played. Elizabeth couldn't say for sure when it had started, but anytime something came up that alluded to his age, their exchange was always the same.

Elizabeth's mom got out a stack of plates and cups and silverware, and her dad set the table. Elizabeth washed up some of the cookware while her mom put the meal on the table. Roast beef, baked potatoes with butter and sour cream, green beans, and homemade dinner rolls. The three of them sat down together and joined hands.

"Dear Heavenly Father," her dad began. "We thank you for the bounty of the earth and for the nourishment it provides. We thank you for the hands that prepared this meal. And we thank you for the opportunity to be together this evening as a family. Bless each person around this table and help each one of us to live out our faith boldly, no matter the circumstance. Amen."

Elizabeth's heart warmed at the prayer. Her parents listened when she was sharing something from her life, and for that she was grateful. Then a lump formed in her throat as she thought about the time to come when they'd no longer be here to share her life with. She swallowed it down quickly and blinked to keep tears from forming. It made no sense to mourn right now, because right now, they were still together.

12

The weather was rainy and uncooperative in the days following Thomas's pitch to his father, and it kept him away from the carport and his project. On the one hand, he was okay with that, because he was still smarting from the exchange and needed a little distance. On the other, he was going stir crazy in the evenings. He spent a great deal of his time thinking about his workspace and his finances, but he still couldn't figure out how to fix either one of them.

The balance of his time he spent daydreaming about Elizabeth. Seeing her every Sunday morning added a spot of color to his otherwise gray life. It's just that it was such a very small portion of time that he got to be with her, a couple of minutes on the walk from Sunday School to church each week. Back when they were teenagers, she had always seemed so far out of reach that he'd never even considered trying. But now...was that still true? He didn't know.

When he awoke that next Saturday morning and the weather was clear, he didn't waste any time. He got right out to his parents' house and started working on the car. He felt his phone buzz sometime about mid-morning, but he ignored it. At noon, when he took a bathroom break, the house was quiet. His parents were gone somewhere for the day—he didn't know where—and wouldn't be back until late. Karen was still asleep.

Back out at his truck, he grabbed the sandwich he'd brought along and checked his phone. It was a text from JB.

Go-karts?

He texted back,

Working on my car

and then put his phone in his pocket. He went back to work and forgot all about it.

He realized his mistake—too late—when JB pulled into the yard not fifteen minutes later. Thomas sighed. *Shouldn't have told him what I was doing*, he thought.

JB slammed the door of his car and walked over to lean against the hood. "Don't you ever get tired of fixing cars?" he asked.

Thomas didn't answer.

"Come on, bro. We gotta have some fun sometimes."

Thomas kept right on working. "Weather's nice today. I'm taking advantage of it."

JB sighed. "Fine. We'll just hang out here." He walked to the house and banged on the back door. "Karen! Wake up!" He kept on pounding until Thomas wondered if the neighbors would complain.

Finally Karen yanked the door open. "What?" she said, and yawned. She was still in pajamas. Her hair was tousled and her eyes puffy.

"Oh, man, you look great!" JB said, laughing at her.

"Shut up," she said and started to close the door.

"Hey, come on," JB said, pushing his weight against it to keep it open. "We're gonna have a party."

"Where?" Karen asked, brightening visibly.

"Right here," he said and gestured into the back yard. "Tommy's too busy working on his car to go anywhere else, so…"

"Cool!" She stepped out the door, wrapped her arms around him, and nuzzled her face against his neck.

He pulled back. "Hey, get us some snacks."

"There's nothing good to eat in there!" she complained, jerking a thumb toward the house.

"Then go to the store," JB told her.

"Come with me," she said, and twirled her hair around her finger.

"You'll be fine, baby," he said, giving her a kiss on the lips and a swat on the butt.

"Ugh," Karen said, and stomped back into the house.

Thomas was rifling through his stash of car parts, but he heard the entire exchange. He could have kicked himself for even responding to JB's text. Although it probably wouldn't have made any difference. His friend knew where he spent all his free time.

JB pulled a cooler of drinks out of his car. He lugged it to the cement pad under the carport and scooted a toolbox out of the way before plunking it down.

"Hey, don't move my tools. Put that somewhere else," Thomas said.

"I don't want it to get dirty!" JB protested.

Thomas looked at the grungy cooler and said no more.

Next JB produced a portable speaker, and by the time he got his playlist up and running, Karen had emerged from the house, fully clothed, hair combed. "Hey, Tommy, you got any money?"

He stopped sorting parts as he considered. He couldn't bring himself to lie. "Yeah," he finally said and went back to his work.

"Can I have some?" Karen asked.

"No," Thomas said.

"Why not?"

"I'm just here working on my car," he said.

Karen huffed. "Fine, then you can't have any of my food." She spun around and faced JB, who was grinning at this exchange. "Last chance to come with me."

"See ya," he said and sniggered.

Karen stomped over to her car, slammed the door behind her, and tore out of the yard.

JB pulled a beer from the cooler, popped the top, and chugged down half the can in one gulp. He smacked his lips. "Want one?" he asked.

"No thanks," Thomas said. He found what he was looking for and moved back to the engine block to work. JB sauntered over and leaned against the car again—this time, right in Thomas's light. "Can you move?" Thomas said. "I can't see what I'm doing."

"Why don't you quit for the day?" JB said, not moving.

"I don't want to quit for the day. Move it."

"Fine." JB only scooted down about a foot, but it was enough for Thomas to be able to see.

A couple minutes later JB sauntered over to the back porch and poked around. When he came back he said, "Hey, where are the chairs?"

Thomas looked around the yard. "Probably in the garage."

JB tried the side door and finding it unlocked, went inside. He came out with several chairs in hand and leaned the extras up against one of the posts of the carport. The other he arranged near the cooler, sat down, and propped up his feet. He grabbed his phone and turned up the music.

About a half hour later, Karen pulled in the driveway. Another car pulled in right behind her. "Look who I found at the grocery store!" Karen called.

Dee Dee.

Great, Thomas thought.

Karen grabbed a bag of food from her car and together they crossed the yard.

"Thought you had to work on Saturdays?" JB asked Dee Dee.

"Told 'em I was sick. Had to leave."

"Dude, you're gonna lose your job," JB said.

"Who cares?" Dee Dee shrugged. "I hate that place."

She hates every place she works, Thomas thought. Which, over the course of time, had been just about every minimum wage job in town.

"Where'm I gonna put this food?" Karen asked.

"Put it on the trunk of the car," JB suggested.

"No," Thomas said. "Go get a table out of the garage."

"Will you get it for me?" Karen asked Thomas.

"No."

Karen glared at him and then turned to JB.

"Uh uh," he said.

Dee Dee shoved JB's feet off the cooler. "Go get the damn table," she said. JB huffed and headed back to the garage. Karen turned her back on Thomas and leaned against the trunk of the car, arms folded, waiting for the table. Dee Dee grabbed a beer out of the cooler and held it out to Thomas. "Want one?"

"No thanks," Thomas replied.

"I'll take one," Karen said. Dee Dee tossed it to her and got another for herself.

She popped the top and took a huge gulp. Then she looked around. "Tommy, will you get me a chair?"

He looked up. She was standing right beside them. "I'm busy."

"Aw, come on."

Thomas ignored her. It wouldn't do any good to argue. Finally Dee Dee got her own chair. She arranged it as close to Thomas as she could get it.

JB came back dragging a table. He set it up and Karen dumped out the bag. "Have at it," she said. "But not you." She glared at Thomas.

"Fine by me," he said.

Things continued on. His friends eating, drinking, and horsing around. Him working. By late afternoon, Thomas had a headache. It was the loud music and loud friends—and the constant badgering to participate.

But it was more than that. Like Thomas, Karen had had it drilled into her from a young age not to drink. And with good reason. They had the dubious distinction of a grandfather who'd managed to get himself and their grandmother killed by driving drunk. They'd never known them; it happened before they were born. But they lived with the fallout every day of their lives in the form of their father.

Over the past few months, the bad habits of both Dee Dee and JB had finally started to rub off on his sister, and today she was nearly keeping pace with them. Thomas watched with growing concern, but what could he do? She listened to no one, especially him. If he said anything, it'd just make it worse.

As for himself, alcohol had never appealed. He had no idea why. It was one thing he agreed with his father on, even though his father didn't believe it. He still grilled him regularly about his habits.

Alongside all these wonderful and unwelcome thoughts, Thomas had been making a mental list throughout the day of all the next car parts he needed to source. While he wasn't ready for any of them just yet, getting out of there for a while, away from the chaos, sounded more appealing with every passing moment.

This was exactly why he wanted a shop space of his own. He didn't have to let anybody in if he didn't want to. And he wouldn't have to depend on the weather to be able to work. It made him mad to waste even a part of the one good day he'd had this week by going to get parts instead of working, but he had to get out of there. All because his friends had no respect for what was important to him.

Decision made, Thomas quietly put his tools away and cleaned up. The others were so drunk by then that they didn't notice until he was walking to his truck.

"Where ya going, Tommy?" Dee Dee called out, her voice slurred.

"Gotta buy some parts."

"Ooh, I'll go with ya," she said, and stumbled after him.

Thomas turned back. "No!" he said. "You won't."

Dee Dee stopped in her tracks, mouth agape. If Thomas had momentarily felt guilty for speaking so sharply to her, it vanished when he saw its effect.

He stowed his toolboxes in the back of his truck, climbed into the cab, and drove away.

Thomas knew every junkyard in the area, and there were several close by, but since his goal was to get away for a while, he decided to visit one that was south of Mansfield. He didn't get down there as often.

Wandering through a graveyard of cars was, in some ways, more satisfying than visiting the pits at the racetrack. At the junkyard, he could come home with treasures for his own projects instead of just watching other people work on theirs.

On the drive down, he left the radio off, rolled down his window, and let the wind blast through the cab. When he arrived, he was so focused on the hunt that he forgot all about his earlier woes. The end result was that when he came away after more than two hours of parts hunting, his headache was gone.

Famished, he drove through McDonald's on the way back and fully intended to go straight home. But as he came into Sutton, he thought better of it and decided to swing back by his folks' house to see how things stood.

It's a good thing he did. The yard all around the carport was trashed and so were his friends. He sat in his truck, engine idling, desperately wanting to back out and drive away again. But there was no way he could leave such a mess for his parents to find. And there was no way his sister would clean it up.

JB and the two girls had spent plenty of time out at the carport in the past, but they'd always kept it lowkey before. It occurred to Thomas that it must have something to do with the presence of his father. For the first time in his life, he almost appreciated the older man's stern attitude. Almost.

Sighing, Thomas turned off the engine and got out of the truck. He went over to where all three of them lay sprawled in the grass, staring up at the sky. He nudged JB with his foot. "Hey," he said.

JB groaned and rolled onto his side.

"Get up," Thomas said.

"No. Lemme alone."

"It's time to go. Take Karen into the house and then I'll drive you and Dee Dee home."

Dee Dee snorted and pushed herself upright. "You're going to drive me home?"

He had no choice. "Help JB get Karen into the house first."

He finally got the three of them headed in the right direction. While they were working on it, Thomas pulled the keys from their cars. Then he went into the house and helped them get Karen to her bed.

"Should we—you know—?" JB asked, nodding his head toward Karen's comatose figure.

"No, we shouldn't," Thomas said, disgusted. But he did make sure she was on her side and unable to roll back over. He'd have to check on her later. The other two were on their own once he got them home.

"Let's go," Thomas said. He ushered them out the door. Dee Dee stumbled toward his truck, but he grabbed her arm and redirected her to JB's car.

"I wanna ride in your truck," she whined.

Thomas ignored this and put JB in the passenger side while hanging on to Dee Dee. Then he opened the back door and finally convinced her to get inside.

She giggled and patted the seat. "Why don't you join me, Tommy? Come on, we could have some fun." She hiccupped and looked up at him with blurry eyes.

Thomas closed the door and got in the driver's seat. He inhaled deeply and blew it out between his lips. Then he started the car and took its occupants home.

When he got back to his parents' house, he killed the engine and for a moment, just sat. He couldn't do this anymore, but how could he prevent it? He had no idea. Finally he pulled the keys and then set to work cleaning up the yard.

When that was done he poked his head inside the house long enough to see that his sister was still breathing. Satisfied, or least knowing he'd done all he could do, Thomas got in his truck and went home.

13

E lizabeth, meanwhile, was having friend problems of her own. Or at least, acquaintance problems. Ever since their little spat at church, Tracy was being aloof. *Childish, even,* Elizabeth thought with annoyance. Every time she entered the teacher lounge, Tracy made a point of leaving.

"What'd you do to make her so mad?" Gavin finally asked one morning after Tracy flounced out.

"Called her out for being rude."

"Yeah," Paul said. "She really doesn't like that."

Elizabeth looked at him curiously. "Nobody likes that."

"True, but Tracy has a way of, well, making your life miserable if you cross her."

"She's already making my life miserable." While that might have been an overstatement, Elizabeth was trying to make a point. "Why should she get to say anything she wants and I can't? How is that right?"

"All I'm saying is be careful," Paul said, raising a hand in surrender.

Gavin chimed in. "I agree. Probably wise to pick your battles with that one."

"Hmm," was all Elizabeth said. She thought back to the day it happened. She hadn't made any effort since then to set things right. Seemed easier not to. But it bothered Elizabeth. It wasn't like her to do that, and exhausted or not, she didn't like how things were.

The question was, could she do what it'd take to fix it?

In Sunday School that next week, they continued their discussion about faith and hostility. Elizabeth found herself thinking about Tracy throughout the lesson.

"Why does hostility exist? What does the Bible tell us?" Roger asked.

"It's because of sin, right?" one of the students asked.

"That's right," Roger said. "Romans 8:7 says, 'The mind governed by the flesh is hostile to God.' When we're hostile to God, it follows that we're hostile to each other as well. The Bible is filled with examples of this." He looked around the room. "When we experience it, it's nothing new."

"I hadn't thought about it like that," another class member said.

"When we put it in this proper perspective, it helps us to—not accept it, exactly—but to understand it," Roger said. "When we understand the reasons why people behave the way they do, that helps us to shape our response in a more appropriate way."

Elizabeth wandered out of the room at the end of class, deep in thought. For whatever reason, Tracy, who was always in church but never in Sunday School, was being hostile. But Roger's words made a lot of sense. Elizabeth needed to remember the source and respond accordingly. She got her chance to try almost immediately.

Despite Tracy's coolness all week, Elizabeth still sat in the same pew with her in church. Her other teacher friends were all married and sitting with their spouses, so in her mind, it made sense. She slid into her seat, but before she had time to say a word, Tracy leaned over and said, "Where's your boyfriend?"

Elizabeth turned abruptly, and Tracy flinched. Elizabeth smiled and said, "You and I don't know each other very well." A flash of annoyance crossed Tracy's face and she looked away. Elizabeth wasn't deterred. "But the woman who came to school early on my second day of teaching, just to give me a little encouragement, is someone I'd like to know better."

She could tell Tracy was listening, so she continued, "The problem is, I don't know where she went. Is she still around?"

For a moment, Tracy said nothing. Then she threw these words over her shoulder. "I was just having fun with you."

"Teasing?"

Tracy shrugged. "Sure. You didn't have to get defensive."

Elizabeth thought about this. "Maybe not," and then fell silent. Tracy didn't know her history or the reasons why she had responded the way she did. Even Elizabeth hadn't known right at that moment. But it still didn't excuse Tracy thinking she had the right to treat her however she wanted, just for her own kicks.

She spoke up again. "The thing about teasing," she said, tipping her head to make sure she had Tracy's attention, "is that it's often hurtful to the other side. One person's fun should not be another person's pain."

Tracy pressed her lips together.

Elizabeth continued anyway. "If you were unaware of that, it's okay. But now that you know, maybe we can move forward in a better way."

Tracy turned to face her. Her eyes were flat, expressionless. "And if I did it on purpose?"

Elizabeth held her gaze. "If that's how you roll, then there's no chance for us." Tracy didn't react. "Personally, I'd rather be friends," Elizabeth said, "but it's your call."

The music began and Elizabeth turned to face the front of the sanctuary. She had no idea what Tracy would do next, but at least she had confronted the situation head on instead of continuing to let it fester. She didn't know about Tracy's life experiences anymore than Tracy knew about hers. Not that it mattered. The ultimate reason why people mistreated each other was the same for everyone. Including herself.

In the middle of the song, the door to the education wing opened and Thomas, Roger, and Nancy slipped through. Elizabeth watched as Thomas made his way around the sanctuary and joined his family in their pew. *I hope everything's okay,* she thought. She'd been so focused on the issue with the woman sitting next to her that despite Tracy's dig, she hadn't thought about where he was—or that he hadn't walked with her—until now.

Tracy leaned over to Elizabeth and this time, Elizabeth flinched. Tracy didn't seem to notice, but whispered, "I shouldn't have said what I did about him. Sorry."

Startled, Elizabeth whispered back, "Forgiven." At the time it didn't occur to her that she knew exactly what Tracy was talking about.

Tracy scoffed and shook her head, but moments later when Elizabeth stole a glance at her, she looked thoughtful.

14

When Thomas had arrived at Sunday School that morning, he didn't have a plan. By the time the lesson was over however, he did. And so, as much as he hated to do it, he gave up walking with Elizabeth to the sanctuary in order to talk with Roger and Nancy privately after class.

He took his time gathering up his books. Then he tidied up the chairs around the table, waiting for everyone else to leave. Finally it was just the three of them.

"How are you, Thomas?" Roger asked, extending his hand as he came around the table.

"I'm okay," Thomas said.

Nancy came over to give him a hug. "Everything going well at work?" she asked.

He nodded but said nothing more. He knew what he wanted to do; he just didn't know how to do it.

Roger studied him for a moment. "It was a good discussion today in class."

Thomas nodded again. "Never really thought about all that stuff before."

"It's a good thing we're studying about it, then. We can all use some help when it comes to dealing with relationships."

Thomas looked down at the floor. "I think I need a lot of help with that."

"Do you have something particular in mind?" Roger asked.

"There's a thing with my friends, and I don't know what to do about it."

"If you like, we could get together and talk," Roger offered.

"That'd be good."

"Would you like to come over for lunch after church?" Nancy asked.

Thomas hesitated, rubbing the back of his neck. "My folks always have Sunday dinner. Kind of expected to be there."

"Of course," Roger said. "Tell me what works for you."

"Maybe after that? Sometime this afternoon?"

"That sounds fine. Come on over when you're ready. Okay?"

"Thanks."

Nancy made sure Thomas had their address and then together they slipped into the sanctuary.

His mind was so full of the Sunday School lesson and the discussion which followed that he barely registered his parents' disapproving looks as he arrived late to worship. In fact, he had trouble getting focused on anything at all until the pastor started announcing prayer requests.

"Ted Johnson is asking for prayer for his wife, Jane. Her cancer has returned."

A murmur went through the congregation. Ted was a local businessman—a financial advisor who did much in their community to help both businesses and families succeed. Jane had waged war against breast cancer about five years ago and won. She had talked continually about her desire to see their son graduate, marry, and have a family of his own. The graduation had happened but rather than marrying, he'd joined the military, so Ted and Jane still had no grandchildren.

The request brought Thomas to attention. As difficult and—to be honest—hostile as his own family often was, he couldn't imagine losing them. As the pastor prayed, he lifted his own simple prayer to God for a second victory for Jane Johnson.

Thomas excused himself from the family dinner table pretty quickly that afternoon, causing his father to raise his eyebrows and his mother to look hurt. Karen would have smirked, but she was still too hungover to antagonize her brother. Instead she just ignored him.

He briefly wondered if she had even a moment of gratitude for everything he had done to clean up after their little party yesterday. But all that thought did was add to his distress, so he let it go.

Once out the door he headed straight for Roger and Nancy's house. Roger opened the door and said, "Thomas, welcome! Come on in."

Nancy offered coffee and then disappeared into another part of the house after serving. The two men took their seats in the living room, Thomas on the couch and Roger in a recliner. Their coffee cooled on the table in front of them. Thomas got right to the point, at least as best he could.

"I need to figure out how to deal with a situation."

"Okay," Roger said. "What kind of situation?"

Thomas stared across the room, trying to find the words. After several false starts, he finally said, "I feel like my friends don't care about what matters to me."

Roger nodded thoughtfully. "What do they do to make you feel that way?"

"Whenever I'm working on my car they're always there, trying to get me to go with them somewhere. And pay for it." He huffed. "Yesterday, because I wouldn't go with them, they showed up where I was and spent all day drinking while I was trying to work." He shook his head. "It ruins it."

"I can see how that would be frustrating," Roger said. "Who are your friends?"

"JB, we've been friends all through school. He works at the shop. He and my sister are together, so Karen's there. And then her friend, Dee Dee." His voice dropped at her name. He stopped and looked down at his hands.

"Tell me about her," Roger said. He picked up his coffee mug from the table and tested its contents. It was still steaming hot so he set it back down.

Thomas stared at his own mug, not sure how to answer.

"It's just the four of you?" Roger asked. Thomas nodded, and Roger continued. "Is Dee Dee more than your sister's friend?"

"No!" Embarrassed, he shook his head. "She wants to be. I don't."

"Ah. And you get paired up by default."

"I guess."

"Have you told her how you feel?"

Thomas exhaled sharply through his nose. "All the time."

"Mmm," Roger mused. "How do you say it?" When Thomas furrowed his brow, Roger added, "What words do you use?"

Thomas thought for a moment. "Well, when she—" he stopped and bobbed his head from side to side. "—gets too close, I tell her to stop. I move away, or push her hands away from me." He could feel the heat rising. He'd never talked about this before.

"Okay, that's good. You don't accept her advances."

"No. Never." Thomas grimaced at the thought.

"Anything else?" Roger asked.

Thomas shook his head.

Roger leaned back in his chair and crossed his arms, tapping a finger against his lips. Thomas twisted his hands in his lap, waiting for the older man's reply. As much as he liked and respected Roger, he wondered if he'd made a mistake telling him all this.

"It sounds to me like you've got two situations going on," Roger finally said. "The one with your friends disrespecting your choices, and the other with a girl you're not interested in."

Thomas nodded miserably.

Roger leaned forward in his seat. "Which to you is the bigger issue?"

"Dee Dee," he answered without hesitation and then looked up in surprise. He'd come here seeking help about his friends. He hadn't even considered the possibility of getting help with Dee Dee.

Roger nodded. "Okay. From what you've said, I think you might need to have a talk with her, one on one, and tell her straight out how you feel." When Thomas looked mortified, he smiled and continued. "It's not an easy thing to do, but it is important since she hasn't taken your hints."

Thomas mulled this over. "Have I been handling it wrong?"

"Not wrong. Maybe just not straightforward enough for her to get it."

"It goes back and forth," Thomas said. "I push her away and she gets mad. Then I do something nice, and she comes back again." He leaned back against the couch cushion and sighed.

"Nice like what?"

Thomas pursed his lips. "Open a car door. Tell her I'm glad she's feeling better. I'm just trying to be decent, but..." he stopped and shook his head.

Roger closed his eyes. "It sounds like this is a young woman who may not have much 'nice' in her life. And the little bit that comes her way, she latches on to." He opened his eyes, and at the horrified look on Thomas's face, held up a hand and added, "I'm not saying you're responsible to fix her life, Thomas. I was just noting that quite often there's more going on than what we see at surface level. Either way, if this situation is unacceptable to you, then it must be dealt with. You'll want to be as kind as possible, but also absolutely clear about what needs to change."

Thomas ran his fingers through his hair and scrunched up his face. "Do you think it'll work? I mean, will she stop..." Thomas couldn't bring himself to say, "throwing herself at me," but it's what he was thinking.

Roger took a deep breath and scratched his ear before answering. "I'd say it's not likely if the four of you keep spending time together, which leads right into the other situation you're dealing with."

"Yeah." Thomas finally picked up his coffee and took a sip. It had cooled, almost too much, so he took another. "I'd like to have a shop where I can work in peace, and no matter what the weather is. Out in the open where I am, I don't have any control."

"Have you looked into making a change?"

Thomas nodded. "I talked to my dad about the extra bay in the shop, but he said no. And I don't have the money to rent a space."

"I see," Roger said. "Well, one thing at a time. If your main concern is Dee Dee, best to start there."

"Okay." Thomas no longer felt worried that he'd made a mistake by talking to Roger. On the contrary, he felt a sense of relief. Hope, even, that things could get better.

"Tell you what," Roger said. "How about we pray together, and then we can start working out what you need to tell this young woman." He looked questioningly at Thomas.

Thomas nodded. "Thank you."

15

On Monday after work, Thomas dialed Dee Dee's phone number. His stomach was in knots and he'd barely had enough time to practice what he wanted to say, but he needed to get this over with as soon as possible.

"Dee Dee, it's Thomas. I need to talk to you. Will you meet me over at the rec center?"

"Ooh, Tommy! Why don't we go get pizza instead?" He could hear the excitement in her voice and kicked himself for not making his purpose more clear.

"This isn't a date. I just need to talk to you."

It was crazy; Thomas could hear her pouting through the phone. Finally she said, "Well, yeah, but we gotta eat."

No way Thomas was going to a restaurant with her. "This won't take long. Will you meet me?"

Dee Dee let out an exaggerated sigh. "Fine," she said, and hung up

Assuming that meant now, he grabbed his jacket and his keys and headed out the door.

He was right. She was leaning up against her car when he arrived.

"Let's go in and sit down," he said. Dee Dee said nothing but trailed along behind him.

They headed for the bleachers in the gym, where a couple of youth basketball games were going on side by side. Thomas was grateful for the noise and for the people. He figured Dee Dee might be less likely to pitch a fit in front of all of them.

"First off, thanks for coming. I appreciate it."

Dee Dee just shrugged and looked at him from beneath her heavy eyebrows, arms crossed, apparently still sulking over the missed pizza opportunity with him. He looked down at the bleachers just beyond where she sat and took a deep breath.

"I haven't done a good job being clear about my feelings. We're friends, and that's it. That's how I've always felt and it's not going to change. I need you to stop—" This was the part that Thomas had the hardest time saying. "—trying to make it more. I don't want to hurt your feelings, but I want you to stop chasing me."

When he finished speaking, he looked up at her. He caught a fleeting glimpse of her mocking stare, the one she got when she wasn't going to listen to anything you had to say. Then it was gone, and Thomas saw something in her face he'd never noticed before. *Is that pain?* He recalled Roger's words, but before he had time to consider them, the look was gone. In its place was the much more familiar flash of anger.

"You're a real jerk, you know that?" she yelled, pointing her finger at him. Beyond Dee Dee sat a young mom with a small child. At this outburst, she turned to look at them both, and then just as quickly turned away again.

"All this time you been leading me on and now you tell me we're just friends?" She huffed and turned her head away. Then she whipped back around and Thomas flinched. "I can't believe I wasted my time on you. I'm glad you finally *told me how you feel*." Her face was contorted in anger and she spat the words at him.

"Gotta make sure Tommy gets what he wants! Well, fine! Just don't ever come crawling back to me when you realize what you're missing." With that parting shot, Dee Dee jumped to her feet and stomped her way down the bleachers and out the door.

Thomas was frozen to his seat. It happened so fast. The young mother stole a glance at him and smiled apologetically.

He'd thought she'd argue. Cajole. Come on to him, even. Those things he had expected. But for her to walk away? Never. Part of him thought she'd come stomping back in to give him another earful.

But she didn't. He sat, willing his heart rate to slow, desperately trying to control the shaking of his hands. The basketball games continued on as though nothing out of the ordinary had just taken place among the spectators in the stands. The squeaking of shoes, grunting of players, and slap of the ball had covered the outburst from all but the nearest one. For this, Thomas was grateful.

He watched them play for a bit, then once he'd collected himself, made his own way down the bleachers and out the door, stopping briefly to see if she was waiting to ambush him. Satisfied she was not, he walked to his truck, replaying her words in his mind. Out of all the things she'd said, there was only one he wished he could respond to.

"Thomas," he said out loud to no one. "My name is Thomas." Then he went home.

Thomas took a long hot shower, ate some supper, and slept well that night. His stomach had unknotted and he was beginning to feel a sense of relief over finally having addressed the situation with Dee Dee.

His peace was short-lived.

"What the hell, Tommy!" This was JB, eight o'clock the next morning at the time clock in the shop breakroom.

"What?" Thomas asked, knowing full well what. The knot of dread returned.

"Dee Dee spent all night crying to Karen, and now she's bitchy! What'd you gotta go and do something stupid like that for?"

Thomas just shook his head and muttered low, "Had to be done."

"Oh—!" JB sputtered and shook. "Couldn't you have just left well enough alone? We were supposed to go out last night and instead, guess who got to sit at home all by himself?" He huffed and stomped off to his bay, jerking open the lid of his toolbox and slamming around its contents.

Well enough for who? Thomas thought. *Not me, that's for sure.* He finished clocking in and headed to his own bay. As he got busy rotating the tires on a truck, he thought about what his friend had said. JB didn't care about Dee Dee. He was just mad that his own plans were ruined.

Well, Thomas didn't care about JB's plans. He felt bad that Dee Dee was upset, but he wasn't sorry he'd done it. She just never would take the hint. He only wished he'd done it a long time ago. *Thank you, God, for Roger,* he silently prayed.

JB didn't talk to him the entire day. At noon he stomped out of the building and Thomas ate lunch by himself in the break-room. He and JB were the only ones who used it. His mother worked mornings in the office, and at noon she and his father left together to go home for lunch. Karen's shift to clean the building and stock parts was supposed to start mid-afternoon, but she seldom showed up until everybody else was gone.

As he ate, the only sound was of the analog clock ticking on the wall behind him. The peace and quiet was welcome, but Thomas did find himself wondering just how long JB would stay mad.

16

"**M**orning." Tracy stopped and leaned against the doorframe of the teacher's lounge.

Elizabeth looked up from the table where she was reviewing her lesson plans for the week. "Morning," she said distractedly and then went back to work.

Tracy came in and poured herself a cup of coffee and then sauntered over to the table. She looked over Elizabeth's shoulder. "Lesson plans?"

"I keep trying to figure out how to make it all fit together better."

"Mmm." Tracy wandered over to the window to look out at the very first students who were arriving. It was the hardy souls who had early morning clubs or small music group rehearsals, along with the handful who simply preferred being at school to being anywhere else.

Then she turned around to lean against the sill, sipping at her still steaming coffee, and watched Elizabeth work. A few moments later Gavin barreled through the door and slid a box of doughnuts across the table. "Morning, ladies!" he called.

Elizabeth looked up again. "Hey, Gavin."

He cast a glance at her book. "Still planning, I see."

"There's got to be a way to make this work better."

"Eh, don't knock yourself out. It'll be better next year."

Elizabeth was starting to be frustrated by that pat answer. Yes, she would have a year of experience under her belt, and yes, she'd get lesson planning figured out eventually. But there would always be papers to grade. How could you teach writing without generating papers to grade?

Why doesn't anybody get that? she thought. All she said by way of reply was, "I know."

Tracy pushed off the sill and headed for the door. "Good luck with the adjustments." With that statement, she was gone.

Gavin gawked at the doorway where a moment later, Paul appeared. "Morning," he said, and laid his jacket over the back of a chair. He pointed back toward the hallway. "Still not socializing, I see."

Elizabeth looked up again and finally it hit her. "Actually, she did speak to me this morning." She made a face at the two men. "I think we're making progress."

Gavin had regained his senses by this time. "I saw you two talking before church."

Elizabeth nodded. "I knew it needed to be done. I just hadn't done it yet." She tapped her pen against the table. "That's not like me."

Paul looked thoughtful. "There's a lot that can be chalked up to being a first year teacher," he said.

"I know," Elizabeth said, leaning back in her chair and stretching her arms overhead. "But there's other stuff too. It's not right to blame all of it on the job."

"Oh, I don't know," Gavin said and reached for a doughnut. "It's a handy excuse."

Elizabeth laughed. "Seriously?"

"Yup," he said and stuffed the doughnut in his mouth.

The tweaks Elizabeth had been working on in her lesson plans had to do with the literature unit she was currently in with her sophomores. She wanted to employ more of the discussion method from Sunday School that she enjoyed so much, but so far, the results were mixed. The big problem? Nobody was reading.

"Morning, everybody," she said to her yawning first hour students. "Pop quiz." The groans were audible from every corner of the room. She raised her eyebrows. "Just need to see how you did with your reading assignment."

A few minutes later she collected the papers and said, "Let's open to chapter five. We're going to read aloud today."

More groans. "I'm not forcing anybody," Elizabeth said. "I know some people aren't comfortable with it. But it's important you read the book one way or the other, and I hope this will spark some interest. Now, who wants to go first?"

The students shifted in their seats and refused to make eye contact. "Extra credit if you do." Half a dozen hands immediately shot into the air. She grinned and took down names. "Excellent."

Elizabeth had no problem bribing her students for cooperation. A little bit anyway. The few points she offered weren't going to make or break a grade, and the students who liked extra credit were also the ones who didn't need it.

At the end of the day, she was happy enough with the discussion they'd generated by reading aloud that she figured she'd use the technique again, at least occasionally. Over supper that evening, she rifled through the quizzes. The results were dismal, of course, but some of the answers were hilarious, and she had to give silent praise for their creativity. Writing was writing, after all. Wasn't it?

By midnight, however, she had moved on to junior essays and was a great deal less amused. Plus, she was nowhere near the end of the pile. On a whim, she dashed off an email to her English advisor back at UC.

Hey, Professor Martens! How is everything going for you this fall? I'm enjoying teaching but am overwhelmed by grading. Any suggestions for how to keep it manageable? I appreciate any ideas you might have.

Thanks,
Elizabeth Shepard

Then she dragged herself off to bed. *Please God, let this get easier,* she thought just before dropping off to sleep.

17

The whole week passed without JB coming around. Thomas was surprised; he'd figured his friend would blow it off after a couple of days. But on Friday, when Karen deigned to come in at her regularly scheduled time to clean, he discovered the reason why he hadn't.

Every time she passed by where Thomas was working, she threw dagger glares at him. Every time she passed by where JB was working, he'd reach out to make contact and she'd slap his hand away. If Karen was mad at Thomas and taking it out on JB, then in JB's mind, it was Thomas's fault.

Of course.

The upside to it all, which Thomas didn't think about until he went to bed that night, was that they didn't ask him to go out with them—or to pay. So it was that he had the entire cold and rainy Friday evening at home free from his friend group. While he would have preferred to be working on his car, at least this was better than spending all his money being out with them.

He watched a movie instead. It was a good break, even if it was a little bit lonely.

The next morning was sunny, and he got half a day of work on his car before the rain started again. As he packed up his tools and headed home, he wondered what he should do with the rest of the day. On a whim, he dialed Roger's number as he was eating his lunch.

"Thomas! Hello. How are you?"

"Pretty good. I wanted to update you on how things went."

"Of course. Would you like to come over?"

"That'd be good."

When Thomas arrived, they sat in the living room again, but this time Nancy brought out cookies with the coffee. "I apologize," she said, "I didn't have any made the last time you were here."

"Oh, that's okay," Thomas said, surprised by her words. He hadn't expected cookies. He hadn't even expected coffee.

She went back into the kitchen, and Thomas told Roger about the meeting and about how things had been at work all week. "At first I thought it was a bad thing JB was mad, but maybe it's not."

"How so?" Roger asked.

Thomas sought the right words. "It's kind of like both problems got dealt with at once."

"It does seem that way, doesn't it," Roger mused. "Do you value your friendship with JB?"

"Well, yeah."

"And your sister?"

Thomas felt obligated to answer the same.

"Then at some point you'll have to address the issue." He held up his hand. "I know it's convenient, because it took care of the other problem, but it has created a new one."

Thomas crossed his ankle over his knee and fiddled with his boot laces. "Is it wrong to just want the break for a little while?"

Roger shook his head. "No. We all need time away sometimes from the people we care about. Even husbands and wives."

Thomas blinked in surprise. "Really?"

"I'm not talking about separation or walking out in anger or anything like that." He stopped and thought for a moment. "On occasion, when Nancy and I are discussing something and we think differently about it—and we do—" he added, looking at Thomas, "—sometimes we'll take a time-out. We'll each go to a different part of the house so we can pray and think and calm down." He leaned forward in his chair. "But the important thing is that it's only for a time. We always come back together and address the issue later on."

This was a totally new idea to Thomas. His parents didn't discuss things at all. It was more like his dad spoke, and that was it. Anything his mother said came after the fact in the form of grumbling and complaining, usually while she was carrying out whatever her husband had decreed.

Thomas was pretty sure he liked Roger and Nancy's way better. "It makes sense," he finally said. "But it sounds hard."

Roger chuckled. "It's not easy, but it's worth it."

The two of them checked their coffee. It was cool enough to sip, but just barely. Roger offered the plate of cookies and Thomas chose two. Then Roger set the plate back down, selected his own, and said, "Nancy wasn't feeling too well on Sunday, or she would have come home from church and made cookies then too."

Thomas stopped chewing and swallowed quickly. "Then why did she invite me to lunch?"

Roger's eyes crinkled as he smiled. "That's how she loves and serves others. We both knew you had something important on your mind, and she was willing."

Thomas looked off toward the kitchen. "Is she feeling better?"

"Oh, yes," Roger reassured him. "She has some back problems and whenever they flare up, the best remedy is for her to lie down for a while."

Thomas took another sip of his coffee and then looked down at it. "It makes me feel bad she even made coffee, if she was hurting."

Roger studied him for a moment. "That's kind of you, Thomas. But you know, just as Christ made the sacrifice of his life on the cross for us, we each have sacrifices that we make in living out our faith. Ours are much smaller, of course..." He took another bite of his cookie and chewed thoughtfully.

Thomas was reminded of how he'd felt at church camp the summer he was thirteen. When the youth leader had explained about salvation and Thomas had prayed the prayer to accept Christ as his savior, it was like someone had given him an unexpected gift. He felt guilty and unworthy, but also incredibly grateful. Just like now.

Then another thought sprang to mind. *Am I making any sacrifices in my life? For my faith?* He furrowed his brow.

"What are you thinking?"

Startled, he looked up. "What? Oh." He set down his mug. "I was trying to figure out if I'm doing that in my life. Sacrificing anything. I'm not sure."

"It's a good question to ask ourselves on occasion. It helps us to walk more closely with God."

"I'm gonna have to think about it some more."

Roger nodded and set down his own mug. Then he leaned back in his chair and said, "I was curious how you plan to spend your free time now that you're not going out with your friends?"

Thomas bobbed his head. "I always want to work on my car."

"Yes," Roger said simply.

"Last night I watched a movie."

Roger nodded. "I wonder if it's time to work on building some new friendships."

Thomas hesitated. "I don't know how to do that."

"Well," Roger said, "as Nancy and I have been praying for you, we've had the idea of hosting a fellowship gathering for the Sunday School class. It'd be an opportunity for everybody—" he spread his hands wide, "—to get to know each other better."

Thomas heard all the words, but his brain zeroed in on just one sentence. *They prayed for me?* Before he realized what was happening, he said it out loud. "You guys prayed for me?"

"We did."

"I didn't even do that for myself." He felt embarrassed to admit it. After all, Roger had prayed with him last Sunday afternoon. Thomas just hadn't thought to do it on his own.

"God longs to hear from us," Roger said. "It's one of the main ways we're in relationship with Him."

"I mean, I do pray, just not about stuff like that." Thomas thought for a moment. "Does He really care? About stuff like that, I mean?"

"Oh, Thomas, God cares about every single aspect of your life, clear down to the very number of hairs on your head. He wants to hear about everything."

Thomas had never thought of God as someone he could talk to. He wasn't used to having anyone in his life he could do that with. It was only sheer desperation that had driven him to seek out Roger, and even that had been hard.

"I guess that's something else I have to work on," he said.

"Just remember, this is a lifelong journey we're on. We'll all be working on this stuff the whole time." Roger winked at him.

"Yeah." Thomas ducked his head.

"So what do you think of the fellowship idea?"

"Oh, yeah, sorry. I like it."

"Excellent! I'll talk to Nancy and we'll get the ball rolling." Roger paused for a moment and then said, "You know, it's just like God to work in this way. He brings together the people and the circumstances to accomplish His will and to take care of each one of us."

Thomas pondered this for a bit and then said, "I don't get it."

Roger inhaled deeply. "Well, I think that all these things are working together for good, like it says in Romans 8:28. All the life events that caused you to reach out to me. The prayers, the idea for a fellowship gathering—even the backache." He raised his eyebrows and shrugged. "God is using all these things to teach all of us and draw us closer to Him."

Thomas swallowed hard against the lump that had formed in his throat. "I never thought about God being close before. He—" He stopped and sighed. "He always seems pretty far away." Thomas looked down at his boots.

"It could be that He's reaching out to draw you closer to Him now," Roger said gently.

Thomas looked up and locked eyes with the older man. "I'd like that."

Roger nodded. "Keep praying, Thomas, even when you're not sure what to say to Him. In fact, let's pray together right now and then we'll talk more about this next time we get together." He stopped and raised his eyebrows. "If you want to, that is."

"I do," Thomas said.

On his way out the door, Thomas poked his head in the kitchen. It reminded him of doing the same on Sunday afternoons at his parents' house. The difference was that Nancy's kitchen had a sunny warmth that emanated from within, even on a cloudy day.

"Thanks for the cookies, Mrs. Beck," he said.

Nancy wiped her hands on a towel and came over to give him a hug. "You are most welcome, Thomas. And it's Nancy." She held him at arm's length. "You know that."

Thomas grinned. "Yes, ma'am."

"You also know you're welcome here anytime, right?" Nancy asked.

Thomas was touched by this. "Thank you."

18

At the beginning of class on Sunday, Nancy handed out fliers for the fall fellowship gathering. "Roger and I will provide the meat. You all get to bring the sides. Oh, and if anyone wants to pitch in, we'd welcome the help!"

"Ooh, I'd love to!" Becky Fleming said. She looked at her husband and he nodded in agreement.

"Anything we can do to help," he said.

Normally Elizabeth would have been glad to lend a hand too. But right now the thought just seemed overwhelming. Was it right for a job to take so much of her life that she couldn't do all the other things she loved? She was sure of the answer to this question but not of its solution.

The next thing she knew, Roger was closing in prayer. She had zoned out for most of the lesson. Mortified, she bowed her head just in time to hear him say, "Amen." Sighing, she gathered her things and headed for the door. Thomas met her there and fell into step beside her. "Hi," he said.

"Hey."

"Sounds like a fun event."

For a moment, Elizabeth was blank. Then it registered what he meant. "Oh, the gathering. Yeah, it does."

They walked a few more steps in silence and then Thomas asked, "Everything okay?"

"Oh, yeah. I'm just tired."

Thomas regarded her thoughtfully. "You've been tired a lot."

Elizabeth looked up at him in surprise. *He'd noticed that?*

"How come?" he asked.

"First year teaching. It's about to kill me." She chuckled self-consciously. "Not really." Then she wrinkled her nose. "Sort of."

"Sounds like you need a fellowship gathering. Take your mind off work." He grinned and then looked away.

"Maybe," Elizabeth mused. "It does sound fun." She glanced over at him again and saw him still smiling. It was a good look on him. "It's nice to see you smile," she blurted out.

Thomas looked back at her in surprise. Elizabeth felt her face grow warm and grabbed for the sanctuary door. Thomas helped pull it open. "After you," he said, motioning her through.

"Thanks," she replied, grateful for the redirection. She stepped inside and went straight to her usual seat in the teachers' section. She tried not to watch as Thomas continued on his way through the sanctuary to join his family.

Before long, Tracy slid in beside her. All week she'd been returning to her normal self, bit by bit. At least, the self that Elizabeth had first met. She was surprised, honestly, and had she been a betting woman, would not have laid money on this outcome. Still, though, she was glad for it.

"Morning," she said.

"Hey," Tracy replied, casting an appraising glance her way. "You look sleepy."

"Pfft, always." Then, "Hey, we're having a fall get-together for Sunday School. You should come."

Tracy wrinkled her nose. "No, thanks."

"Why not? It'll be fun."

"When is it?"

"Uh." Elizabeth pulled out the flyer. "Week from next Saturday."

"Well, there you go. I have plans."

Elizabeth raised an eyebrow. "Really?"

"Really."

"You always have plans."

"Nothing wrong with that. You should too." Elizabeth squinted at her. "You know," Tracy said, leaning in close. "Like going out on dates. Having fun."

The twisty knot tightened in Elizabeth's gut. *Dang it,* she thought, deflated. *That really is it. One mention of dating and that's my response.* The fact irritated her, but exhaustion soon turned that irritation to despair. She simply had no capacity to deal with it right now.

Elizabeth sighed and almost shook her head, then remembered who she was talking with. She waved a hand breezily. "Can't. I'm a workaholic."

Tracy scoffed. "Right." She paused and then said, "You can't let the job take over your life, you know."

"Can't be helped," she said, still being flippant. "The English classroom generates a lot of assignments to grade."

"Well, stop it."

Elizabeth laughed and then turned serious. "It's kind of hard when the very thing I'm supposed to be teaching is writing."

"Mmm. Maybe you need to hire somebody to grade all the papers for you."

Something clicked in Elizabeth's mind. *Wouldn't that be fantastic? To let someone else do all that work?* But before she could consider it any further, the music started. Elizabeth shook herself to attention and filed the thought away for later. She didn't want to miss the church service too.

19

On the Saturday morning of the party, Elizabeth made her mother's creamy coleslaw and a homemade chocolate cake. Even that small bit of work in the kitchen felt good. Normal. She hadn't been cooking much since school started. To her surprise, it also helped the afternoon of grading papers to feel less like drudgery. She couldn't be sure, though, if it was the cooking itself or the event she was cooking for that made her feel better.

The first people she saw when she walked through Roger and Nancy's door that evening were Becky Fleming and Paul's wife, Sabrina. Becky motioned her over, and after dropping off her food in the kitchen, she joined them.

"Elizabeth, hi! How are you?" Becky gave her a big hug.

"I'm good. How about you?"

"Fantastic! Hey, you've met Sabrina, right?"

"Briefly, yes. You're Paul's wife, right?"

"That's right."

"I have to tell you how grateful I am to him, and all the teachers," Elizabeth said, motioning to Becky. "Everyone's been so supportive, helping to keep me sane. So far, anyway." She made a face.

Sabrina smiled. "I know when Paul first started teaching, he was working all the time and so tired! Poor guy. But he finally figured out how to manage."

"I hope I do too," Elizabeth said.

"Oh, you will," Becky reassured her. "It just takes time."

"So, I can't keep this to myself any longer," Sabrina said, wriggling with excitement. "You guys want to know a secret?"

Elizabeth wasn't one for gossip, but she didn't even have time to answer.

"I'm pregnant!" Sabrina half-whispered and then gave a tiny squeal.

"Oh, my gosh, Sabrina! That's fantastic!" Becky embraced her friend.

"Thank you!"

"Wow, congratulations! This is your first?" Elizabeth asked.

"It is. Now, we haven't actually started telling anyone yet, so—" Sabrina put a finger to her lips.

"Of course," Becky said and turned an invisible key against hers.

"I won't say a word," Elizabeth agreed.

"Well, I gotta scoot," Sabrina said. "I'll talk to you guys later."

Becky and Elizabeth watched her bounce across the room to find another group of female friends. Elizabeth wondered how many people would be sworn to secrecy before the night was over.

"That's so awesome," Becky said, turning back to Elizabeth. "Daniel and I are ready to start a family too."

"Really? That's great!" Then Elizabeth shook her head. "I can't even imagine adding a family into the mix of teaching. How will you do it?"

Becky smiled, her face shining. "It'll all work out. I can't wait."

Becky's enthusiasm was infectious, and Elizabeth had a huge smile on her face when she looked up and saw Thomas coming in the front door. She raised a hand in greeting. His eyes lit up, and he returned the gesture.

Becky saw the exchange. "You two seem like you know each other."

"A little. He and his dad do farm service calls. My folks are older, so my dad has been calling on them for a long time. He's glad not to have to do the repairs himself. Anyway, that's how we met."

"Oh, that's nice. I bet it was good to have a familiar face when you moved to town."

Elizabeth hesitated. "We don't know each other all that well. He and his dad were only out two or three times a year. Then in high school we'd run into each other at sporting events when our two schools played each other, but that's about it."

"I see." Across the room, Becky's husband was shaking Thomas's hand and welcoming him into a group of men who were talking together. "You said your parents are older?" Becky asked.

"Yes." After a pause, she added, "My dad's seventy-seven."

Becky's eyes widened. "Oh, my!"

"And my mom is sixty-five."

"Do you have older siblings?"

Elizabeth shook her head. "No, it's just me. My folks always wanted children but could never have any. Then one day, long after they'd given up hope, Mom got sick. Not even thinking about pregnancy, they thought it was the flu, or cancer, or who knows what. You know how the mind works."

Becky nodded.

"Anyway, they went to the doctor, bracing for the worst, and came home with the best." Elizabeth smiled as she reminisced. "They're great parents."

"That's an amazing story, Elizabeth."

The familiar sting of tears was behind her eyes. "I do worry about them, though."

Becky put her hand on Elizabeth's arm. "Well, of course you do!"

"It's part of the reason I wanted to move back to this area. To look out for them."

Becky's eyes crinkled and she gave Elizabeth a little squeeze. "I imagine they're very happy to have you so near."

"I know I am. Cincinnati was too far away."

At that moment, Roger called for everyone's attention and they gathered around to pray over their meal.

Thomas had been surprised to find himself looking forward to the party on Saturday. Maybe Roger was right. Maybe it was time to find new friends. It seemed like so many things had been changing in his life recently. Many of them were good changes and he was grateful, but he was still trying to get used to them all.

One change was that he was praying more. Trying to, anyway. It wasn't easy because he had no model for it. For as long as he could remember, Thomas had never seen his family pray for anything except a meal.

Another change was the picture of God he carried in his head. Before He'd always seemed so distant, but what was it Roger had said? That God cared about even the number of hairs on his head? Somehow, that felt good. It made Him feel closer.

When he woke up on the day of the party, the weather was good, so he decided to venture out to work on his car. Before he got out of bed, though, he prayed. "Dear God, I hope it goes okay with me working on my car today. And at the party tonight." He thought for a moment, wondering if God knew what he meant. Unable to figure out any better way to say it, he closed. "Amen."

Perhaps God did understand, because his day went off without a hitch. He worked until mid-afternoon and then cleaned up. Under normal circumstances, he would have kept on working until dark. But today was not normal circumstances. Today, he had a party to go to.

So far so good. That's what Thomas was thinking after Roger's prayer over the food. Upon arrival he'd been drawn into a group of men and actually joined the conversation. Some, anyway.

Now they were filling plates with food and settling down to eat. Tables had been set up wherever there was space for them.

"Hey, Thomas, why don't you join us over here?" Daniel Fleming motioned toward a round table where Becky, Sabrina, and Elizabeth were already seated. Paul, Sabrina's husband, was behind him in line.

"Sounds good." Pfft, who was he kidding? It sounded great. He never could have made that happen on his own—to get to sit at the same table with Elizabeth and with the guys he'd already been talking to.

He balanced his plate while selecting a cup of cider and headed toward the table. The seat next to Elizabeth was empty. As he set his plate, silverware, and drink down, Elizabeth glanced up at him. "Hey, how are you?" she asked.

"I'm good. How about you?"

"Doing all right."

"Glad to see you decided to come," he said as he sat down.

"Eh, you were right. I needed some time away from work."

Thomas grinned bashfully. "Yup." Then he picked up his hamburger.

"You work at the automotive shop, right, Thomas?" This was Sabrina. Thomas nodded, since his mouth was already full. "I thought so. I'm going to have to bring the car in sometime soon."

"Why, what's wrong with it?" Paul wanted to know.

"You know, it's got that noise," Sabrina reminded him.

"Oh, right. I forgot."

"The infamous noise." Daniel nodded knowingly. He turned to Thomas. "Any idea what that might be?"

Thomas grinned again. "Nope. But I'm sure we can figure it out."

"It's kind of like when I get a phone call and somebody says, 'My pipes started gurgling. Why is that?'" Daniel said.

"Oh, Daniel!" Becky chided. "Be nice."

"I am. It's just funny to talk about." Becky made a face at him, but her eyes were twinkling.

The conversation continued to swirl around Thomas, and he was content to let it. He especially liked hearing Elizabeth laugh.

The next time he joined in was with this question from Becky. "So Thomas, what do you do outside of work?"

"Uh, well, I fix cars."

Sabrina wrinkled her nose. "Really? You fix cars all day and then go home and fix cars?"

"Sort of," Thomas said. "I buy old junkers to fix up and resell."

"Oh, nice!" Daniel said. "What're you working on right now?"

"It's an old Honda..." At this point Paul and Daniel tuned in to what Thomas was telling them about his work, and the women drifted off into their own conversation. Pretty soon people were getting up for second helpings and then dessert.

When stomachs were full and meal trash discarded, several of the women went into the kitchen to help cover what remained of the food. Roger directed the guys to take down the tables and rearrange the chairs. Becky was right beside him, making sure everything was just so, because she had organized games.

Once everyone was back in the main room, she clapped her hands and called them to attention. "Okay, everybody, listen up! We're going to play some games." The response was a mixture of groans, some real and some affected. Thomas didn't know what to think; he wasn't used to playing games.

"Oh, stop it!" Becky said. "It'll be fun. The goal is to get to know each other better. So here's what we're going to do." As she talked, she handed a pen and three note cards to each person. "Write one question on each card, something you'd like to learn about someone else. And make sure it's NOT a yes or no question."

After a few more moans, the scuffle and chatter died down as people began thinking and writing. Thomas sat for a moment, wondering what to ask. He thought of the things he'd like to know about Elizabeth. Things like, what was college like? Did she miss it, or was she glad to be back and living in Sutton? But those were too specific. Then he thought how glad he was that she hadn't married somebody. He wondered if she'd come close but quickly pushed the thought aside. It wasn't a good question to write down either.

He tried again. *What kind of questions do you ask people you want to get to know?* He had no idea. The only questions he ever asked strangers were, "What's going on with your car?" and "When do you want to bring it in?" Then he thought about the things he'd like Elizabeth to know about him. As he pondered this, he looked around and saw that he wasn't the only one struggling. Mostly it was the guys. The girls were all writing furiously.

Finally Thomas bent his head and scribbled down three questions that he thought were reasonable to ask in a group.

Once everybody was done writing, Becky gathered up the pens. "Now we're going to pair off and ask each other one of our questions. When you're both done answering, you trade the cards and change partners. Does that make sense?"

"Wait, we don't keep our same cards the whole time?"

"Nope," Becky said. "That way we learn a whole lot of different things about people! Now, to make it easy to pair off, we're going to draw numbers. After that, it's up to you who you switch with."

Thomas was relieved to find that his first partner was Paul. At least it was somebody he'd already spoken to. Paul, while he didn't seem to be uncomfortable with the game, also didn't seem to care too much about it. "What's your favorite food?" he asked Thomas.

So many to choose from! Thomas had thought the hard part was writing the questions, but now he had to answer them. And this one should have been easy! Finally he chose one from among his many favorites. "Fried chicken and mashed potatoes."

"Oh, yeah," Paul said. "I love KFC."

"Sunday dinner at Mom and Dad's," Thomas said.

Paul's eyes grew big. "Every week?" Thomas nodded. "Wow, can I come over?"

Thomas chuckled. "Sure." Then he selected one of his cards. For a moment he grew self-conscious, but then he plucked up his courage. "What's your favorite memory from growing up?"

"Oh, wow. That's a good question." Paul thought for a moment and finally offered up his answer. Then Becky rang a small bell. The two men exchanged cards and moved on to the next person. By the time they'd rotated through half a dozen partners, Thomas found that he was enjoying himself. The game got easier with practice.

Then the bell rang again and he found himself face to face with Elizabeth.

"Hi," he said.

"Hello," she replied.

They stared at each other for a moment, Elizabeth smiling and Thomas feeling completely at a loss for what he was supposed to do.

"You want to go first?" she asked him.

"Oh, okay." Thomas shuffled through his cards, trying to decide which one to ask. Abruptly he said, "What's your biggest fear?" and glanced up at her.

Elizabeth's smile faded and her eyes grew serious. For a moment, Thomas thought he'd made a big mistake. Then Elizabeth tried to smile again. Her eyes were bright and when she spoke, her voice was choked. "Losing my parents."

Thomas exhaled in relief and then immediately felt guilty. What she'd said had registered. "You worry about them, don't you?"

Elizabeth swallowed and then nodded. She looked down at her cards and rotated through them. Then she sucked in a breath and said, "What's yours?" She peered back up at him.

Thomas blinked in surprise. Could she really have that question written on her card? What were the odds?

And how on earth was he supposed to answer?

Being without you.

Startled, Thomas exhaled. It was an honest response from the depth of his being, but there was no way he could say it out loud. Instead he stared at her, his jaw working as he tried to figure out a reply.

The bell rang. They both flinched at the sound. Thomas looked down at the cards in his hands and selected the top one. "I didn't really have that question on my card," he said and handed it over.

Elizabeth looked sheepish. "Neither did I." She handed him a card, they traded partners, and the game continued on.

When Thomas got home that night and slid between the sheets, he laced his fingers together behind his head and thought about the evening he'd just experienced. It was so different from the time he spent with JB and Karen and Dee Dee. He'd had fun, and the games had helped. He'd talked to so many people and said more during this one evening than he often did in an entire week.

And Elizabeth. His heart was full as he pictured her in his mind. For a long time he lay there, still and quiet, savoring the feeling. *Thank you, God,* he thought, and then was glad he'd thought it.

As he turned over to go to sleep, one more thought occurred to him.

Maybe, just maybe I could ask her out for a date.

20

When Thomas woke up the next morning, he knew that's what he wanted to do. He wanted to ask Elizabeth Shepard for a date. And he didn't figure there was any reason to wait. He'd do it right after Sunday School.

What he hadn't counted on was the increased camaraderie among his classmates since the party. He enjoyed it before and during class, and even participated a little bit, but after class was a different story.

Things started out normally enough with Thomas waiting for Elizabeth at the door. When she walked up, she grinned. "Isn't this fun? I'm so glad Roger and Nancy decided to host a party!" They left the classroom and headed toward the sanctuary.

"Me too," he agreed. "But Elizabeth, I did want to say sorry if my question last night made you sad."

She looked up at him in surprise, and then her eyes softened. "That's very kind of you, but not necessary. It was a great question." Then she added, "It just has a hard answer."

"Yeah." It made Thomas sad for her—and that he could do nothing to change it for her.

"You know you never answered mine," Elizabeth said. Thomas looked over at her, startled. Her eyes were full of mischief.

"I—" he began and then stopped. He still had no idea how to answer that honestly, at least not without embarrassing himself.

Elizabeth laughed good-naturedly, and before either of them could say anything else, more students from class caught up and engulfed them in their post-party chatter. The whole group swept through the door of the sanctuary as one and then peeled off to find their seats, including Elizabeth.

Thomas stood a moment just inside the doorway and watched her go. His opportunity had been swept through the door along with his classmates. *Now what?*

The fellowship was good, but—well, he enjoyed being with Elizabeth more. As he pondered what to do next, he moved across the sanctuary to where his family sat, as silent and segmented as the Sunday School class had been connected.

Thomas hardly noticed, though. He was still thinking about Elizabeth. *Maybe I can talk to her after church,* he thought. He never had before. And if asked why, he would not have been able to say.

"Hey, girl," Tracy called as Elizabeth slid in beside her.

"Morning. You should have been there last night. It was fun!" Elizabeth said.

"Been where?"

"At the Sunday School party."

"I thought there was something different about all the people who just came in." Tracy looked up and followed Thomas with her eyes as he made his way across the sanctuary. "Even him."

"Who?" Elizabeth looked up from the bulletin she'd been perusing.

"Thomas." She dipped her head in his direction.

"Oh, right. I think he talked more last night than I've ever heard him before."

Tracy turned to scrutinize her. "Really?"

"Mm hmm." Elizabeth was bent over her bulletin again. "We were sitting at the same table for the meal," she explained. "Later the whole group played games; it was great. I'm glad I went."

When Tracy didn't respond, Elizabeth looked up. "What?" she asked.

"Nothing."

Elizabeth paused, wondering if she should push. But things had been going well between them, and she didn't want to ruin that. "Okay," she finally said.

She couldn't help but be curious, though. In the couple months she'd known her, Tracy had always spoken her mind. If she didn't, what did that mean?

When the music started, Elizabeth worked hard to focus her attention on worship. Struggling, she said a brief prayer and then pushed the exchange with Tracy from her mind.

"Hey, you wanna grab some lunch?" Those were Tracy's first words after the benediction.

Surprised, Elizabeth said, "Sure." They'd never done anything together outside of school and church before.

The two women scooted out quickly to beat the lunch crowd at a local restaurant. Once they'd placed their orders and gotten their drinks, Tracy said, "There is something I want to talk to you about."

I knew it, Elizabeth thought. Out loud she said, "Okay."

"It's just, last time you got pretty defensive."

Elizabeth squinted. "You mean last time when you were teasing?"

"Yeah, then." She said no more.

"Well, are you teasing now or do you want to have a serious conversation?"

"A serious one."

Elizabeth dipped her chin. "Okay, then. Let's do it."

Tracy took a deep breath and exhaled. Then she pierced Elizabeth with a steady gaze. "You always walk out of Sunday School with Thomas."

Elizabeth nodded. "He always waits for me."

"You know why that is, don't you?"

The twisty knot came back into her gut. "Tracy—"

"Look, all I'm saying is that he's crazy about you."

"I—" Elizabeth stopped and pressed her fingertips against her forehead. Then she sighed. "I think he has been for a long time."

"Well, then!"

"But he's never acted on it."

"Maybe he just needs a little encouragement."

"That's not—"

"Not what, Elizabeth?" Tracy interrupted. "Not what you want?" She raised one eyebrow and said in a singsong voice, "That's not how it looks to me."

Elizabeth's jaw dropped. "I enjoy his company, walking from Sunday School. What's wrong with that?"

"Nothing."

"Then what's this all about?"

Tracy just shrugged her shoulders and smirked.

"Tracy!"

She raised her hands in surrender. "I'm just saying, you got a guy right there ready to go. What are you waiting for?"

"I—" Again Elizabeth stopped. She closed her eyes and a thought popped into her head. *What am I waiting for?* Startled, her eyes flew back open and she stared across the table at Tracy, who gave her a sideways glance. "I'm not ready to date anybody," she said.

Tracy frowned. "Why not?" When Elizabeth drew in a shuddery breath and let it back out again, Tracy's eyes widened. "Did you have a bad break-up?"

"Sort of. A guy from college. We dated for two years, but we had different goals. It wasn't going to work, but he just wouldn't let it go." A chill ran up her spine and she exhaled sharply to get rid of it. "It was a rough summer. I just need a break, that's all." Then she threw out her hands. "Which makes me mad, because I like going out!"

Tracy leaned forward eagerly. "Then you need to just do it! Find someone to push all those bad memories out of your brain!" She tipped her head and grinned suggestively.

Elizabeth shook her head. "I don't think that's the solution. Not for me." Tracy quirked an eyebrow but Elizabeth ignored her. Instead she picked up her iced tea and sipped. She could not see how playing fast and loose with a nice guy's feelings could possibly make her feel better. On the contrary.

Tracy leaned back in her seat, and then grabbed her own drink. She sucked down a third of her pop while eyeing Elizabeth closely.

Elizabeth was lost in her thoughts, but she did stretch, and yawn, and then rub her face. "Oh, man," she said, as the last of the adrenaline rush from the prior evening drained away and left her feeling tired once again.

Tracy set her drink down abruptly. "Are you still not sleeping?"

Elizabeth grimaced. "Nothing's changed. I'm still trying to survive my first year of school. Remember?"

"Well, there's your problem, E!"

Elizabeth raised an eyebrow at the new nickname. "What do you mean?" she asked, and then promptly yawned again.

"You start getting some sleep," Tracy said, tapping the table between them, "and I guarantee you'll be ready to date again."

Elizabeth scoffed. "Oh, okay. I'll just magically start getting all this grading done faster."

Tracy chuckled. "I get it; the first year is hard. But it will get better."

"How? I can see it for you and Paul and Gavin in your subject areas, but I'm always going to have all these papers to grade! How does that ever get better?"

"Hmm." Tracy rested her chin in her hand and drummed her fingers against her cheek. "I don't know, but you can't let it ruin your life."

Elizabeth groaned and leaned her head back against the booth.

The waitress appeared and placed two sandwich and salad platters in front of them. Elizabeth offered a brief prayer over their food. She then placed her napkin in her lap and said, "I know you're right; I just haven't figured out how to do it yet."

Tracy raised her chin in acknowledgement but said nothing because she was already chewing. Elizabeth poked at her salad and then said, "I liked your idea of hiring graders. I also reached out to my advisor at CU." She paused. "I haven't heard back yet."

Tracy swallowed. "Reach out again. Sometimes people forget."

"I will." She finally took a bite of salad and then asked, "Does that have to be approved, you suppose? To use graders?"

Tracy bobbed her head. "You could always just do it and claim ignorance."

Elizabeth scoffed. "And lose my job in the process."

"Just get another one."

She couldn't believe her friend's cavalier attitude. "With no references? No thanks. Besides, this location's perfect for me, and honestly, I like the size of the school."

Tracy tipped her head back and exhaled. "Not me."

This took Elizabeth by surprise. She'd not heard Tracy say anything about being unhappy in her position. "Really? What are you looking for?"

Tracy shrugged. "I don't know." She turned her attention to her salad and said no more.

Elizabeth started on her sandwich. *Why does she stay here if she doesn't like it?* she wondered. She decided against asking that question out loud, though. Instead she said, "There is one thing I miss about my time in Cincinnati."

"Oh, yeah? What's that?"

"Theater."

Tracy looked up. "Really?"

"Yeah. I loved going, whenever I could afford it. That's the only bad thing about living in a small town. No options."

Tracy snorted. "Oh, I can think of a lot of bad things about living in a small town."

Elizabeth wrinkled her nose. "Then what are you doing in one?"

"Biding my time. But, listen. If you like the theater, then you should go." She leaned forward in her seat. "Take a date."

Elizabeth pointed her finger at her. "No." Tracy snickered. Then Elizabeth had an idea. "You come with me."

"Yeah, right." Tracy laughed. Then she thought for a moment and said, "You serious?" When Elizabeth nodded, she stared at her for a moment and finally said, "Sure. Why not?" Then she picked up her sandwich and polished it off.

The two women spent the rest of their lunch in lighter conversation, talking and laughing—and looking up theater events to go to.

Elizabeth followed up on her email to Professor Martens that afternoon and was rewarded with a same-day reply.

Elizabeth, it's wonderful to hear from you! I'm sorry I didn't get back with you sooner.

I'm glad you're enjoying your job, but I certainly understand the stress of grading. I feel like it's something we should cover better, especially for English teachers.

At any rate, there are several things you can try, including rubrics, a coding system, and outside help.

Let's get together by phone and talk. Let me know what works for you.

Hang in there,
Prof M

They scheduled for later in the week, and Elizabeth came away with some great tools she could implement on her own, as well as great advice on how to approach her principal about hiring graders. The problem was, it was going to take time to get all of that established, so for now she just had to keep plugging away.

The net result was that she came to the Sunday School class that next weekend as tired as ever.

21

When Elizabeth hustled out of church the week before, Thomas was disappointed but not discouraged. He figured he'd just try again next Sunday. But as he thought it over during the week, he realized it might not make sense to ask her in the hallway between Sunday School and church after all. After worship, they would have more time and could find a less busy space to talk. So that's what he planned to do.

They still walked to the sanctuary together, though, after Sunday School. Elizabeth was quiet, and he thought, looked tired again.

"How's your job going?" he asked.

She yawned and then shook it off. "Sorry. Same as always. Too much grading to do."

Thomas thought this over for a minute. "I would've been okay with less writing in English. Bet your students would be too." He grinned mischievously and looked away.

"Very funny," she said. "I'm sure you're right, but..." She shrugged. "It's my job."

"Yeah." Thomas pulled open the door to the sanctuary, and they parted ways.

He planned to catch back up with Elizabeth right after worship, but instead, Daniel and Paul hailed him from the next section over.

"Hey, Thomas," Daniel said. "We've got a question."

"What's up?"

"After class this morning, I was talking with Roger," Paul said. "We'd like to start a men's Bible study. Would you be interested?"

Thomas had never been in a Bible study before. When he was in school, he had participated in youth group. For him, it was much like Sunday School; he listened but said little. This seemed like a good opportunity to learn—and to spend more time with other people.

"Yeah, that sounds good."

"All right! Are there any evenings that work better than others?"

The only thing Thomas ever did in the evenings was work on his car—or hang out with his friends. Since that second one wasn't happening anymore and the first one was starting to give way to the season, his schedule was pretty free. "No, I'm flexible," he said.

Daniel spoke up. "If there's any topics you're interested in studying, let us know. Roger asked us to collect ideas."

"I'll give it some thought."

The trio continued to talk as they made their way out the door and into the parking lot. Eventually Becky and Sabrina made their way over, and for the first time in his life, Thomas stood around after church with a group of friends and talked. Much to his surprise, he liked it.

Then he saw Elizabeth exit the building and head toward her car. "Excuse me," he said to the group and headed toward her.

Elizabeth's brain was foggy and she couldn't wait for her nap when she got home. Maybe even before lunch this time.

"Hey, Elizabeth."

She turned to see Thomas walking toward her. "Hi. What's up?"

"I wanted to ask you a question."

"Okay. Do you mind if we keep walking? I am so ready to get home and sleep."

Thomas furrowed his brow. "Is it really that bad?"

"Yeah, I guess. I dunno." She waved her hand in the air. "I've got some ideas to make it better, but they're gonna take time."

"I wish I could help."

Elizabeth stopped and turned to look at him. She could see the concern on his face. For a brief moment, she felt something tugging at her insides, but it didn't feel quite like the twisty knot. Then she smiled and said, "That's sweet of you. You want to grade papers?"

"What? No!" He looked horrified and Elizabeth laughed.

"Oh, well. It was worth a shot." They walked past a few more cars and then Elizabeth stopped. "This is me. What did you want to talk about?"

His face was serious. "Maybe you just need to take a break from it sometimes, you know, like you did for the party."

Elizabeth bobbed her head. "Maybe." She looked down at her car, ready to climb in and get home to her nap.

"Like, maybe go out to eat. With me."

Elizabeth froze. Then she turned, almost in slow motion, to look up at him. "W—what?"

Thomas gave her a shy half-smile, but he held her gaze. "I'd like to go out with you, Elizabeth."

Stunned, Elizabeth couldn't speak. Exhausted, she couldn't think. She just stared.

"What do you say?" Thomas finally asked.

What do I say? she thought. *What DO I say?*

"I can't believe you asked me out," she said. *I can't believe I just said that!* she thought.

A small crease lined his forehead. "Why not?"

"You never did before. In high school."

"I know." Thomas dipped his head.

Elizabeth looked out across the parking lot. She still couldn't think.

"Elizabeth?" She turned back and saw him watching her, calm, serious, hopeful. Waiting patiently for her reply.

"Oh, Thomas. I don't think I'd be a very good date right now."

The light in his eyes faltered. "Why not?" he asked again.

"Well this, for one thing." She held out her hands. "I'm exhausted. I just don't have the bandwidth to give to anything else right now. I—" She stopped and blew out her breath.

"It's okay," Thomas said. He looked away, but the disappointment was evident on his face.

"I'm sorry," she said in a small voice.

"I hope you can get some sleep," was his reply. He directed the words to her shoes.

At a loss, Elizabeth unlocked her car. Once she was inside, Thomas closed the door for her and then walked away across the parking lot. She watched him go, the twisty knot lodged firmly in her gut.

Or wait—was it the twisty knot? She couldn't tell. Her hand shook as she put the key in the ignition. *I'm a basket case when I'm tired,* she thought.

Elizabeth was starving when she woke up three hours later. Starving and groggy and—oh yeah. The parking lot memory came screaming back into her consciousness.

So that wasn't a dream.

She still couldn't believe it. She could not believe that Thomas Schaefer had worked up the courage to ask her out. After all this time! Elizabeth stretched her arms over her head and yawned. Then she got up and went into the bathroom. As she splashed cold water onto her face, it occurred to her how coincidental it was that he asked her out so soon after she and Tracy discussed how he'd never asked her out in an entire decade.

She scowled into the mirror. Would Tracy really have done that? Would she have talked to him despite what Elizabeth said? While she didn't think so and didn't want to think so, the truth was, she wasn't sure.

Now she had to decide if she was going to confront Tracy about it or let it go.

Elizabeth went to the kitchen and got some lunch. As she was reheating leftovers from the night before, another thought occurred to her. Thomas had been kind even though she said no. Quite gentlemanly, in fact, closing her door for her. Elizabeth blew her breath out between her lips. More so than anybody from college had ever been. Especially—

Oh, there it was. The other reason for saying no. Chad. Elizabeth shook her head in frustration. When was he going to quit ruining her life?

Elizabeth grabbed her plate out of the microwave. *How exactly is he ruining anything here? It's not like I was actually thinking of saying yes.*

Was I?

It had never been a real question before. Not with Thomas Schaefer. People had crushes all the time and never acted on them. You didn't have to make decisions on those. You just enjoyed them. But Thomas had changed the game. He had acted.

And now Elizabeth had no idea what she was supposed to do.

22

Even though Thomas was always quiet, at this day's family dinner he was also distracted. So much so that his father noticed and spoke sharply to him when he wasn't attentive enough to his mother's chatter.

Karen's head popped up, always on the alert for any chance to tear him down. "Go ahead, Mom," she said. "*I'm* listening." She stared at him, eyes glittering, daring him to fight back.

But he didn't. Instead he just said, "Sorry, Mom."

"Oh, it's all right," she said, raising her eyebrows and poking at her mashed potatoes. "I know you have more important things on your mind than listening to me."

You have no idea, he thought.

Thomas left right after the meal, knowing full well that by doing so, he was offending his parents yet again. But he just couldn't do it. He couldn't stay. He needed to get alone with his thoughts so he could sort them out.

As it was, he didn't stay at home, either. He changed clothes and then immediately drove back over to his parents' house. The weather was decent, and he needed to be busy too. He went out to the carport and got to work. Not five minutes later, the back door opened and his father came out.

"You working on Sunday, son?"

"Yep."

"You know I don't—"

"Let me be, Dad. I just need to—be here." He looked up at his father and then back down at his work.

Jack stood with his arms crossed and stared at him for a few seconds, brow furrowed. Then he said, "All right," and turned to go back into the house.

Thomas could scarcely believe he'd spoken to his father that way. He was equally surprised that his father had let him.

He poked around under the hood of the car for a few minutes and then decided he wasn't in the mood to do anything major. Instead, he got out his sanding kit and set to work on some of the smaller patches of rust that were on the car's body. The motion was so familiar he could do it in his sleep. Eventually he relaxed and his thoughts started flowing.

Thomas had never asked anybody out on a date before. Taking Dee Dee to prom his senior year didn't count.

I don't want to think about Dee Dee.

Thomas dropped the sandpaper. He grabbed a rag to wipe away the grit and see where he stood. Still some rust. He set to work again.

He knew Elizabeth was tired from her job. She had said so repeatedly.

Maybe I should have waited to ask her.

Until when? Next summer?

Thomas frowned at a particularly stubborn spot. He was hoping to get the surface rust off without damaging the paint too much, but it looked like this one might go deeper than that.

What if it was an excuse and she just didn't want to go out with him?

How am I supposed to figure out the answer to that question?

Thomas left the stubborn spot for another time and moved on to the next section of the car.

He wondered what should happen next. Like, could he still talk to her after Sunday School? Or would she not want him to?

Maybe that's how I'll know if it was an excuse. If she lets me talk to her.

He had hoped not to have any major paint job repairs on this project, just because it meant he for sure wouldn't get this vehicle finished until next spring. If the weather had been better—or if he'd had a shop—he could have flipped this one before Christmas.

Thomas sighed. The truth was that right at this moment, he just felt bad. In his mind, thoughts about Elizabeth had always equaled possibility. Now they simply felt like dashed hope.

Why, God?

As he uncovered additional rust spots that needed repair, Thomas resigned himself to the fact that this car was going to take more time and more labor than he'd hoped. It wasn't the end of the world, but he was just going to have to be patient and work through it.

23

"Morning," Tracy said as she walked into the teacher lounge. Elizabeth was at the counter, pouring a cup of coffee.

She looked up at Tracy, contemplating, so it was a moment before she replied. "Morning."

Tracy got a mug out of the cupboard and looked over at her. "You good?"

"Not sure."

Tracy raised an eyebrow. "What's up?"

Elizabeth leaned toward her and spoke softly. "Did you talk to him?"

"Who?"

Elizabeth tipped her head and pressed her lips together.

Tracy looked bewildered for a moment, and then recognition dawned. "Do you mean—" She looked around the room and then whispered, "Do you mean Thomas?"

"Uh huh."

"No! I wouldn't do that. I was just joking when I said it."

Somehow, Elizabeth believed her. She had to ask the question, but she was sure this was the truth.

"Why?" Tracy sucked in her breath and peered into Elizabeth's face. "Did he—?"

"Uh huh."

"He asked—" She lowered her voice again. "He asked you out?"

Elizabeth nodded.

"Oh, my gosh! What'd you say? You said yes, right?"

"I did not."

"What?" Tracy almost shouted. "Are you insane?"

A couple of teachers from across the room who were seated on the sofa and chatting together stopped and looked up at them. Tracy waved them off.

"Are you crazy?" she whispered.

Elizabeth exhaled heavily. "No, I'm tired."

"Elizabeth!"

"I don't—I can't—" She raised her hands to her head and then thrust them into the air. "—do it right now." Then she leaned her forehead against the cupboard.

Tracy reached across to grab the coffee pot and fill her mug. "If you weren't tired would you have said yes?"

"I don't know." Elizabeth huffed and turned around to lean up against the counter. "If he'd asked in high school I probably would have said no. He was really quiet. So shy."

"You're not in high school."

"I know that."

"And you've been away at college. You're both grown-ups now."

"I know that! But you're missing the point. I'm not in dating mode right now. I told you before."

"Because of your job."

"Yes." For a brief moment, Elizabeth felt the absurdity of the statement. Now that she was—as Tracy had so helpfully reminded her—an adult, there was always going to be a job. Was it going to keep her from ever living a life? Or was it just an excuse?

Then Elizabeth yawned. The day hadn't even started yet, and she was tired. Her exhaustion was definitely real. Everybody kept saying, "First year." She was ready to start replying, "English teacher."

Equally as real, however, was the fact that she could not let it rule her life. At least not forever. She had to figure out how to make the job manageable, and that was her priority right now. Everything else just had to wait.

Tracy turned to lean against the counter next to her and tested her coffee. Then she said, "Just don't let him slip away, Elizabeth."

Elizabeth frowned. Her friend was still focused on Thomas. She turned toward her. "After all this time you think he'll suddenly get over it?"

"Stranger things have happened."

Elizabeth pondered this. It did seem that some people flitted in and out of emotional attachments as easily as they changed clothes. But not Thomas. This was ten years they were talking about, so it didn't seem likely. Then she was annoyed with herself. Why did it even matter?

Did it matter?

"Why do you care about this so much?" she asked abruptly.

Tracy shrugged. "I don't know." Then she turned to face Elizabeth. She had the same smirk on her face that she'd had at church when they first spoke of him. "I think it's cute how much he likes you."

"Very helpful, Tracy. Thanks."

Tracy clicked her tongue and winked. "Anytime."

24

On Tuesday afternoon, Thomas pulled a newer model car into his bay. He needed to check codes, but the diagnostics tool wasn't in its usual place.

Without giving it any thought, he said, "Hey, JB, you using the scanner?"

JB looked up in surprise. The two of them hadn't spoken in over a month. "Yeah. I mean, I'm done with it." He disconnected it from the truck he was working on and handed it to Thomas. "Sorry."

"No problem."

On Wednesday, Thomas clocked out at noon and went into the breakroom for lunch. He bowed his head in prayer, and when he looked up, JB was standing in the doorway. "Hey," Thomas said.

"Mind if I come in?" JB asked.

"Nope."

JB plunked his lunch box down on the table and sat across from Thomas. "I was getting tired of fast food."

Thomas grinned. "Yup." Then he took a bite of his sandwich.

On Friday afternoon at five, they met up at the time clock. JB paused and looked at Thomas. Then he punched his card and put it in the slot. As Thomas punched his, JB said, "Kinda miss hanging out."

Thomas nodded. "You should come over sometime. We could, I don't know, watch a movie."

"Just me?"

"Yes. Just you," Thomas said, looking him straight in the eye.

JB nodded. "Maybe...go-karts?"

Thomas thought this over. He did like go-karts. "You pay your own way."

JB dropped his head and chuckled. "Yeah. Okay."

On Sunday morning, Thomas rounded the corner on his way to Sunday School class and almost ran into Elizabeth.

"Oh! I'm sorry," he said.

Startled, Elizabeth chuckled. "It's okay." She hesitated and then said, "Good morning."

Thomas regarded her solemnly. "Good morning. How are you?"

She bobbed her head. "I'm doing all right."

"Getting any more sleep?"

Elizabeth pursed her lips. "I'm sorry," she whispered.

Thomas was embarrassed. "I shouldn't have asked that."

"No, it's okay. I really am trying to figure out how to do this job and not let it kill me. It's just going to take some time."

Thomas thought for a moment as they walked toward the door. "Do you like teaching?" he asked.

She looked up at him thoughtfully. "I do. I really do."

"Then I know you'll figure it out." He held out his hand for her to enter the room ahead of him.

After worship, Daniel and Paul caught up with him. "Bible study's a go," Paul said.

"Tuesday evenings at my house," Daniel added.

"Okay," Thomas said. "That sounds good."

"I know we're getting close to the holidays, but what would you think of starting this fall anyway? Or do you think we should wait until after the first of the year?" Paul asked.

Thomas had never really felt the frantic hustle of the holiday season that people talked about. His life was pretty much the same day in and day out. Holidays were just longer Sundays at his parents' house.

"I say start now," he said.

"My man!" Daniel said, holding out his fist to bump. "That's what I thought too. By the way, did you have any ideas for what to study?"

"Uh," Thomas hesitated, uncertain what the two men would think of his suggestion. But it was something he was very interested in, so he gathered his courage and said it anyway. "Yeah, I kind of thought I'd like to learn more about prayer."

"Oh, that's a good one," Paul said.

"Yeah, it is. I think we could all stand to learn more about that," Daniel agreed. "Okay! I'll check in with Roger and we'll start a week from Tuesday."

When Thomas arrived home after Sunday dinner, he turned off his truck and for a moment just sat. So much had been happening lately—at least from his perspective—that he wasn't sure what to make of it all. He wasn't used to things happening in his life.

He decided to call Roger.

When he picked up his phone to dial, he thought back to their last meeting and realized it had been a month.

"Thomas! Hello," Roger said.

"Hi. I know we haven't talked in a while. Sorry about that. I thought maybe we could catch up today."

"No need to apologize. I'd love to catch up," Roger said. "Do you want to come over?"

Thomas hesitated. "How is Nancy feeling?"

"Nancy?" Roger asked. "She's fine. Why?"

Thomas was embarrassed. "I just didn't want her to go to any trouble if, you know, her back was bothering her."

It was a moment before Roger replied. "That's very nice of you to think of her," he said, his voice soft. "Today, she is doing well. And I think she would love to have somebody to feed cookies to."

Thomas chuckled. "Okay. I'll be right there."

After Nancy served the coffee and cookies, Thomas shared with Roger what had taken place at work that week. "All I did was ask for a tool."

"God can work through a tool."

Thomas blinked. "You think that was God?"

"Do you?"

He considered this for a moment. "I don't know. I hadn't thought about it like that."

"God is always at work in the lives of His people, even when we don't recognize it."

Thomas picked up his coffee and took a sip. Then he said, "How do you know?"

"That God's at work, you mean?" When Thomas nodded, Roger continued. "The Bible assures us of this truth in many places." He pulled a book toward himself that was sitting on the coffee table. It was a black, leather-bound Bible. When he opened it, Thomas could see pencil markings and notes written in the margins on lots of pages. "In Philippians Paul tells us, 'It is God who works in you, both to desire and to work for his good pleasure.'" Roger looked up. "In other words, when we accept Christ as our Savior, the Holy Spirit comes to dwell within us. He begins changing us to want the things that God wants, and then He guides us toward doing those things."

Keeping his finger in Philippians, Roger turned to the Old Testament. "One of the promises God gave to His people, the nation of Israel, is in Jeremiah. 'I know the plans I have for you, plans for good and not for evil, to give you hope and a future.'" Roger paused to pick up his coffee mug and take a sip. "These words continue to bring hope and comfort to those of us in His church today as well."

Thomas had never felt like there was much hope for his future. For most of his life, things always just continued on as they were, in ways that Thomas didn't necessarily like. Even his own recent efforts to bring about change had mixed results.

Roger set down the mug and turned back to Philippians. "Then Paul reminds us of this, 'He who began a good work in you will bring it to completion at the day of Christ Jesus.'"

"What does that mean, 'at the day of Christ Jesus?'" Thomas wanted to know.

Roger paused in his page turning. "Ultimately it means when we're with Him in eternity."

"So...not in this life," Thomas said.

"Well, we're moving toward it in this life. We seek to know God here so we can enjoy Him there."

When Thomas furrowed his brow, Roger said, "As Christians we still go through difficult things in our lives, but God reassures us in Romans that 'for those who love God all things work together for good.'"

"For good," Thomas mused. "For knowing God."

"Yes," Roger said simply.

Thomas inhaled deeply and let it out slowly as he thought. It seemed crazy that all the troubles with his friends—and even his family—could draw him closer to God. He didn't feel like they had. But then again, he was here talking to Roger because of those very things.

"It'd be nicer if we could know God without things being so hard," he said.

Roger closed his eyes and nodded. "I think we all feel that way, but the wisdom of Proverbs reminds us to 'trust in the Lord with all your heart, and lean not on your own under standing.'" He stopped and thought for a moment. "God is all-knowing; we are not. Plus, when things are going well, we tend to forget to lean on Him."

Thomas brushed his fingers through his hair as he thought. "Does God allow bad things on purpose, just so we'll lean on Him?"

Roger didn't answer immediately. He tapped his finger against his Bible as he thought. "I want to be careful here. God doesn't orchestrate bad things for that purpose, but He does work through them when they happen. He uses them for good—to help us recognize our need for Him and to draw us closer to Him."

So life, thought Thomas, *even my life, is filled with opportunities to draw closer to God.* This was a brand new way of thinking about things. To him life had always just felt...difficult. But to consider there was the possibility for good in all of that?

Roger turned some more pages in his Bible. "Let's see," he said, skimming to find what he was looking for. "Ah, here it is. In John, the writer gives us the words of Jesus himself, 'I have said these things to you, that in me you may have peace. In the world you will have tribulation.'" Here he looked up at Thomas and raised his eyebrows before finishing the quote. "'But take heart,' says Jesus. 'I have overcome the world.'"

Thomas could have thought those words were written just for him. For twenty-three years, he now realized, he had been living hopelessly, even after he'd accepted Jesus as his Savior.

But all the passages Roger was sharing with him from the Bible spoke of—promised, even—peace and hope, no matter what his everyday life was like.

Roger's eyes crinkled when he smiled at him. "In other words, none of our trials can change our eternity with God when we have Christ as our Savior. Peter writes of this promise, that we can cast all our anxieties on God, because He cares for us."

Roger stopped and thought for a moment and then flipped again to where he was holding his place in Philippians. "There are so many promises in God's Word, but I want to share just one more for now. Paul reassures us, 'Do not be anxious about anything, but in everything by prayer and pleading, with thanksgiving, let your requests be made known to God. And the peace of God, which surpasses all understanding, will guard your hearts and your minds in Christ Jesus.'"

Roger closed the book and ran his hand across the cover before gently placing it back on the coffee table. "It's a lifelong journey and a daily—sometimes even a moment by moment—rededication to trusting Him, in all things."

Thomas picked up a cookie from off the tray and took a bite. Then he said, "So, prayer."

"Indeed," Roger said. "That's the best way to communicate with God."

"I'm not very good at it."

"Thankfully, God's not grading us." Roger smiled. "And honestly, pretty much everyone feels the same way you do. The key is to start wherever you are and seek to grow in your prayer life—not to worry about how well you do it."

Thomas nodded. "I gave that to Paul and Daniel this morning as an idea for Bible study." He looked up, uncertain what the older man would think of this.

"To study about prayer, you mean?" When Thomas nodded, Roger said, "That's a good idea. Hmm." He then selected a cookie from the tray and said, "Why don't we pray together now? Then we can get serious about finishing off these cookies. What do you say?"

Thomas grinned. "That sounds good."

25

In the weeks that followed, Thomas and Elizabeth each got busy on Sunday mornings. Thomas, for example, got taken up with the men's Bible study group. They were enjoying their new camaraderie and were on fire for what they were learning about prayer. For her part, Elizabeth was beginning to work on her proposal for hiring graders, and it consumed her thoughts. She spent a lot of time talking about it with her fellow teachers, asking questions and getting feedback.

Thomas wasn't sure how to manage both things—his desire to connect with the other men and his desire to connect with Elizabeth. When she so easily filled up the space he used to inhabit with conversations of her own with other teachers, Thomas thought maybe she didn't want to talk to him anymore. Uncertain if it was okay to try talking with her anyway, he didn't.

When Elizabeth saw Thomas so readily give up their brief time together after Sunday School to spend it talking with some of the men, the seed planted by Tracy took root in her mind, and she thought he was avoiding her. Unwilling to trifle with him if she was in fact not ready to date, she didn't try to entice him back into it.

It didn't prevent her, though, one Sunday morning when they happened to make eye contact across the table in class, from greeting him. It was her natural inclination to be friendly, and before she even thought about it, she smiled and lifted a hand.

When the greeting wasn't returned, she felt it must be validation of Tracy's claim and concluded that Thomas truly was no longer interested. Somewhere deep in her sleep-deprived brain, this made her sad.

The actual truth, however, was that Thomas wasn't even aware that he hadn't responded. He was thinking about the *no* behind the smile and wondering if, all along, the smiles had been nothing more than general friendliness, the kind she would show to anyone.

On Thanksgiving, Elizabeth headed out to the farm to spend the day with her folks. Usually she loved this day, but this year everything just felt wrong.

For his part, Thomas never would have said holidays felt right to begin with. The added loneliness he felt this year was just more of the same. He wasn't sorry to have an emergency tow call come in. It got him out of the house and gave him something to think about other than Elizabeth Shepard.

At least for a little while.

Part Two

Elizabeth came back from Christmas break rested, and that made all the difference. She had her finished petition in hand, lesson plans outlined for second semester, and her new grading toolkit ready to go.

In other words, she felt like herself for the first time in months.

All except for her lingering sadness about Thomas. That was new. But Elizabeth tried not to spend much time thinking about it. She couldn't. She knew what she was facing this semester, even with the grading tools she intended to use. Long-term, she was hanging all her hopes on that petition and praying it would be approved. If it wasn't, she didn't know what she'd do.

When she pulled open the door to the old high school building on the first day back, Elizabeth felt like a pro. She knew what to expect this semester, and she was ready to get to it.

But first things first. She walked down to the principal's office and knocked on his door.

"Come in." Mr. Brownlee looked up from a stack of papers. "Miss Shepard! Did you have a good break?"

"I did! Much needed."

He smiled knowingly. "What can I do for you?"

"I wanted to give you this petition. I'm hoping the district will approve hiring graders for my English classes next year." Mr. Brownlee opened the folder and skimmed the contents as Elizabeth continued. "Besides keeping me sane, I believe outside assessment will be good for the students. All my research is in there."

"Looks very thorough." He closed the folder. "I'll read it over more closely once we get back in the swing of things." He looked up at her. "I'm glad you value having your students write."

"Oh, yes! Honestly, I think it's the most important thing we do in my classroom."

"I agree," Mr. Brownlee said. "Now I can't promise anything, but I do think the school board will be interested in helping you to succeed in that—and not burn out in the process."

"Thank you, Mr. Brownlee."

"You're welcome. Now let's have a good semester!"

They did in fact have a good semester, and for Elizabeth it started off first thing in January with her junior unit on *The Catcher in the Rye.*

"Welcome back, everyone. We're going to start this session with literature." Groans came from every corner as Elizabeth handed out the books. "Cute, but you don't need to worry. There will be plenty of writing to go along with it." She stifled a smile as some of the students wilted in their seats.

She returned to the front of the room. "Okay, first impressions. Let's look at the cover. Tell me what you think."

At first there was nothing more than uncomfortable silence. Elizabeth waited. Finally, one of the braver souls raised her hand and said, "It's a horse, right?"

Elizabeth nodded.

Another student blurted out, "What's rye?"

"It's a grain. What else?"

The students were beginning to warm up a little, and more questions came out.

"Why does the horse have a pole through his neck?"

"Yeah, and why is the cover so red?"

"The horse is dying."

"Gross!"

"Idiot, if the horse was dying the blood would be underneath him."

Elizabeth intervened. "All right, comments welcome, name-calling not. Great questions, everyone. As we're reading this book, we'll try to answer them. What I want you to do now is write one paragraph—"

The groans were louder this time. Elizabeth raised an eyebrow. "Really? If the hardest thing you ever have to do in life is write a handful of sentences, you've got it made." She scanned the room, daring anyone to disagree. Satisfied, she continued. "—one paragraph on why you're going to absolutely hate reading this book."

She got her response and smirked at her students. "After that, you can start reading."

Over the next several days, the juniors spent their time reading the novel and writing additional unexpected paragraphs, including this one on the day they finished: *how I think differently about this book now than I did a week ago.*

"Pfft, I don't," one slouch in the back said.

"Oh, you do," Elizabeth reassured him. "You either hate it more or you hate it less." That comment got a few laughs. "Either way, you know more about it now than you did a week ago, and that in itself changes your thinking. Tell me how in your paragraph."

The next day, Elizabeth said, "All right, let's talk about your post-read impressions. Who wants to start?"

After a moment of thoughtful silence, the comments started rolling in.

"I wish I could disappear for a weekend."

"What happened to him at the end?"

"Yeah, like did he get sick and die?"

"No, dope, he was telling the story afterward."

"No name-calling," Elizabeth cautioned. "What else?"

"He sure had a lot of freedom."

"Pfft. I didn't think he had any."

Elizabeth's pulse quickened. Some of these kids were thinking.

"I didn't like Holden."

"Why not? I did."

And on it went. Elizabeth went to the board and began writing down their comments. "Okay," she said when they were finished, "for today—" A ripple of laughter moved through the room; they knew a writing assignment was coming. "—take one of these topics, and write about it. That's all the direction I'm giving you."

Throughout the unit, Elizabeth enjoyed reading the written assignments in a way she had not all last fall. She was staying up way too late doing it again, but somehow she didn't begrudge it.

The next morning, Elizabeth opened with this question. "Some of you liked Holden. Others didn't. Whichever way you felt, tell me why."

"I could never decide if what he said was true or not."

"Yeah, that was weird."

"But I think he thought what he said was true."

"What about when he said stuff like, 'I don't want to talk about it,' and then turned around and said, 'I want to talk about it'."

Elizabeth jumped in. "Why do you suppose he did that?"

A quiet young man spoke up for the first time. "I think he was kind of full of himself, telling this story, and he was talking to hear himself talk."

Elizabeth nodded thoughtfully at this. Another student added, "I kind of felt like he wasn't really sure what he thought."

She stopped for a moment. "Almost like he said something he thought he believed, and then as he talked about it, realized he believed something completely different."

"Yeah, but he did it over and over again!"

Elizabeth responded. "It sounds like you feel the character, in this sense, never changed throughout the book. Is that accurate?" The girl nodded. "Anybody disagree?"

The class was quiet on this one. Elizabeth wasn't surprised.

"Was he supposed to change?" someone finally asked.

"What do you think?"

The class was silent for so long that Elizabeth changed tack. "Tell you what, let's use this to write about today. It's obviously a tough question, so just write your thoughts as they are now, even if they're scattered. Just get them down on paper."

Elizabeth watched as her students got busy, a satisfied smile on her face. This unit was another thing she had worked on over Christmas break, and she could not have been happier with how it was going. She'd seen more engaged writing and heard more thoughtful discussion than on any unit she'd taught last semester. Her sample size was small, of course, but she was sold. She planned to use this model again with her other classes.

The next day she handed out the final writing assignment. "First, I want to commend you all for your work on *The Catcher in the Rye*. You've read, written about, and discussed this book. Now it's time to think about it in relation to yourself. Your last paper on this unit is to be a discussion of your final valuation of the book—and of your study of it—along with its impact on you."

The sigh of disbelief was audible.

"I know it sounds like a big undertaking. That's because it is. But studying anything is a waste of time if it doesn't impact us in some way. Sometimes we have to fight to understand what that impact is. That's what I'm asking you to do now. Cement this in. Love it or hate it—it really doesn't matter. Just make the time we've spent on this unit mean something."

"Miss Shepard?" It was the quiet boy. "What did you think of this book?"

Elizabeth opened her mouth and then closed it again. "How much of an answer do you want?"

"I really want to know!"

Elizabeth was surprised to hear several murmurs of assent from among his classmates.

"All right," she said. "I'll share my thoughts with you, but only after you've written your papers."

"You should write one too," Slouch called from the back.

Elizabeth raised her eyebrows. "That's a good idea. I think I will."

2

The Catcher in the Rye
by Elizabeth Shepard

Believe it or not, I had never read The Catcher in the Rye until last summer when I was preparing to teach this year. My first impression was shock. I hadn't expected to encounter that much strong language in a book on the high school reading list. It's not that I mind strong language in a book—as long as it serves a purpose. I do, however, mind if it's overdone or added just for shock value. In those cases, it doesn't add to the story but rather gets in the way of it.

My final impression, at the close of the book, was annoyance. When I read a work of fiction, I want to join the main character on a journey. Physical or emotional, it doesn't matter. It just needs to be a trek in which our hero is dealing with his tough issues in such a way that he changes. That doesn't mean he has to solve every problem. It doesn't even require a happily-ever-after ending. The hero just needs to grow in some way before the story comes to a close.

And come to a close it must. Whatever the author's purpose in sharing this slice of life with us, at the last page we want to be able to say within ourselves, "Yes, that was the right place to end our journey together," even when we don't want to end our journey together.

Catcher, in my opinion, ended with no apparent character growth and no closure. Some might argue the opposite, that Holden recognizes he can no longer stay on the carousel of childhood. I don't see it. When our narrator, Holden himself, steps out of his story to say goodbye in chapter twenty-six, he's still the same Holden he's always been. I see nothing but hopelessness in this small slice of his life.

And that left me at a loss for how to present this literature unit in any meaningful way. I wrestled with it for a long time because I failed to see the value in presenting such a pointless struggle.

Then last fall I experienced a struggle of my own in trying to survive this job. Going through that difficulty, seeking help from others, and taking action to fix it—those things have value, and they changed me. When I compare my experience with Holden's, I find that I much prefer my own. But, if I must find value in this work, then let it be this: that the study of hopelessness might encourage us not to give in to it. Rather, may it spur us on to seek hope for our own lives wherever it may be found.

3

The congregation cheered the day Ted Johnson announced he was offering a financial management class at the church once again, but not because they were excited about financial management.

"Jane tells me it's time to get out of the house," Ted explained from the lectern. "She says I'm driving her crazy." After the polite titter, they couldn't help but break into applause. Jane was done with chemo and in remission once again.

Thomas was as happy as everyone else about that news, but he was also interested in the class. He recalled hearing about it in years past, but he'd never paid attention before. Now he was thinking about money all the time—and how he didn't have any. Maybe the class could help him with that.

He signed up right away.

That evening, when he prayed over his supper, he included his thanks to God for the opportunity to take the class. As he ate, he sort of felt like it was an answer to prayer, only he'd never actually prayed it. Then he wondered if God sometimes counted our thoughts as prayers and answered them anyway.

It was a cool idea, but Thomas came down on the side that he wanted to actually pray the prayers. To remember to lift things like that up to God. He was trying, but sometimes it was hard.

The very next week, Paul approached him about starting a men's prayer group. It would be separate from Bible study and give the men of the church a place to pray together and support one another for anything they wanted to lift up. As he spoke, Thomas had the distinct feeling that God had answered his thoughts once again.

"So what do you think?" Paul asked.

"I think it'd be good. I know I can use all the help I can get when it comes to praying." He watched Paul closely to gauge his response.

"Amen to that," Paul said. "It's why I want to do it. Our Bible study made me realize how important it is—and how much we all struggle."

"Yeah," Thomas agreed.

"You want to help me talk to the guys, see who's interested?"

Thomas blinked. He'd never helped plan before. "Sure. I'd be happy to."

Right then and there Thomas offered a silent prayer of thanks to God for answering his thoughts about praying. Then he asked God to help him remember to go beyond thinking and lift it all up to Him.

As he left worship and drove to his parents' house for Sunday dinner, he thought back to something Roger had said. Living out his faith was a lifelong process; there would always be something more to learn. He needed to remember that, both to encourage himself to keep learning and also to keep himself from despairing over what he did not yet know.

That night, Thomas got a piece of paper and wrote down the things he wanted to remember to pray about. It included his class and the new prayer group as well as the men's Bible study. He stopped and thought for a moment, and then wrote down the word, "Elizabeth." She was never far from his mind but again, he wanted to be purposeful about praying for her. For them. He wasn't sure if there was a them or ever would be. He just knew it's what his heart wanted.

Thomas placed the paper on his bed stand and used it every night to talk with God.

The financial class that winter and spring was everything he prayed it would be. By the time it ended, he had learned how to track his expenses and plan his purchases, and for the first time in his life, he was saving money.

And the best part? Thomas knew exactly what he was saving for.

4

Mr. Brownlee appeared in the open doorway of Elizabeth's classroom during her planning hour a few weeks into the semester. "Knock, knock," he said. "Can I bother you a minute?"

"Sure; it's no bother." She put down her pen. "Unless I'm in trouble. Then I'm busy." She grinned.

Mr. Brownlee chuckled. "No, nothing like that." He leaned up against the wall just inside the door and crossed his arms over his chest, tucking his hands into his armpits. "I took your proposal to the school board meeting last night. I wanted their input and blessing since this is something new for our district. They'd like to hear from you about it at their next meeting."

Elizabeth blinked. "Really? Are they interested or...?"

"Oh, they're interested. They were impressed with your research on what other districts are doing, and they liked that you included costs. I answered a few questions for them but really they want to talk with you." He pushed off the wall. "They meet again in two weeks. I'll touch base with you before then." He headed out the door.

"Thanks, Mr. Brownlee," Elizabeth called after him. He raised a hand in acknowledgement as he strode toward whatever was next on his list.

Elizabeth waved her fists in the air. *Maybe this is going to happen after all!* she thought. *Thank You, God, for bringing it this far.* As she silently said the words, she realized she hadn't actually prayed about her petition before now. So she prayed again. *God, help me to remember to lift this up to you over the next couple of weeks.*

She wasn't usually nervous about public speaking, but this was something new and she had a lot riding on the outcome. In the days leading up to the meeting, every time she started to worry, she prayed. *Funny how that helped me to remember,* she thought.

On the night of the meeting, she and Mr. Brownlee sat for an hour and a half before their item came up on the agenda. Elizabeth couldn't help thinking about how many papers she could have graded in that amount of time.

"Okay," said the board chair. "Next up is the petition to hire graders for high school English writing assignments." She paused and shuffled some papers. The other board members took the opportunity to lean back in their chairs and stretch—or check their phones for messages. "I think we have one of our teachers here with us this evening?"

Elizabeth took a deep breath and stood up. "Yes, ma'am. Elizabeth Shepard. I teach freshman, sophomore, and junior English."

Her introduction produced an audible response from the board members. One portly gentleman leaned forward in his seat and said, "Well, no wonder you want help grading. That's a lot of students!"

At that comment, Elizabeth relaxed a little bit. "Yes, sir, it is." She moved to the aisle and walked to the podium. "I understand the board has some questions for me."

"Yes we do," the chairwoman said. "First, we've all read over your proposal, and I must say, it was well done. It makes me confident that your students have a very capable teacher guiding them." She paused and looked up and down the row to her fellow board members for their agreement.

"Thank you," Elizabeth said.

"Yes, the proposal was fine," said another member, a local business woman. "And I understand that reducing time on task is the main reason for it, but what I want to know, Miss Shepard, is what do you see as the drawbacks of this request?"

Elizabeth warmed to the task. "I love that question," she said, "because every methodology for completing this part of the job comes with trade-offs. The first was getting no sleep." A couple of the board members chuckled. "My entire first semester is a blur because of it. Hired graders will allow me to be more rested, but at the cost of being more disconnected from my students' work."

"Exactly," the business woman said, leaning forward as she spoke. "And how is that okay?"

"Well, communication for one," Elizabeth said. "The graders will alert me of concerns as well as outstanding work. Plus, I will still be grading some of the assignments myself. Just not all of them."

The woman bobbed her head to the side and sat back in her chair.

Another member spoke up. "My question has to do with ensuring that the graders are doing a good job. Who will assess them?"

"I think that will come from several places," Elizabeth said. "For one, I as the teacher should review a random sampling of their work. Second, I'm sure they should answer to Principal Brownlee. And third, I think it'd be worthwhile to get feedback from the students."

"You want the students to grade their graders?" This came from the fifth and final member of the board.

"In a sense," Elizabeth said. "Between my classes I've got about 150 students. I'm sure there will be a few who won't take it seriously, but aside from those, we should be able to get a pretty reasonable picture of how the graders are doing from that number of responses."

The board fell silent and after a few moments, the chair spoke up again. "Are there any other questions?" When none were given, she said, "Thank you for joining us this evening, Miss Shepard. It's always heartening when we see a teacher who is dedicated to helping her students succeed."

"Thank you for your time," Elizabeth said.

She left the podium and rejoined Mr. Brownlee. He leaned over and whispered, "Nice job."

"Do you think so?" she whispered back.

"Oh, yes. I'm sure of it. But hey, I'm ready to get out of here. How about you?"

"I am. Believe it or not, I have papers to grade."

Two weeks later Mr. Brownlee stopped by Elizabeth's classroom to tell her the school board had voted unanimously to approve the hiring of graders for the district's English teachers. "It won't happen until next fall," he cautioned.

"I'll take it!" Elizabeth exclaimed. She jumped up from her desk and went over to shake his hand. "Thank you so much for your help with this."

"Of course," he said. "Like I told you, we want to see you succeed and be happy here."

"So far so good," Elizabeth said. Mr. Brownlee gave her a wink and then continued on his rounds.

Sutton had a tradition of hosting a district-wide, end-of-year picnic in the city park for both faculty and staff on the final workday of the year. It was a nice way to end. Elizabeth enjoyed having time to chat with her fellow teachers without having to worry about the clock.

There was a brief meeting tucked in amongst the food, fun, and fellowship. It was light-hearted, though, and mostly for entertainment. Just before closing, the superintendent called Mr. Brownlee to the microphone.

"Thank you, Steve. As you all know, working with students is an important but sometimes overwhelming job. It doesn't matter if we're teaching, policing, or cleaning up after them. Because we've all made it through another school year, I think we should give ourselves a round of applause."

The hooting and hollering went on longer than Elizabeth would have expected. She had to admit, however, that it was a good way to release pent up steam at the close of the busy and oftentimes stressful school year. When the masses finally quieted, Mr. Brownlee continued. "On occasion, we have reason to offer special recognition to a teacher or staff member whose contributions during the school year have risen above normal expectations."

At this pronouncement, the crowd grew quiet. Sutton didn't automatically hand out awards every year, as if to fill a quota. They were indeed occasional, and as such, carried the honor of being truly earned.

"So often in our work, we are about getting through the week, the day, or even just the hour, and we don't have time to solve problems or devise long-term solutions. This is true for any of us, let alone a first-year teacher. And yet that is exactly what took place this year. Faced with the overwhelming burden of grading that every English teacher experiences—"

Elizabeth flinched. *Is Mr. Brownlee talking about me? Why would he be talking about me?* Her brain froze on the question. Then the people nearby started turning to look at her, to see her response, and she knew that he was, in fact, talking about her. Between her brain freeze and the vacuum created by so many eyes looking her way, Elizabeth missed everything else Mr. Brownlee said, until this:

"Please join me in honoring our Excellence in Education award recipient, Elizabeth Shepard! Elizabeth, come on up!"

The crowd erupted once again. For a second Elizabeth remained frozen, and then someone gave her a gentle push and she made her way to the platform. Mr. Brownlee shook her hand and handed her a plaque. Then he leaned in so as to be heard over the cheering and said, "It's been an honor to work with you this year. I hope Sutton gets to keep you for a long time to come."

"Thank you, Mr. Brownlee." She looked up at him and in that moment shook herself free from her shock. "Truly, thank you."

The town newspaper had a photographer on hand, and she and Mr. Brownlee had to pose for a shot. Then Elizabeth walked among her fellow teachers, shaking hands and receiving their congratulations.

"Elizabeth!" Becky Fleming squealed and wrapped her in a hug. "Oh my gosh, I'm so proud of you!" She held her at arm's length. "This is well-deserved."

Elizabeth was touched. "Thanks, Becky."

"We have to celebrate." Other people were leaning in to congratulate Elizabeth so Becky said, "We'll talk."

"Whoo hoo!" Gavin threw one arm around her shoulder and gave her a hug.

Paul was more restrained, offering a hand. "Nice work, Elizabeth."

"Thank you, Paul."

"You know what this means, don't you?" Gavin asked.

"No, what?" She couldn't imagine.

"Next year you get to bring the donuts!" Elizabeth laughed and wrinkled her nose at him.

Eventually people began drifting away to enjoy the summer. Elizabeth was about to do the same when she saw Tracy.

She was leaning up against a table about fifteen feet away, her hands clasped in front of her, a slight, but also slightly mocking, smile on her face. Elizabeth walked over.

"Excellence in Education, huh?" she said, taking the plaque from Elizabeth's hand. "Very nice."

Elizabeth exhaled through her nose. "It should say 'Tracy, Paul, and Gavin' on it too because I couldn't have made it through without you guys."

"Oh, please." Tracy rolled her eyes as she handed back the award. They turned to walk toward the parking lot.

"So what are you doing this summer, Tracy?"

"Eh, spending as much time on the beach as possible. You?"

"I'll probably be out at the farm."

"Working?" There was a note of derision in her voice.

"Of course! I've got to keep my fingernails dirty." She held out her hand. They locked eyes and Tracy grinned before looking away. Elizabeth continued, "But hey, there's some good theater around over the summer. Maybe we can hit a couple?"

Tracy shrugged. "Sure."

"Excellent. I'll see ya," Elizabeth said, stopping by her car.

"Later," Tracy replied and walked on.

The story came out in the paper later that week. Everyone at church and in Sunday School offered their congratulations. Elizabeth was touched by the acknowledgements, but she also felt a little silly being the center of attention just for doing her job. That's what it felt like to her, but she didn't say that to anyone at church. She did mention it to her parents when she saw them next.

"Well, now, people like to recognize good work. There's nothing wrong with that," her father said.

"I know, but we set the bar kind of low, don't we? I mean, it feels like we honor regular good ole' hard work because it's rare. That's just wrong."

"Mmm, it does seem to be the way of things these days," her mother mused. "But it doesn't change the fact that it's right to offer praise for a job well done. Just enjoy the recognition and let it spur you to continue doing a good job, even when it's difficult."

Elizabeth thought this over. "I guess you're right."

That night she hung her plaque on the wall right across from her bed where she could see it every single day.

5

Elizabeth was still enjoying the tingle from the whole affair as she worked in the flower beds around her house one morning. It felt so good to be back in the dirt. She let her thoughts roam freely as she cleared out the debris of winter and ended the neglect these spaces had endured.

She wondered how next year teaching would be different with graders on board and could hardly wait to find out. Then she scoffed at herself. *Don't wish the summer away too fast, girl!* She wondered if she could plant a vegetable garden in her backyard. *I'll have to ask the landlord.* Ever since the *Catcher* essay, her fingers had been itching to write again. *Maybe I'll do that this summer too.*

Newly unburdened by a schedule, Elizabeth felt free to embrace it all. She wanted to spend time out at the farm, take care of her home, and enjoy church without the threat of falling asleep...she would miss Sunday School, though.

Sunday School reminded her of Thomas and her thoughts shifted, focused. Despite the passage of months since they'd regularly spoken at church, she still missed that. And now that school was out and she had time to think about it, she longed for it. There was something about talking with Thomas that just seemed right to her. It didn't matter if the conversations were short; they were always meaningful.

If only she'd realized that before they ended.

The thing was, when they did end, Thomas did not fade into the background of people for her. He was always present and visible. She wondered if she'd made a mistake saying no last fall, but every time her thoughts went there, she remembered her situation at that time, both personally and professionally. There was simply no way she could have done it.

And now he seemed to have given up. It made her sad to think that simple timing could ruin what she now, finally, was starting to see as a possibility.

Her thoughts drifted again and she realized that out of all the people who had congratulated her on her award, he was not one of them. He hadn't said anything at all.

Elizabeth stopped thinking after that.

Instead, she focused on her garden. With the weeds and old leaves gone, she was pleased to find the soil soft and pliable. She worked it up with a trowel and then planned her layout. After that she dug a hole, placed a flower, and added water. Over and over again all along the front and side of her house.

Near the end of the last bed, Elizabeth jabbed her trowel into the soil to make the next hole and hit a rock. After a few failed attempts to remove it, she enlarged the space. No matter how far she dug outward, the rock was still there. She removed the topsoil until she finally came to the rock's edge and then started digging out around it. Only, it wasn't a rock; it was a boulder.

When Elizabeth finally dislodged the piece, it turned out to be nearly two feet across and several inches thick. It was flat and smooth on the top, and she brushed the dirt away easily. The underside, however, was rugged. Soil clung to its surface, filling crevices and hiding the true shape of the stone. Elizabeth brushed at it, but it was stubborn.

Inexplicably curious about what lay underneath, she hauled it over to the spigot and turned on the hose. The spray only removed a portion of the dirt, however. She went into the house to retrieve a scrub brush and then set to work once again.

The combination of time and effort finally paid off. Elizabeth turned off the water and stared. Gently undulating bands of color had appeared where darkened soil had once lived. It was beautiful. "I think you deserve a spot among the flowers," she murmured.

Elizabeth perusen the beds in front of her house until she found just the right location. She hauled the boulder over and set it in place. Then she stepped back to take a look. "I love it," she whispered.

The sun was high in the sky by the time Elizabeth finished her work. She was sweaty and tired, but satisfied. Her phone pinged just as she was putting away the last of her gardening tools. She quickly threw all the trash into the bin and then pulled off her gloves to check the message.

Hey, beautiful.

Elizabeth sucked in her breath. *Chad Somers? What the heck?*

He apparently saw when she opened the message because he immediately typed back.

Saw your award. Congrats! I'm in town. Thought we could have lunch to celebrate.

Elizabeth shook her head and then read the message again. *He's in town—in Sutton? What on earth for?*

She scoffed and went into the house. She threw the phone on her bed and headed for the shower. After she got out and dried off, she went back to the bedroom and picked up her phone.

Hey, come on. I know you're seeing my messages.

Elizabeth groaned. *How very typical. I'm supposed to be available at any moment to indulge his whims.*

Elizabeth dropped the phone back onto the bed and turned to her closet, where she selected a fresh pair of jeans and a t-shirt. As she slipped sandals onto her feet, she noticed there was dirt residue under her fingernails, despite the gardening gloves she'd worn. She smiled.

Then she picked up her phone again and contemplated the messages. *I'd be a fool to reopen this can of worms. Better just to ignore it,* she thought. She went back into the bathroom and blew dry her hair.

Still though. Why did he reach out after all this time?

As she put her hair up into a ponytail, her stomach grumbled.

Then she thought, *It's just lunch. What could it hurt? It might be fun to see what I gave up—or avoided.* Elizabeth rolled her eyes at herself.

Then she frowned. It *was* just lunch, but it was with the guy she blamed for messing her up last year.

So why am I even thinking about this?

Elizabeth scrutinized herself in the mirror, searching for the answer. To her surprise, she did not see, in the image staring back at her, the hurt that Chad had inflicted. She also did not see sorrow from wasted time, or insecurity for moving forward.

No, what she saw was herself as she was now, living where she wanted to live and doing what she wanted to do. A person who had survived a grueling first year of teaching. She wasn't the same person he had injured last summer.

She smiled at her reflection. This Elizabeth could handle one lunch with a guy who, in the space of three text messages, had revealed himself to be exactly the same as he had been back then.

She marched to the bedroom, grabbed her phone, and dashed off a note.

> *Hey, thanks. Sorry; my hands were full.*
> *Sure, we can get lunch. When and where?*

Twenty minutes later, she pulled open the door to Maddie's Diner. The noon rush was in full swing, but she managed to snag a table toward the far end of the dining room. A few minutes later the door opened and in walked Chad. He was dressed in a business suit and tie and had every hair combed perfectly into place. More than a few heads turned.

Yep, Elizabeth thought. *Still Chad.*

He looked around the room, caught her eye, and lifted his chin in recognition. Then he cast another glance at the modest accommodations and began picking his way through the tables. Elizabeth's practiced eye picked up on it right away. Maddie's Diner was not quite up to his usual standards.

"Hey," she said brightly, as he approached. She held out a hand to shake and he reached out to hug. "Oop," she said.

Chad then took her by the shoulders and leaned in to kiss her cheek. "Hi, Lizzy," he said. He slid his hands down her arms and grabbed her fingers, then leaned back to give her an appraising look.

Elizabeth pulled away and motioned to the table. "What brings you this direction?" she asked, taking a seat. She resisted the urge to swipe at her cheek. Chad didn't answer; he was busy wiping down his chair and then the table with napkins from the dispenser.

Satisfied, or at least convinced he could make it no better, he wadded up the napkins and then sat down. Still he did not answer. "You look—" he tilted his head to the side. "—comfy."

Elizabeth shrugged. "Same as I always looked."

"Yes," he agreed drily and moved the crumpled napkins to the edge of the table. "I was in Sandusky for a business meeting," he said, finally in answer to her question. "I figured I might as well stop in to say hello. Tell you there were no hard feelings."

Elizabeth pressed her lips together to stifle a grin. "Good to know," she said. *Oh, my word,* she thought.

Chad looked around the room and signaled for service. Elizabeth looked up in time to see Maddie scowl in his direction. *Oh, dear,* she thought. *It's going to be tough to keep a straight face.* She covered with another question. "So how's your job going?"

Satisfied Maddie had seen him, Chad looked over at Elizabeth. "Oh, it's going perfectly. I've already been promoted to Engineering Manager." He leaned forward over the table—after checking that there was nothing sticky to attack his sleeves. "The meeting I had this morning was with a new potential client, someone I know personally. If I land this account for the company, that's going to put me in a really sweet position with the boss." He leaned back in his seat, apparently satisfied with this report of his accomplishments.

"Wow, that's great. Congratulations." Elizabeth had forgotten how this felt—to always be cheerleading his accomplishments. Not that there was anything wrong with celebrating; it was just the expectation that grew stale.

Maddie appeared beside the table. "What can I getcha to drink?" She slapped down the menus and whipped out her pad.

"Iced tea for me, Maddie," Elizabeth said. Maddie nodded and turned to Chad.

"Same for me," he said. "And do you have lemon?"

"Iced tea with lemon," she said and wrote on the pad.

"I want the lemon on the side, not in the glass." Maddie nodded and started to walk away. Chad called after her, "Oh, and can you please take away these napkins?" He motioned dismissively at the pile. Maddie turned back and swiped up the napkins all in one motion and then was gone.

Elizabeth nearly died from repressed laughter. She so wished she were in the audience for this comedy, instead of the cast. Then she could laugh out loud whenever she wanted.

Instead she took a deep breath and exhaled slowly to steady herself. Chad didn't notice; he was busy looking all around the room once again.

After that, the conversation lulled. He had yet to mention the award he'd originally claimed as his reason for being there, and Elizabeth was certainly not going to bring it up.

Maddie returned with two glasses of iced tea—lemon on a plate for Chad—and a pile of napkins. Elizabeth covered a guffaw with a small cough and then quickly sipped her drink.

Thirty minutes, a burger and fries, and a half-eaten Cobb salad later, Elizabeth and Chad stepped out onto the sidewalk.

"Ugh, finally," he said. "I needed some fresh air."

That was it. She'd had enough. The lunch was over and Elizabeth had satisfied her curiosity. He'd never once asked anything about her job, and there was simply no reason to endure him any longer. She turned to face him. "It was interesting to see you again, but I've got to be going." Again she held out her hand to shake, but again he didn't take it.

Instead, he gave her another appraising look. "You surprise me, Lizzy."

Elizabeth squinted at him and dropped her hand. "Really. How so?"

"I think it's a waste. You, in this place." He gestured all around them at the small downtown. "You could have done so much better."

Elizabeth laughed out loud this time. "Well, Chad, you know everybody has their own preferences."

"Yes. I just never thought yours would be so...common." He clicked his tongue, then turned on his heel and walked away.

Elizabeth laughed again as she watched him go. She was so glad she'd decided to come to this lunch. It had been enlightening in a most unexpected way.

She walked to her car, and as she stuck the key in the ignition, took note once again of her dirt-stained fingers. Then she said out loud to herself, "You know what, Elizabeth? I think it's time we figure out what to do about Thomas."

6

By the time Elizabeth was gardening and dreaming of how else she'd fill up her summer, Thomas was back in full swing working on his car in the evenings. The Honda was finished and sold. Now he was working on a mid-90s Camry. His goal was to complete two more restorations this year before winter shut him down.

It had been a couple of weeks since the award article came out in the paper, and the excitement had died down. Thomas wanted to congratulate Elizabeth, but so many people surrounded her at church and Sunday School that he didn't try. He didn't want to be one of the crowd when it came to Elizabeth.

He left work and headed to the carport as usual. He took an indirect route as he sometimes did so he could drive through town. He liked to envision where he could have a shop space of his own.

Someday. He was making progress toward that goal now, thanks to the class, but it was slow. He was going to be working from the carport for a long time to come.

On this particular day, he drove down Pinewood by the dog park. He was almost past when out of the corner of his eye, he saw Elizabeth. She threw a tennis ball for a golden retriever and the dog bounded after it.

Thomas stomped the brake. He checked his rearview mirror, then backed up and u-turned into a parking spot. He turned off the engine and unbuckled his seatbelt.

The dog bounded back to Elizabeth, who scratched his head and took the proffered ball. She threw it again and when the dog took off, turned to chat with the dog's owner, a woman Thomas recognized from church.

He hadn't made a conscious decision to stop. His foot had kind of acted on its own. Now his body followed suit, and he got out of the truck and went to lean on the low stone wall that surrounded the park.

Elizabeth looked up and saw him. A slow smile spread across her face. She raised a hand in greeting, and Thomas responded in kind. Suddenly he found it hard to breathe.

Elizabeth kept her eyes on him and spoke to the woman over her shoulder. Then she walked to the wall.

"Hi," she said.

Thomas's insides quivered. "Hello."

Elizabeth opened her mouth to speak again and then closed it.

"I was just driving by and saw you, so I stopped to say hi," Thomas said quickly.

"I'm glad you did." She studied his face. "It's been forever since we've talked."

Thomas ducked his head. "I know."

Elizabeth moved forward to lean her elbow against the stone wall. "How's everything going?"

"Good." Thomas looked up. "Congratulations on your award."

Elizabeth blinked.

"I wanted to tell you before, but there were always a lot of people around."

She smiled again. It reached up into her eyes and made them crinkle. "Thank you." Then she shook her head. "It was crazy. I couldn't believe they did that."

"I could," Thomas said. "I know how hard you worked last year. You deserved it."

Elizabeth's eyes grew bright. "Thanks."

"You wanna get some pizza?"

The words were out of his mouth before he even realized he was going to say them. He looked over at her, horrified for a moment that he had ruined their first conversation in months.

Then even more words came out of his mouth. "Unless you've already eaten. I was just thinking we could, you know, celebrate."

Thomas swallowed hard. He wanted to look away, but he couldn't. She was staring at him—not frowning, also not laughing. Her eyes were—soft.

"I would love to."

It took a moment for her words to register.

"Really?" he asked, hardly daring to believe.

"Mm hmm," she said and scrunched up her shoulders. Then she looked down at herself and added, "As long as you don't mind how I'm dressed."

"Pfft." Thomas gestured at his own work clothes. They both grinned. Elizabeth walked over to the gate and exited the park.

Correction. Elizabeth floated over to the gate and exited the park. *How did that happen?* she wondered. It was just a few hours ago when she sat in her car and wondered how to make this very thing happen.

And now here it was, happening!

She looked up at him as she rounded the corner. His eyes were hopeful, but questioning. Almost as though he thought she might change her mind and walk away.

She did not.

Together they walked to his truck where he opened the passenger side door for her. She got in, and as he walked around to the other side, took stock. The cab was much cleaner than she had expected for a working man's truck. She felt oddly satisfied by this. It still showed some evidence, though, and when Thomas got in, he must have felt it because he gathered up a couple of tools and stowed them behind the seat. "Sorry. I grabbed these from work to use tonight."

"No problem. What were you going to do?"

"Work on my car."

"Oh, right. I remember you talking about that. Is it the same one from last fall?"

Thomas checked for traffic before backing out. "No. I sold that one and now I'm working on another."

"That's cool. How long does each one take?"

"It depends on what needs done—and on the weather." Elizabeth looked at him questioningly. "I only have a carport to work under, so I don't get to do much in the winter."

"Oh…" Elizabeth rolled down the window and propped her arm on the ledge as she pondered his answer. "I bet that's frustrating."

Thomas closed his eyes for a moment. "It is. Someday I wanna have my own shop."

"Nice." She thought for a moment. "Are you looking for a place?"

"I like to drive around and look at buildings, you know, imagine if they'd work for a shop." He signaled for a turn and then pulled into the pizza place. "I've started saving up money for it too, but I've got a long way to go."

Elizabeth unbuckled her seatbelt. "It's cool that you're working toward it, though."

"Yeah." Thomas turned off the ignition. "I wish I'd started a long time ago, but I didn't know how." He looked over at her. "Then I took that budgeting class at church this spring."

"Oh, I read about that. Was it good?"

"Yeah! It helped me a lot." Elizabeth nodded and reached for her door. "Hold on," Thomas said. He got out, came around, and opened the door for her.

"Thank you," she said, touched by the gesture.

It didn't take long for the two of them to discover they both preferred pizza with lots of toppings, so they ordered a large supreme from the menu.

As they waited, Thomas said, "So, your award. The paper said it was because you worked out a system for grading?"

"That's right." For a moment, Elizabeth was distracted from the conversation, because he'd actually brought it up again. *Unlike Chad, who had not*, she thought.

I don't want to think about Chad.

"I'm glad," Thomas said. "I know you were struggling with that last fall."

"I was." She looked away. That memory always felt sad.

"Sorry. I shouldn't have—"

"No, it's okay," she said, waving a hand to stop him. "The struggle was real, but it messed up a lot of things..." She felt tears forming and blinked quickly. "I'm the one who's sorry."

Thomas studied her face until Elizabeth squirmed and looked away again. "You don't need to be," he said. "It couldn't be helped."

"Next year will be better." The waitress dropped off their drinks and Elizabeth immediately grabbed hers.

"I'm just glad I don't have to do it," Thomas said.

Elizabeth nearly spit out her pop. "What, you don't want to apply to be a grader?"

"No, thanks." His grin was bashful, directed toward the table, but he looked up at her from under his lashes and caught her eye anyway.

Soon after, their pizza arrived and with it, plates and forks. Thomas served up the slice Elizabeth wanted and then one for himself. He set the spatula down and they looked at each other uncertainly.

"Should I pray for us?" he asked.

"That'd be wonderful."

They bowed their heads and Thomas offered a simple prayer. "Father, thank you for this food. And thank you for this chance to...be together." He huffed. "Amen."

"Amen." When Elizabeth looked up, Thomas's head was still down but she could see that his cheeks were reddened. "I'm glad you asked me," she said softly. He glanced up at her. "I've missed talking with you, ever since you asked me the first time—" She looked down. "—and I said no." She picked up her fork and sliced off the tip of her pizza.

Thomas took a bite of his own before answering. "I wasn't sure if you wanted to talk to me after that."

Elizabeth looked up in surprise. "I always like talking with you." She opened her mouth to speak again but then wasn't sure what to say. Instead, she put the bite of pizza in her mouth.

They were both silent for a bit, but then Thomas furrowed his brow and asked, "Why?"

Again Elizabeth looked up in surprise. "Why do I like talking with you?" She chuckled. "I don't know. Let me see." She cast about in her mind, trying to figure out exactly why she took pleasure in such brief conversations with this quiet man. She studied his face as she thought, which obviously embarrassed him.

He's so gentle, she thought.

I can't say that.

Then a memory popped up.

"Okay, here's one," she said. "My first day back in town, when I brought the car into the shop?" He nodded. "In less than a minute, you reassured me about my parents."

Thomas blinked in surprise.

Elizabeth thought some more and then continued. "You've done that so many times. We have this tiny little conversation and somehow you find a way to make me feel better about things." She looked away, embarrassed. "That's probably selfish."

"I don't think so."

Elizabeth looked back at him and then tipped her head. "See what I mean?"

After pizza, they drove around town and Thomas showed her some of his favorite spaces. They were all residential.

"So, you want to set up a private shop," Elizabeth said.

"Yeah."

"Which means you're really looking for a house too."

"Yeah, I think so." Thomas sighed. "Even more money."

"Mmm," Elizabeth mused. "Don't give up, though. It'll happen when it's God's perfect timing."

Thomas was quiet for a moment and then said, "I hadn't thought about it like that."

Elizabeth smiled ruefully. "It's always easier to remember God's perfect timing for somebody else's life. Much harder for your own." She paused and then added, "Which I guess is why we need other people—to help us figure these things out."

"I've been talking with Roger from Sunday School."

"You mean as a mentor?"

"I guess so."

"That's cool. He's such a good teacher."

"Even better in Bible study."

"Really?"

Thomas grinned in reply.

They both fell silent as Thomas drove to Elizabeth's house. When he pulled in the driveway, she undid her seatbelt and said, "You know, I should find a Bible study to join. I think I'm ready to do stuff like that again."

Thomas looked over at her. "Maybe...stuff like this too?"

"Yeah," she said, her eyes shining. "Stuff like this too."

$$7$$

Thomas didn't even care that he didn't get to work on his car that evening. Spending the time with Elizabeth was so much better.

It was the longest amount of time they'd ever been together, the most they'd ever talked. It was amazing and Thomas wanted more. She'd said yes to that idea, but he couldn't rest on just the words. He needed confirmation, and so he stopped by Elizabeth's house later that week.

She was working in the yard, surrounded by bags of mulch. When he pulled to the curb, she looked up, smiled, and waved. It was the same motion from across the table in Sunday School, but this time, Thomas knew it was just for him. Just as it had been at the dog park.

He got out of the truck and headed up the walk. "Hi," he said and leaned against the post of the porch steps.

"Hello." She removed a glove to swipe a hand across her forehead. "How are you?"

"I'm good." He gestured to the flower beds. "Those look nice. I like the rock."

"Thank you." Elizabeth surveyed her work. "It was buried on the side of the house. When I cleaned it up and saw how pretty it was, I thought it needed a place among the flowers."

"Nice."

"What are you up to this evening?" She stood and stretched her back.

"Going to work on my car, but I wanted to ask if you'd go with me to the racetrack on Saturday. You ever been?"

Elizabeth shook her head.

"There's tons of races and a show at the end of the night. Plus, you can walk through the pits and look at cars."

"Sounds right up your alley." Elizabeth's eyes twinkled.

He grinned. "Yeah."

"What time?"

"I can pick you up at nine."

"Nine...a.m.?"

Thomas nodded.

"Oh." She thought for a moment. "Didn't you say there's a show in the evening?"

"Yeah, it's all day."

"Wow."

Thomas's eyes were shining. "What do you say?"

Elizabeth chuckled. "Sure. Why not."

Thomas rang her doorbell at exactly nine on Saturday morning, but Elizabeth was ready and waiting. When they reached the motorsport park, she couldn't believe how many people there were. Not only were the nearby fields filling up with spectator cars, but there were also tons of campers. It was much like the county fair, only with cars instead of cows.

Once they got parked, they made their way to the pits. "We'll watch the races later," Thomas said. "Now's the best time to look at cars, before the place fills up."

Elizabeth was glad she hadn't said anything about how many people were already there.

To her unpracticed eye, most of the cars looked normal at first glance, but as she watched alongside Thomas, she saw that they really weren't. They had different tires, and they emphasized aerodynamics, and of course they had sponsorship logos all over them.

"So—" she stopped, feeling a little foolish for her ignorance.

"What?" Thomas asked.

"I was just curious. Are these cars specially made for racing?"

"Some are. Others are modified street cars. And then there's the really specialized ones."

There was no hesitation, no trace of shyness as he spoke. Elizabeth was intrigued as he continued. "There's different race classes for each type. Even street legal cars."

"What do you mean?" Elizabeth asked.

"Well, for example, you could sign up and race your car here if you wanted to."

She laughed out loud. "I don't think that'll be happening."

Thomas just grinned.

She thought for a moment "Have you ever raced?"

"No." He shrugged. "I'm not interested in that. I just like to see what they're doing under the hood."

Thomas pointed out some of his favorite features to her. By the end of the morning, Elizabeth was amazed by two things. One, how much Thomas knew about cars and two, how much he had talked during the past two hours. It was fun to see his passion. Of course, she'd never be as excited about all that horsepower as he was, but that hardly mattered. She could appreciate it at some level just because he did.

At noon they made their way to the food court and got lunch. Afterward, they got ice cream and wandered around the grounds to enjoy it. Elizabeth saw that a lot of families had brought coolers and wagons for their kids and were making a day of it.

"Wow," she murmured.

"What?" Thomas asked.

"People really get into this."

"Yeah, they do."

During the afternoon Elizabeth watched her first ever drag races and Thomas explained how it worked. It wasn't always as simple as fastest car wins. "How do you keep all this straight?" she asked, laughing.

"I don't know. I just do."

Out of everything she experienced that day at the track, by far her favorite was the jet truck. It was a thrilling end to the day—a fun day spent with Thomas, but a very long day spent at the track. By the time they were leaving the park with hundreds of other spectators, Elizabeth was yawning. "Sorry," she said, embarrassed.

"It's all right."

When they returned to Sutton and Thomas pulled in her drive, he got out and opened the door for her. "Thanks for going with me today," he said.

"Thanks for inviting me. I'll see you in the morning." She turned and headed up the walk.

"Yep, see you."

He didn't pull away until she was inside. Once she was, she dropped her bag on the chair and headed toward her bedroom, peeling off clothes as she went. She threw on pajamas and collapsed into bed, not even bothering to brush her teeth.

8

Thomas couldn't have imagined anything more perfect than spending the day with Elizabeth at the track. It was so much better than going with anybody else. Even JB.

Elizabeth had asked questions and been interested in the answers. Thomas had talked more than he ever had before in his life, even all this past year with Roger and Bible study and his class. It was easy with her. He liked that.

As he got ready for church the next morning, he felt more secure about things with Elizabeth. But he also wondered what came next. For example, how would it be at church? Sunday School was out, and for worship they sat in different sections of the sanctuary.

Thomas arrived first and took his usual seat with his family. When Elizabeth arrived and got settled in her regular spot, she looked up and caught his eye. She smiled and raised a hand in greeting.

For him.

After worship he slipped out of the pew and passed by his friends with just a brief wave. He made his way to the back of the sanctuary, and Elizabeth did the same. "Good morning," she said.

"Morning. Did you get rested?"

"I did. Crazy how a day like that can wear you out."

"Eh, you get used to it."

Elizabeth laughed. "I can work outside all day at the farm and not be that tired."

Together they walked toward the exit. "What are you up to today?" Thomas asked.

"I'm going to my folks'. Have some dinner, relax for a while. I usually go on Saturdays and help them with whatever they're working on for the day." They stepped through the doors and out into the sunshine. "How about you?" she said.

"Mom always has Sunday dinner."

"Oh, nice."

Thomas shrugged.

Elizabeth squinted at him. "Or...not?"

He looked away, embarrassed. "No, it is. It's just kind of expected and..." His voice trailed off. He wasn't comfortable saying anything more.

Elizabeth pursed her lips. "They don't want to give up their time with you?"

"I guess not."

Elizabeth was silent as they walked through the cars. Thomas had no idea what she was thinking, but his own thoughts were uncomfortable. He'd almost spoken about things in his family that he never mentioned to anyone. Who would he have talked to about them, anyway? JB didn't care, and Karen was part of the problem.

There is Roger.

Thomas stopped. He hadn't thought of that. After that first problem he'd taken to Roger, mostly they'd talked about matters of faith. Talking about personal concerns was difficult, even with someone he liked and respected as much as Roger.

"You okay?" Elizabeth had turned back.

"Hmm? Oh, yeah. Just thinking." He caught up with her.

"So was I—about what you said about your family."

He hoped she wasn't going to ask questions. As much as he struggled with his own feelings about his family, he certainly didn't want to color hers by revealing too much. Then he heard what she was saying.

"It's hard to balance, isn't it? For example, I moved back here on purpose to be near my parents."

He nodded. "To look after them."

She closed her eyes and exhaled. "Yes, exactly. But they seem more concerned that I'm around TOO much." She stopped when they reached her car and frowned. "I know that's the opposite of what you're saying, but it's still about figuring out balance."

Balance wasn't something Thomas had ever thought about. For most of his life he'd found it easier not to rock the boat when it came to his parents.

He looked up to find Elizabeth lost in her own thoughts.

Until lately, he thought. *I've been rocking the boat more lately, maybe even starting with that old carport.* Not to mention all the decisions he'd been making—or trying to make—this past year. Thomas furrowed his brow.

"Hmm," Elizabeth said, startling him from his reverie. "I better scoot. I hope you can enjoy your family dinner today, in spite of it all." Her eyes crinkled when she smiled.

Thomas felt a warmth spreading inside his chest. "Thanks," he said. "You too."

9

As she drove to the farm, Elizabeth thought about Thomas and the conversation they'd had after church. After all those months of silence between them, they'd transitioned so easily to dating.

Dating. That's what they were doing, after more than a decade of knowing each other. It was different from any other time Elizabeth had dated. Different from when you met a brand new person. In that situation, you knew basically nothing about them and had to start from square one.

But she and Thomas already had history, small as it was. He understood, somehow, her concern for her parents, and he accepted it. Then today he'd given her a glimpse into his own family dynamic. Just a snippet. She only knew a little about his dad from farm calls...and she wondered what life was like for Thomas, growing up.

However it was, he seemed to have come out of it okay. In this past year, she had found him to be kind and considerate, patient, and even-tempered. A decent man with passions and interests. None of that had been visible beneath the outward covering of shyness that she'd always assumed was his defining trait when they were in school.

As she pulled into her parents' driveway, Elizabeth lifted a prayer of thanks to God for sending Thomas by the dog park that day she was there.

Gardening around her house in town, even with a small vegetable patch in the backyard, didn't take nearly as much time as the garden her mother planted every year, so Elizabeth was easily able to start on one of her other summer projects.

Back in college, when she first declared her major, one of her professors said, "English, huh? You'd better be planning to teach because nobody makes a living writing."

Stunned by that unexpected declaration, Elizabeth had quietly added an Education minor to her course load and proceeded to get her certification. Not that she regretted it; she really did enjoy teaching. But she also enjoyed writing, and despite her professor's bleak outlook on the profession, it was one of her main goals for the summer.

Elizabeth didn't have the next great American novel in mind, but she did have lots of stories from the farm. Animal stories mostly. In fact, that's what she was working on when Thomas rang her doorbell just after five o'clock on Tuesday.

"Hey!" she said. "Come on in."

But he didn't. "I'm still in my work clothes."

Elizabeth looked him over. His clothes didn't seem too bad, but she liked the fact that he was mindful of it. She stepped out the door.

"I was on my way over to the carport to work," he explained, "but I wanted to see you first." He glanced at her, suddenly shy again.

"I'm glad you did." Now that she was beginning to understand him better, she found his shyness to be more meaningful.

Thomas looked around and said, "Looks like you got your mulching done."

This too pleased Elizabeth. "I did. And a vegetable garden in the back. You want to see it?" They went down the steps and walked around the side of the house. "I asked the landlord if it'd be okay because it meant tearing up some of the yard, but he didn't care. Less to mow, I guess."

"Makes sense." They looked over the garden patch and then took a seat on the back steps. "So what do you do over the summer, besides gardening?"

She ran down her list of activities and then added, "I also want to go to the theater. I've only gone a couple times since I've been back."

Thomas just nodded.

"Speaking of which, there's a show on Friday I'd like to see. I was wondering if you'd go with me?" Elizabeth glanced over as she asked the question and was surprised to see a look of discomfort settle on Thomas's face. "You okay?" she asked.

"I—yeah." He squirmed a little and then finally said. "I don't want to. I don't really like plays."

"Oh," Elizabeth said, taken aback. She sat for a moment, saying nothing as she tried to wrap her head around his answer. *What does that mean?* she wondered. She hadn't expected him to decline an opportunity to go out together. It didn't make sense.

As she was pondering this, she heard him say, "But I was hoping we could go to the track again on Saturday."

It took a second for Elizabeth's brain to switch gears and register what he was asking. In her confusion she said, "In the evening?"

"No, it's all day."

That's when it clicked. He had declined her invitation to a Friday night show and then turned around to invite her to an all-day Saturday event. *What does that mean?* she wondered again.

A tiny little tooth began to gnaw on the inside of her gut. She rubbed the spot with her fingers. "I'll be out at the farm on Saturday."

"Oh," Thomas said.

They sat for a moment, each lost in their own disappointment.

"I could come in the evening," Elizabeth offered.

Thomas frowned and shook his head.

Elizabeth frowned and wondered why that wouldn't work.

Finally, he spoke. "I guess we could skip this one."

Elizabeth turned to study his face. *Oh my gosh,* she thought. *He means this as a regular thing.* She hadn't realized. She could see it for the evening show. That had been fun and would be similar to a movie or a concert or a play. She frowned again.

Apparently not a play. But all day, every week? *There's no way,* she thought. "The thing is," she said, "I work out at the farm every Saturday."

He looked confused. "You didn't last week."

"Well, no, I changed my plans so I could go with you."

"You could do that again."

Elizabeth blinked in surprise. "Technically yes, but I didn't realize you meant for the track to be a thing every week."

"Not every week. Just a couple times a month. Usually."

"Still though, that's a lot."

"They're all different," Thomas said. "And I don't understand. You're not working, so you can go out to the farm anytime. Why does it have to be Saturdays?"

The tooth gnawed on her gut again. She pressed against it as she turned to look at him once more. *He's completely serious,* she thought. *Not only did he turn down my invitation, but he also wants me to change my plans so I can accept his.* A thread of memory floated through her brain and for a moment, she saw Chad.

Elizabeth sucked in her breath and turned away.

"Hey," Thomas said, reaching out a hand. "Are you all right?"

She glanced sideways. It was Thomas sitting next to her. *Of course it's Thomas.* Embarrassed, she ducked her head. "Yeah, I'm fine."

He withdrew his hand. "So...are we good?" She looked at him quizzically and he added, "For this weekend?"

Elizabeth considered the question. "If by good you mean that I'll meet you out there in the evening, then yes."

Thomas frowned. "No."

She raised her hand, palm up, and then let it drop in her lap. "Then I guess we're not good."

Indeed they were not. They were at an impasse—already. Hadn't she just been marveling at how easily they'd moved into dating? And now this. They'd each made an offer which the other had rejected. Elizabeth had even made a counter-offer, which had also been rejected.

She had the feeling that no matter what she suggested, it would suffer the same fate.

Was the track really that important? Was she going to have to add *stubborn* to her list of Thomas's traits? She'd never seen it before, but here it was.

"Okay, look," she said, fully serious. "Maybe we need to take a break for today and think about this individually. Then we can talk about it again."

Thomas straightened. "Yeah. That'd be good. Maybe tomorrow?"

"That sounds perfect."

Thomas stood up. "Okay, I'm gonna go work on my car then."

She looked up at him. "Have fun."

He gave her a crooked smile and took off around the corner of the house.

Elizabeth sat for some time, contemplating what had just transpired. It wasn't right to compare—she kept telling herself that—and yet the comparison kept creeping in. Chad had grown more self-centered the longer they'd dated, but she'd never seen that behavior in Thomas at all. *What does it mean?* she wondered for the third time.

Once back inside the house, she tried to return to her writing project, but it didn't work. Her thoughts were consumed. Taking a break and talking again tomorrow was smart, but it meant that she had hours to get through before there could be any resolution.

It wasn't until later when she was getting ready for bed that she thought to pray about it. Bedtime, meals, church, those were the times Elizabeth prayed automatically, but it wasn't often she remembered to pray on-the-spot. "I'm sorry, God." she said. "I should have prayed about this sooner. I have no idea how to resolve it. We need your help. Amen."

Thomas had a somewhat different response to the whole thing. When Elizabeth suggested taking a break and talking again tomorrow, it brought to mind Roger's story about him and his wife taking time-outs. *That's what this is!* he thought with satisfaction.

As he got started working on the Camry that evening, he recalled more of the conversation with Roger. "...so we can pray and think and calm down..."

I should pray, he thought. So with his tools in hand and his head bent over the engine block, Thomas closed his eyes and offered this silent prayer. *Lord, we need to figure this out. Will You help us? Amen.*

With that, he focused his attention on the task at hand and worked through until dark.

10

The next afternoon, just before five o'clock, Elizabeth sent a text.

Hey. I'm down at the dog park if you want to talk.

There was something about the dog park that appealed to Elizabeth for their meeting. Maybe it had to do with the fact that they'd gone on their first date from there. Or maybe it's because it was peaceful. She wasn't sure.

At any rate, a few minutes after five, Thomas pulled up. Elizabeth gave the beagle she was playing with one last pat, said goodbye to its owner, and stepped outside the gate.

"Hey," she said as Thomas got out of his truck.

"Hello," he replied. He nodded toward the park. "You have lots of dog friends."

"Gotta get my puppy fix." She grinned.

Together they walked down the sidewalk and settled themselves on the far end of the stone wall. The dog park was several blocks west of Main Street, and beyond it there were only a handful of houses inside the city limits.

"How was your day?" Thomas asked.

"It was good," she said. "I worked on a project, and then spent some time prepping for school." She chuckled self-consciously. "It feels kind of silly to be doing that already, but..." She shrugged. "How was yours?"

"Pretty normal." He looked over at her. "Normal's good at the shop."

"That makes sense."

They fell silent for a few moments, and then Thomas ventured to say, "I was glad you suggested taking a break and talking later. Roger mentioned about doing that sometimes." He glanced over at her.

"That's cool," she said.

"Yeah." Then after another pause, he said, "I prayed about it."

"Me too." Then, "Did you come up with anything?"

Thomas drew in a slow, deep breath. "I feel like the plan we had yesterday was a good one."

Elizabeth cast a sideways glance at him. "Except we didn't agree on it."

"No, we didn't," he said. "But I thought after the break it might look better to you."

Elizabeth opened her mouth and then closed it again. She studied her shoe-clad feet, wriggling restlessly as they dangled beneath her, before she spoke. "What about the ideas I had? Did any of them look better to you?"

Thomas shook his head slowly. The truth was, he hadn't thought about them. After he'd prayed, he put it out of his mind, thinking he'd done what was needed. Now he realized it was more complicated than that. Neither of them had changed their minds, so they were still in the same place they were yesterday.

He wished he'd asked Roger how it went when he and Nancy came back together after their time outs. But he hadn't. Then he wished God would speak to him directly and just tell him what to do. But He didn't. Finally Thomas said, "We both have things we want, right?"

"Yes," Elizabeth said slowly.

"Then we do whatever makes that happen."

Elizabeth didn't answer right away. She drummed her fingers against the stones as she thought, and Thomas waited. "So," she finally said, "what you want is to go to the racetrack a couple times a month, together, for the whole day on Saturdays." She looked over at him. "Is that right?"

"Yeah."

Elizabeth continued. "And what is it you think I want?"

"You said you like to work out at the farm." Thomas looked over at her and she bobbed her head to the side. "If you go to the farm another day, then you still get to go, but Saturday's free for the track."

Elizabeth rubbed her fingertips across her forehead. "It's not quite that simple."

"Why not?"

"Well, for one thing, I feel like I'm the only one who has to make an adjustment. I'm supposed to change my workday instead of going on the day I want to go. But nothing's changing for you." She paused to think for a moment. "Plus, I don't want to spend my entire Saturday twice a month out at the track. It's too much."

Thomas blinked. "I thought you liked it."

"I did like it. I just didn't realize you intended for there to be so many of them. Going to the track all day was fun—once. Doing it over and over again wouldn't be that much fun for me."

"But we'd be spending the day together."

"I know," Elizabeth said, "but there are lots of ways we can spend time together. Like, for example, I invited you to a play on Friday evening." But Thomas was already shaking his head. "What's that mean?" she asked, gesturing toward him.

"I don't want to go."

"Because you don't like plays, right?" He nodded. "Then surely you can understand. I don't want to go to the track so much because I wouldn't like that. It's the same thing."

Thomas was at a complete loss. He had no experience with this. At no time in his own family had negotiation—or even discussion—ever taken place. His dad made the decisions and that was the end of it.

He shifted position uncomfortably. As difficult as it had been growing up in his parents' household—and as much as he didn't want to be like his dad—he found he had a small measure of appreciation for his father's way of doing things.

Elizabeth spoke again. "I think it'd be better if we both made some concessions instead of just me."

With that sliver of appreciation foremost in his mind, Thomas had a hard time accepting this suggestion. Everything would be easier if he made the decision. Besides, wasn't it the man's job to lead?

An image of his mother burst into his mind. With unexpected clarity he saw her, not just as his mother, but as another person who suffered under his father's control. *If it is a man's job to lead,* he thought, *surely it's not meant to be like that.* He swept his fingers through his hair. *What is it meant to be like, then?* He had no idea.

"Thomas?" Elizabeth said, tipping her head to peer into his face.

"Sorry. Just thinking."

"Anything you want to share?"

He shook his head. He still couldn't imagine confessing such family secrets to anyone—not even Elizabeth. Instead he said, "What do you suggest?"

"Let's go for the evening," she said.

That had been her suggestion yesterday, and Thomas still didn't like it. Most of the fun was looking at the cars in the pits. And besides, by her own argument, they were both supposed to give something up. What was her concession by going in the evening?

Thomas's frustration grew. What was so wrong with his plan, anyway? Neither of them had to give up anything with his. Why couldn't she see that? He was certain Roger and Nancy would have figured this out by now.

Another emotion roiled up inside him. For most of his life Thomas had kept quiet and done what was expected of him.

At the time, he didn't know any different; it's how life was for him. But when he'd finally started making more decisions for himself, it made him feel like he could breathe for the first time ever, and he didn't want to give that up. He couldn't give that up. He wouldn't.

Not even for Elizabeth.

"We could both do what we want if you'd just move your workday," he said abruptly.

"Okay, fine," Elizabeth said, smacking the stones. "I'll move my workday and come to the track with you all day on Saturday—if you'll go to the show with me on Friday evening."

Thomas shook his head. "I don't want to do that."

"Why not?"

He sighed. "I told you."

"But why do you hate theater so much? It would help if I could understand."

"I just do." There was an air of finality in his tone that shocked Elizabeth. She was transported back a year to another conversation with another guy...

"Look, Lizzy, it doesn't make sense for you to go north. I'm never going to move up that way. There's nothing there for me. Take a teaching job here."

It hadn't mattered what her reasons were or what suggestions she'd made, none of them were good enough. It was Chad's way or—

—or nothing. When she'd ended it, it hadn't ended. He'd spent the rest of the summer badgering her to change her mind.

Elizabeth's heart was pounding and her stomach was in knots. No way could she go through that again. She jumped off the stone wall and jammed her hands into the back pockets of her jeans. Then she walked a few steps away.

"Hey." Thomas slid off the wall. Elizabeth turned to face him, and he reached out to her.

She stepped back. "This isn't working. We're getting nowhere."

Thomas furrowed his brow. "What do—" but she shook her head.

"I think we need to go back," she whispered. She pulled her hands from her pockets and wrapped them around her elbows.

"Go back where?"

"To how things were before. When we just talked after Sunday School. At least that worked."

Thomas reeled. His chest heaved. He opened his mouth, but no words came out.

"You know I'm right," she said. "If we can't even agree on how to go out on a date, then what are we doing? Let's go back to being friends before we completely ruin everything."

"I don't want that," Thomas whispered.

Elizabeth threw up her hands and let them drop. "I don't know what else to do."

She saw the pain flood his eyes, and her agitation vanished. *He's not Chad.* She exhaled. *I know he's not Chad.*

And yet, it hardly mattered. Different man, same conflict. Just totally unexpected with this one. *Maybe I'm the problem,* she thought.

"I'm sorry, Thomas." She truly was. After a decade of possibility and a mere week of reality, it was over. "I'd better go home," she said.

Thomas deflated. Elizabeth could have cried at the sight, but it didn't change anything. If they couldn't agree, then there was no way forward.

"I'll drive you," he said.

The offer wrecked her. In spite of it all, he could still be a gentleman. How could he be so stubborn and so kind all at the same time?

But it didn't matter. She couldn't be steamrolled. She wouldn't. She'd die inside if she were. "I think it's better if I walk."

He wanted to protest; she could see it, so she spoke again quickly. "Thank you, though. I'll see you in church." Then she turned and walked away.

11

Thomas stood rooted to the spot long after Elizabeth disappeared from view. His breathing was ragged; he ran his fingers through his hair again and again. Finally he got in his truck and drove to the carport. When he arrived, he turned off the engine, but it wasn't until sweat began trickling down his back that he opened the door and got out.

The Camry was ready for an oil change, so that's what Thomas did. Unfortunately, he over-tightened the bolts for the gasket. When he crawled out from under the car and put in fresh oil, it promptly leaked onto the ground. "Dang it," he said. He grabbed a bag of cat litter he kept on hand and spread it over the spill.

He accomplished little in the next half hour and finally gave up and went home. He didn't bother removing his work boots. Instead he wandered into the kitchen, made a peanut butter and jelly sandwich, and grabbed a bottle of pop from the fridge. Then he flopped down on the couch.

He turned on the television and stared, unseeing, at the screen. At first the sandwich languished in his hand, but at some point during the mindless parade of images which passed before his eyes, he mumbled a prayer of thanks and ate without tasting.

The sun was near the horizon by the time his brain started to function again, and the first thought that passed through his mind was, "*You're just like Dad.*"

His sister's words thumped him in the chest. Gasping for breath, he sat up straight. "No," he said.

The conversations with Elizabeth over the last two days replayed in his mind. The conflicting thoughts he'd had bounced off one another. He sank back into the cushions as the truth became clear. Ultimately, he'd demanded his own way.

"Please God," he whispered. "I don't want to be like my dad."

The prayer left him conflicted. His dad was a good mechanic. He'd learned from his dad and he liked that, but everything else about his father was a muddle. He fiddled mindlessly with the edge of the cushion as he stared off into space and the light faded from the sky.

Thomas flinched when a commercial flashed brightly across the screen. He looked around to find that the room was completely dark. He reached for the remote and turned off the TV. Then he unlaced his boots and kicked them off, not caring how they landed.

In the shower he scrubbed the grease off his hands, wondering how much he had ingested along with the grape jelly. Then he simply stood under the stream, head down, hands pressed against the shower wall, until the water started to cool. It felt good, physically, but it did little to settle the anguish in his mind.

After he dried off, he donned a pair of boxers and then returned to the living room, flipping on the light switch as he did so. That's when he saw the boot tracks from door to kitchen to couch. Sighing, he cleaned up the mess and put his boots by the door.

When Thomas went to bed directly afterward, all he felt was—empty.

In the days that followed, Elizabeth poured herself into gardening when her thoughts threatened to overwhelm, both at her house and out at the farm. It was better than being cooped up inside on all these gorgeous summer days, especially after an entire school year of it. Her writing project languished, but she couldn't focus on it anyway. Not after what happened at the wall.

She played it over and over again in her mind. *Was there anything I could have done differently?* she wondered. *Anything I should have?*

She kept going back to the day she had lunch with Chad. She was convinced she was no longer injured by him, yet at the first sign of trouble with Thomas, she'd bolted. She didn't want to; she just couldn't see that there'd been any other choice, because she could not live that way.

And now they were disconnected. Thomas had avoided her at church on Sunday, despite her plea to go back to the way things were.

She couldn't blame him, not really. It wasn't easy to go backward. Neither of them wanted to go backwards. But in Elizabeth's mind, it was better than going forward with nothing.

Because in spite of it all, she found herself still drawn to him. It was confusing. What happened at the wall was so frustrating, and it didn't make sense—why he was so adamant about things being his own way. His refusal to explain why he hated theater so much. His absolute veto of all her ideas. All of them!

Are all guys like that? she wondered. *Surely not. My dad's not. That counts, doesn't it?*

No matter how many times she went over it, she could never resolve the situation in her mind. Since they'd failed to resolve it in real life too, the combination left her unsettled and unhappy.

That was the one good thing about the lunch with Chad—she'd gotten her resolution about him. She'd seen him with clearer eyes and knew she'd made the right choice. Maybe over time she'd be able to have that kind of clarity about Thomas.

Maybe, but in the meantime, the thought was no comfort at all.

Compounding the problem was how isolated she felt from everyone else too. Tracy hadn't been to church since school let out. Her other teacher friends were already in and out with vacations, and her parents kept shooing her out the door to spend time with her friends.

What friends? she thought. *I wish we still had Sunday School.* Then she stopped. *Why couldn't we? Some of the other classes meet year round.* After mulling it over for a bit, she decided to approach Nancy.

"I almost hate to ask because I know how important it is to have a break."

"That is true," Nancy said. "Although teaching Sunday School isn't quite as intense as teaching regular school." She gave Elizabeth a wink. "Mostly we take the summer off because people come and go and it's harder to get continuity on a study."

Elizabeth thought this over. "What about stand-alone lessons each week? That way people could pop in whenever."

"Well, now, that's a good idea," Nancy said. "Tell you what. Why don't you touch base with your classmates and see what they think. I'll talk to Roger and we'll compare notes. What do you say?"

Elizabeth hesitated. It wasn't that she didn't want to. On the contrary, she was fine talking with everyone from class. It's just—Thomas. How was she going to manage that?

She snapped to attention. *What am I thinking? I'll figure out how to manage it!* Maybe it would be a way to get past what had failed and go back to what worked.

"I can do that," she told Nancy.

Within a couple of days she had contacted everyone in class except him. The response was good—enough, probably, to carry to Nancy. But her purpose was incomplete. She wanted to talk to Thomas; she was just anxious about trying, because what if he refused? That would be so final.

She procrastinated a while longer, citing her self-imposed gardening schedule. Then, annoyed with herself for being ridiculous, she marched out of the house, got in her car, and drove down to the shop. Whatever the outcome, she had to try.

When she arrived, it was JB who came to the counter. Elizabeth only knew him by sight. "Hi. Is Thomas here?" she asked.

JB looked her over. "Yep."

Elizabeth raised an eyebrow. "Can I speak with him, please?"

JB smirked. "Yep," and then he sauntered back out to the shop. Elizabeth rolled her eyes and wandered over to peruse the bulletin board, trying to calm her nerves. After a reasonable length of time passed and Thomas didn't appear, she frowned. *Would he seriously refuse to talk to me here?* she wondered. She wouldn't have thought it, not at the business. *Whatever, it doesn't matter. Now that I'm here, I'm not going to let that happen.*

She just wasn't sure how she'd accomplish it if he didn't choose to walk through that door.

Then suddenly, he did.

"Hi!" she said, relieved, and started walking toward the counter, at the same time that he said,

"How can I help you?" He busied himself pulling out the appointment book.

She stopped and stared.

"What do you need done?" he asked and picked up a pen.

"Really?" she said. "Is this how it's going to be?"

Thomas clicked the pen repeatedly. "I don't know how else it should be."

Elizabeth frowned. "Like it was before." The ache in her chest confirmed how much she longed for it to be like it was before.

He looked up at her from underneath his eyebrows.

"Seriously, Thomas. We only went out on two dates." She closed the distance to the counter and stood right in front of him. "We can still be friends."

Thomas huffed and shifted his weight.

"You want to throw away a whole decade of knowing each other just because we have different interests and couldn't figure out how to share them?"

His only response was to doodle along the edges of the book.

So stubborn! she thought. Then she furrowed her brow. *Or hurt.* She changed tack and spoke more gently. "We live in a small town. We need to be able to speak to each other."

"Fine. Just tell me what you want done on your car."

"I'm not here about my car."

Thomas threw down the pen and glared at her. "Then what are you here for?"

Elizabeth stifled a grin. She'd never seen him ruffled before. "Sunday School."

He blinked in surprise. "What about it?"

"I was talking with Nancy about having class over the summer. I miss it." She stopped, distracted because Thomas's eyes lit up. *What does that mean?* she thought.

"Um, anyway, she tasked me with polling everyone about it. So, would you be interested?"

To her surprise, he smiled. "Yeah, I would. I miss it too."

A warmth spread through her. *This,* she thought. *If we can at least have this.*

"Okay, cool. I'll tell her." She gave him a sideways glance. "Thank you, Thomas."

He huffed and tried not to smile.

After enjoying that for a moment, she added, "That's all I needed."

"Okay." He hesitated and then said, "Guess maybe I'll see you at Sunday School." Elizabeth smiled but he didn't look at her again. Instead, he returned the appointment book to its place under the counter and disappeared out the shop door.

Elizabeth watched him go, vaguely amused. *Apparently Sunday School is the balm to soothe his wounded soul,* she thought and then frowned. *Or something like that. I need to get back to writing.*

Thomas went back to work, and outwardly he looked the same as he always did: quiet, focused, productive. But after the completely unexpected visit from Elizabeth, inwardly he was a wreck. He'd been devastated when she walked away from him at the dog park. In the days since, he'd experienced so many emotions—the full range of grief, if he'd been able to name it. But also embarrassment. He'd failed spectacularly at dating the only woman he'd ever loved.

She wanted to go back to being friends—was apparently perfectly fine with just being friends. But he couldn't do it. He couldn't face her at church and do what they'd always done, so he avoided her instead. It didn't feel better, but it was all he could manage.

And then she showed up at the shop.

When he couldn't figure out any way to avoid talking to her, he tried to be professional—to keep his distance and just do the job. But Elizabeth was still Elizabeth, and in spite of it all, his feelings for her hadn't changed.

And so he was also confused. She walked away but wanted to keep him close. *What does that even mean?* he wondered. Were they done, or was there hope? And if there was hope, what needed to happen?

Thomas had no idea.

Don't be like your dad. The thought sneaked up on him. He frowned at the engine block as he continued to work. Karen wasn't completely wrong about him, as much as he wished she were. Sometimes he was just like his dad.

But that's not all bad. Is it? Again, his thoughts were in a muddle.

Demanding your own way all the time is. Thomas sighed. He could understand that. But how was he supposed to give up what he wanted without suffocating in the process? He'd only just learned how to breathe.

You could talk to Roger. Thomas considered and immediately rejected this idea. It would be too hard. There was too much to tell. He couldn't bear the shame.

"God, I need your help," he whispered.

When he got home from work that day, he added the prayer to his list.

12

Daniel and Becky Fleming had picked up the mantle of hosting the fellowship gatherings for the Sunday School class, and the group was gathered for an Independence Day picnic. Theirs was a quaint, two-story century home with a wrap-around porch. It was rough inside and out, but the Flemings had big plans.

"Daniel wants to finish the outside first," Becky explained as she led a group of women, including Elizabeth, on tour through the house. "I know it makes sense, but I can't wait to do up all these bedrooms!"

Everyone was excited when Paul and Sabrina showed up with their two-month old baby girl. The women cooed over her as they inspected fingers and toes. Once the food was set out, Sabrina was perfectly happy to let Becky hold the baby while she filled her plate and ate.

Elizabeth didn't take a turn. She wasn't opposed to babies; she just had no experience with them. Besides, Becky looked quite content with the little girl on her lap. Elizabeth made herself useful by refilling drinks and fetching dessert.

The meal was just winding down when the call came in.

"Elizabeth, honey? It's your dad." Normally Elizabeth warmed with love for her father every time he called, because he still felt the need to identify himself even though cell phones and caller ID made it practically impossible to be unknown. But this time, something in his voice stopped her cold.

"Dad? What's wrong?"

"Well, now, it's probably nothing."

"Tell me," she said.

"You know your mother's had this cough going on. I think it's wearing her out. Plus—" he stopped.

"Go on."

"I can't be sure, but I feel like she's struggling to breathe."

A shudder went through Elizabeth's body, and her breath came in shallow gasps. "Dad, you need to get her to the hospital. I'll meet you there." Elizabeth grabbed her purse and mouthed the words, "I gotta go," to Becky. As she hustled through the house and out to her car, she realized her father had not replied.

"Dad?"

"Can you meet us here?" he said.

Elizabeth stopped short. She heard frailty in her father's voice for the first time. Her hands shook as she tried to unlock the car door. "Of course. I'll be right there. You have her ready to go, okay?"

She made the drive in something less than thirty minutes. She pulled to a stop and threw open her car door. Then she paused to take a deep breath. *I need to be calm for them,* she thought. *Calm, but speedy.* She ran up the sidewalk and into the house.

"Hi, Momma." They were sitting in the kitchen with a small overnight bag. "Let's get you to town, shall we?"

"Okay." Elizabeth was shocked by the thin, wispy voice which answered her. She was glad her father hadn't waited any longer to call.

The next few days were a blur. Laurel was admitted to the hospital for pneumonia, where she received antibiotics and breathing treatments to help her fight the infection. Elizabeth answered a million texts that first evening until Becky insisted that she run point on communications with their church family.

Thanks, Becky. I am so grateful.

Of course! Let me know what else I can do.

There really wasn't anything. Not everyone was comfortable doing farm chores, and once they were back home, her parents' church family more than took care of meals.

The problem was harvest. Even at age seventy-eight, Bob Shepard wanted to be involved in every minute of it. He had a hard time letting his crew work without him while he was at Laurel's side.

And he was by her side every moment. While Elizabeth agreed with him being there, she was startled by the level of stubbornness he demonstrated over the farm work. She decided to pick her battles, though. While harvest was important, her mom was more so. As she ran back and forth to the farm to take care of the critters, she prayed that God would hold off any rains and give them a few more days to get the crop in.

When Elizabeth stepped back into the hospital room on the morning of the third day, the first thing she noticed was her father. He was exhausted. This, now, was their new most urgent need, and Elizabeth shifted her priorities.

"Dad, let me take you home so you can shower and get some sleep. You can come back after that, but if you don't take care of yourself, you're going to end up sick too."

It took several conversations and even a plea from her mom, but he finally agreed. Once they were inside the car, the stress of it all came to the surface, and his tears fell.

"Oh, Daddy. She's going to be okay."

"I know it." He pulled a handkerchief from his pocket and blew his nose. "It's just that—well, I never thought she'd be the one to get sick."

Elizabeth didn't share with him that she'd thought the same thing.

"It made me realize how terrible it would be to lose her." He sniffled and turned away. Elizabeth reached over and took hold of his hand.

When she pulled into the yard, she put the car in park and cut the motor. Then she turned to him. "I understand what you mean. It's horrible to think about losing someone we love. But the thing is, as Christians we know that what's next after this life is eternity with God. That's the very best thing, and we have to keep our eyes fixed on it."

He nodded and then blew his nose again. "You're right, honey. I know that. But it sure doesn't feel good to think about being separated, even for a little while." He looked up at her and smiled weakly. "I didn't know I was such a coward."

Elizabeth shook her head. "You're not a coward. Nobody wants to be alone." She was startled when an image of Thomas flashed through her mind. For a moment, she felt very alone herself.

While her dad showered, Elizabeth put together a simple lunch. They prayed and as they ate, her dad said, "I don't know what I'm going to do about harvest."

Elizabeth gingerly set down her sandwich. "I was thinking about that too," she said, "and you know, we could get the crew back over here. They can cut and I can drive the truck. That way you can stay with Mom at the hospital."

Elizabeth knew how much he loved farming, and she could see him battling his own desire to be involved. "I suppose we should." He sighed, and Elizabeth saw his weariness once again.

"Why don't you go get some sleep, and I'll make the calls to get that going. We'll go see Mom again this evening." Bob agreed and just like that, Elizabeth added grain hauling to her list of duties.

Laurel was in the hospital for a week. Once they were home, either Elizabeth or her father was on duty in the house, and the other was out working harvest. Elizabeth was in the field when one of the crew called to tell her that he'd broken down.

"Oh, we were so close!" she said.

"I know. Sorry."

"Let's trade places. You drive the truck and I'll call for repairs."

13

"**S**chaefer's." Everybody in town knew who they were, and that was all the greeting a phone call required.

"Hi. It's Elizabeth Shepard. We've got a breakdown in the field."

Thomas's insides quivered. "Hi, Elizabeth," he choked out. "It's Thomas."

"Oh, hi," she said. "How are you?"

"I'm all right. Is it the combine?"

"Yes. We're so close to finishing and they're forecasting rain overnight. Is there any chance you're available today?"

"I can be right out." It was his dad's policy to prioritize farm service calls, especially during harvest, and Thomas agreed. A lot of farmers were motivated to keep costs down and do as many of the repairs themselves as they could; after all, the service wasn't cheap. But Schaefer's had their regulars, and Bob Shepard was one of them. There was no way Thomas wasn't going to get him back up and running as soon as possible.

Plus, Elizabeth.

"Really?" she exclaimed. "Oh my gosh, that's great news. Thank you. I'll see you soon."

"Yep. See ya." Thomas hung up the phone and stifled a grin, even as a wave of uncertainty overtook him. How would it be? They hadn't spoken since that day at the shop. At the party, the women had all been busy with Paul and Sabrina's baby before she got called away, and she'd never made it to Sunday School.

But this—this was an opportunity uniquely his. He took a deep breath. He would embrace it.

Nerves settled—as least as much as they could be—he went out to the lot to check the second service truck and make sure it was ready to go. His father was out on calls in the main truck, and this one was parked toward the back, behind the tow, because it wasn't used as often. Once he was satisfied, he stepped back into the shop.

"Hey, JB, I'm headed out for a call. Will you answer the phones?"

JB popped up from underneath the hood of a truck. "What?" he said. "You've got a car torn apart in here."

"Can't be helped. It's a farm call. I'll finish tomorrow—or tonight. Anyway, will you take care of things here?"

"Fine." JB disappeared back under the hood of the truck. "Need a freakin' raise if I'm gonna be the officer manager too..."

But Thomas was already out the door.

When he arrived, it was Elizabeth who greeted him, but it was all business; there was work to be done. She gave him the rundown as it had been given to her, and then he hauled out his tools and got to work.

Elizabeth leaned up against the service truck to watch. She had always watched during repairs, and a decade ago, Thomas had liked to imagine she was really there to watch him. Now he pushed it from his mind so he could focus on the task at hand.

It was an hour before he could get the machine back up and running, and he was drenched in sweat long before he was finished. After he tightened the last bolt, he dropped the tool back in its box and swiped his arm across his forehead. He leaned back, checking his work to make sure he hadn't missed anything.

Then from over his shoulder, Elizabeth offered him a water bottle. He looked up at her in surprise. "Thanks." He twisted the top off and downed the entire thing.

"Want another?" She held out her hand for the empty bottle.

"No, I'm good," he said and handed it to her.

Thomas packed up his tools and loaded them into the back of his truck. Elizabeth texted the crew to let them know the combine was back up and running. Then she leaned against the machine and stared off into the distance. Thomas came around to the side of the truck and leaned against it, just opposite her.

"How's your mom?" he asked.

Elizabeth turned to him and breathed in deeply. "Really weak." She shook her head. "But at least she's on the mend."

"That's good."

She smiled. "Thanks for asking."

Thomas nodded. She looked tired. "Is there anything I can do to help?"

Elizabeth pointed at the machine behind her. "You just did. This was huge. Thank you."

"Just doing my job on that one."

"Still though," she said and then regarded him thoughtfully. "It's funny how things change, isn't it."

"What do you mean?"

She smiled wryly. "I was just thinking back to a decade ago. We were both out here then too, but back then it was with our dads. Now you're the one fixing and I'm the one managing, while my parents are..." She gestured toward the house and then dropped her hand.

"They're okay," Thomas said, praying it was true. Praying they would be for a long time to come, for Elizabeth's sake.

She studied his face, almost as if she were willing his words to be true. There was both worry and longing reflected in her eyes. "I hope so," she finally said.

It occurred to Thomas that Bob Shepard was a regular customer because of his age. That it was his age which made it possible for Thomas to meet Elizabeth all those years ago. And that it was his age which was causing Elizabeth such distress at this very moment. He wished he could take her in his arms and comfort her.

Instead, it occurred to him that even though some things had changed, others were still very much the same.

14

Laurel recuperated steadily, but slowly. At first she was so weak she needed help just to walk across the house to the bathroom. The pressure on Elizabeth and her father eased slightly once harvest was complete, but it wasn't long before Laurel started fretting.

"Elizabeth, have you had a chance to look in on the garden?" she asked.

The garden had been a major part of life for as long as Elizabeth could remember, as important as any field crop or livestock—at least as far as Laurel was concerned. While it was her domain, they all worked together to make it a success.

"Uh, not yet." Not since Laurel had gone into the hospital. She'd only glanced that direction on her way out to the barn, and she could see that the weeds were growing.

"I don't want to lose that produce."

Elizabeth and her father exchanged glances. "We'll take a look today," he said. After lunch, while Laurel napped, they slipped outside. Bob whistled as they approached. "Good thing she's not up to walking this far yet," he said.

"Yeah." Elizabeth sighed and put her hands on her hips. She thought briefly of her own small, abandoned garden at home. *Nothing I can do about that,* she thought. "I can get started on it this afternoon," she said.

"And I'll work some this evening."

Between them they got the garden into passable condition, if not quite up to Laurel's standards. The good thing about it was that she was motivated to get back out there, so she worked hard each day to rebuild her stamina. The day finally came when she could walk the whole distance to the garden. Bob set her chair in the sun, and Laurel supervised while he and Elizabeth worked.

"Just lay those weeds down around the tomato plants. They help to make a nice mulch." Elizabeth smiled to herself. She already knew her mom's gardening habits. She had, after all, grown up with them.

"Bob, I think those green beans are going to need water. They're looking a bit droopy."

"All right, we'll turn the hose on them when we're done here."

More than once that summer, Elizabeth looked out across the endless rows of beans and potatoes and onions, the big patch of corn and head after head of cabbage and wondered, *Why on earth do they need this much produce?*

Every time, she shook her head and kept on working, but thoughts of her dad's many acres of cropland and her mom's large garden always crept back in. She wondered if maybe they shouldn't be working so hard anymore.

Laurel, although still not at full steam, was working along-side her husband and daughter by the time Elizabeth's summer break was drawing to a close. Elizabeth had spent the vast majority of it living back on the farm. She was tanned and fit, but she hadn't written another word all summer, and she hadn't gone to any shows.

It was just as well. Even the thought reminded her of the fiasco with Thomas and brought an overwhelming sense of sorrow. So she chose not to think about it.

The one thing she couldn't help thinking about, however, was the fact that she hadn't made it to a single one of the summer Sunday School classes.

15

While Thomas was glad he'd had the opportunity to see Elizabeth out at the farm and help her family in the process, the aftermath was an increased sense of loss and loneliness. He simply did not know how to move forward.

The thing was, he didn't want to move forward if it meant leaving Elizabeth behind. He had never hoped for any other life for himself, and in the last year since she'd moved home, he'd begun to think it could be a reality rather than just a dream. For that to happen, though, he had to fix what was broken. The problem was, even though he was praying about it, he still didn't know how to fix that kind of brokenness.

And so he threw himself into working on the kind he did know—cars. He spent every spare moment of daylight working on one project after another. If he'd added up the time, he would have realized he was nearly working a second full-time job out there. Of course, that was only possible by working morning to dark on Saturdays too, which meant he wasn't out at the track. It had lost its appeal.

The upside was that, without those expenses, Thomas's finances were improving faster than he'd expected. Even though he'd been working the budget program for several months, it still hadn't hit him just how much money he'd been spending at the track—not until he was able to repurpose those dollars into upgraded vehicle purchases.

That's when he begrudgingly began to consider that *not* going to the track so much *might* have its benefits.

One Friday evening while Thomas was still working on his current project, he received a call from Daniel Fleming.

"Hello."

"Thomas, hey. How are you?"

"I'm good."

"I was wondering if you're busy tomorrow."

"Uh, why?"

"I'm supposed to finish the installation of a steel roof and my help bailed. I need an extra set of hands."

Thomas looked down at the car he was working on. He had hoped to finish this one up tomorrow and then get started on another. He wanted to say no. He had his own work to do. Surely Daniel could find someone else.

But before he could open his mouth, a memory surfaced. It was one of his conversations with Roger, and it was about making sacrifices. Nancy had offered hospitality even when she didn't feel well. At the time, Thomas hadn't thought he'd ever made a sacrifice like that.

Probably still haven't, he thought. *Would helping a friend with his work qualify?* He didn't know.

"Thomas?" Daniel asked.

"Sorry. I was just thinking it through. Yeah, I can help."

"Oh, that's fantastic! Thanks so much. I really appreciate it."

"Sure. No problem." Suddenly Thomas realized how much it meant to Daniel, and he was glad he'd said yes. He sent a silent prayer of thanks to God for bringing that memory to mind and helping him to answer the right way.

Daniel and Thomas were on the job site at first light. Together they set up the workspace and then while Thomas unloaded the steel from the work trailer, Daniel climbed the ladder to install the last of the furring strips. When he finished, he climbed back down, grabbed his circular saw, and headed back up to trim them to length.

Thomas had just pulled the last piece of metal from the trailer when Daniel yelled. He looked up in time to see flames shooting from the saw and Daniel smacking at them frantically. He dropped the metal and ran over to the outlet. He yanked the extension cord from the socket and then scrambled up the ladder.

The flames were out by the time he reached the top. Daniel leaned forward over his knees, panting.

Thomas looked first at the saw and then at Daniel. "You good?" he asked.

"Yeah," he said. "Ruined my saw, though."

"Here, let me see it." Daniel passed it over to him and Thomas went back down the ladder. He carried it to the trailer and sat down to inspect the damage.

Daniel followed him down the ladder. He went to the back of his truck and rifled through his toolboxes, muttering the whole time. "Not gonna get it done today...not enough batteries for the cordless...have to drive to Mansfield...burned my freakin' hands..."

Thomas set the saw down and went to his own truck for some tools. When he returned, he loosened the casing on the handle and removed the power cord. Then he trimmed away the burned area and reconnected the wires.

Daniel had finally located his first aid kit and was taking care of his hands. Then he came around the back of the trailer to see what Thomas was doing. Once Thomas had the saw put back together, he plugged it in to test it.

"Is that safe?" Daniel asked, somewhat dubiously.

"Yeah, the motor's fine." Thomas pointed to the back part of the handle. "The flames were here where the cord is. A wire must've come loose." Turning the saw away from both himself and Daniel, he pressed the lock switch and pulled the trigger. It fired right up. Daniel whistled, and Thomas looked up "Good as new."

"Well, all right!" Daniel exclaimed. Thomas shut it off and handed it over.

Daniel turned it this way and that. "I never would've known how to fix this. Thanks, man. I owe you one."

"No problem."

"I might have to get you out here again next time I have a breakdown." He snickered. "You do job site calls?"

"Yup." Thomas grinned and then lifted his chin toward Daniel. "Your hands okay?"

"Oh, yeah." Daniel sounded annoyed. "They'll be fine." He patted the saw, as if to show how well they worked, and then looked around. "Maybe we'll get this done today after all."

"Let's do it," Thomas said.

And so they did. It was nearly sundown by the time the last piece of metal was in place, but it was done.

Thomas was used to working that late so the long hours didn't bother him. A part of him still lamented the work he didn't get done on his car, but the greater part of him was glad to have spent the time helping a friend.

At the end of the day Daniel pulled out his wallet and slapped some bills into Thomas's hand.

"Oh!" said Thomas.

"What, didn't you think I was going to pay you?" Daniel asked.

"I hadn't thought about it," Thomas said.

"Be careful of that," Daniel warned. "Some people would take advantage."

Thomas stowed the bills away in his own wallet, knowing it would add nicely to his car fund. He did wonder, though, if getting paid somehow undid the sacrifice he'd thought he was making.

The question rolled around in his mind the whole drive home.

Later as he cleaned up and got supper, it morphed into something else. *What if I'd sacrificed what I wanted that day at the dog park with Elizabeth? Would things be different now?*

Probably. Thomas sighed. But the thing was, could he have done it? He wanted to be with Elizabeth, sure, but he also wanted to be able to breathe.

Why did those two things have to be in conflict?

At a complete loss for the answer, Thomas set down his plate, went into the bedroom, and added the word *sacrifice* to his prayer list.

16

Elizabeth was back in Sunday School when the school year started in late August. She was tanned and toned, and Thomas thought she looked good. *Really good.* He hadn't seen her since the equipment repair, and he found himself looking forward to walking with her after class again.

He chewed on his lip as he thought about that. Going back to what they did before wasn't what he wanted—wasn't what he was praying for—but it was better than nothing.

As class ended, they met up at the doorway, almost as if by mutual agreement. "Welcome back," he said solemnly.

"Thanks," she replied, much the same.

They walked in silence toward the sanctuary. It wasn't uncomfortable, but Thomas knew their time was short. He hated to waste it, but he was uncertain what else to say. When they reached the door, he pulled it open but she didn't go through. Instead, she said, "I think it's time for my parents to scale back on their work." She looked up at him. "I have no idea how to tell them that."

Thomas raised his eyebrows. He couldn't imagine trying to tell his parents, especially his dad, to do anything. Then he said, "Probably need to pray about that one."

Elizabeth blinked in surprise, and for a moment, Thomas thought he'd made a mistake. Then she said, "You're right. Sometimes I forget to do that." Her eyes carried a hint of vulnerability as she looked at him, and it startled him. Elizabeth was always self-assured, always confident. "Thank you for reminding me," she said.

"You're welcome," he said, almost automatically. Then he stopped, and with more purpose said, "I'll be praying for you too."

Elizabeth didn't say a word, but he could see her eyes growing moist. At a loss for what to do next, he gestured toward the sanctuary. "After you."

Elizabeth took a seat in her usual spot, and Thomas walked through the sanctuary to join his family. He was busy thinking about his conversation with her and wondering what it meant that she had confided in him. He liked that she had confided in him. But the question was, could he handle that much closeness with her knowing there might never be anything more?

Before he had a chance to answer his own question, Pastor Stephen stepped to the pulpit.

"Brothers and sisters, I just got off the phone with Ted Johnson." A murmur passed through the room. Jane had already beat cancer twice.

"As many of you know, their son Evan is serving in the armed forces. His unit was on a training exercise, and there was a vehicle collision. Evan and three of his fellow soldiers were killed."

There was a collective gasp from the congregation. This was quickly followed by the distinct sound of weeping.

Pastor Stephen looked around the room. "This is a call no parent ever wants to receive. I think the sorrow must surely be multiplied when it's your only child." He paused as his voice broke. For a few moments, he sought to pull himself together, and the congregation quietly grieved. When he spoke again he said, "Can we just take some time right now to lift up this family? If you are willing, please join me at the rail to pray."

Thomas was among those who came forward. It was two and three people deep across the entire front of the sanctuary. As he listened to Pastor Stephen's prayers and those of the elders, he lifted his own silent offering toward heaven. *It just seems so wrong, God, for so much to be heaped on one family. Cancer was enough. Why did they have to lose their son too? Why, God?*

Elizabeth knelt with her church family in stunned silence, listening to the prayers but unable to form her own. All she could envision was what it was like for them to lose their only child. All she could relate it to was the possibility of losing her parents. They were all she had. She had lived with that worry since her freshman year in college, and it was made more real over the summer when her mom was so seriously ill with pneumonia.

That had come out of nowhere, completely unexpected. One day she was healthy; the next day she wasn't. Same for the Johnson's. One day Evan was there; the next day he wasn't. It was just a training exercise. You weren't supposed to die in training exercises.

As the pastor and the elders each prayed and the words penetrated the haze of shock which enveloped her mind, little by little her thoughts turned toward God. She was grateful Pastor Stephen had taken this time for the congregation to pray and process. *Thank You, God, for Pastor Stephen,* she thought.

That thought shook her awake, and then she was finally able to offer this prayer. *Oh Father, I know life isn't a right. It's a gift, and You are in control, not us. It's just that You made us for life, and You made us to be in families. That's why it hurts so badly when it's lost. Please, I pray, help Mr. and Mrs. Johnson to keep their eyes fixed on You, to feel Your love and Your care for them. Amen.*

Elizabeth went straight to her parents' house after worship. She'd been out at the house all day Saturday, but she just needed to see them again. Over lunch, she shared the news.

"The other thing is that Mrs. Johnson has already been through two bouts of cancer. They'd already had their share of trouble, and now this," she told them.

"There are no guarantees about that," her dad said. "Some people experience a lot of heartache in life. Others, not so much.

The point is, no matter what we go through, we keep our eyes fixed on Jesus. Regardless of what life throws at us, eternity with Him is our ultimate goal, and He will help us to endure whatever comes our way."

"I feel like I have to keep reminding myself of that," Elizabeth said.

"We all do, honey," her mom said. "And honestly, God wants us to keep thinking about it, to stay close to Him. He wants this relationship with us. It's why He created us, and it's why He saves us."

Bob helped clear the table after lunch and then went to take a nap. Elizabeth dried dishes for her mom, and when they finished, her mom gestured toward the counter and said, "Would you carry those down to the basement for me?" The jars of beans and tomatoes were the result of Saturday's labor. "I went to bed before they were completely cooled last night."

"Sure." Elizabeth gathered an armload and headed downstairs. As she tucked the jars in at the back of the shelves, she was reminded once again of her concern regarding her parents and the farm. While Laurel always did a good job rotating her stock, there were still hundreds of jars of canned goods lining the shelves. Way more than two people needed.

She also thought about the harvest she and her father had struggled through, even with the help of his crew. When life was normal, both the garden and the field work were fine. But things hadn't been normal this year. And what would happen the next time one of them got sick?

Again Elizabeth wondered if it was time for them to scale back. Then she recalled Thomas's suggestion to pray. She thought about the time of prayer at church for the Johnson's. *God, I need to pray more,* she thought. *I need to come to You with all things.*

So, before she headed back up the stairs, she placed one hand on the shelf, bowed her head, and said, "Father, I don't know if I should talk to Mom and Dad about this—now or ever. I don't want to disrespect them, but I'm concerned for them. Will You help me to do the right thing?"

Elizabeth took a deep breath, exhaled, and then headed back up the stairs. Once she'd made her final trip, however, and struggled to find room for all the jars, she felt less uncertain about speaking up.

"Mom," she said gently on her final return. "You have quite a stockpile down there."

"Oh, yes. It doesn't hurt to have some ahead."

"True, but I think you might be a couple years ahead at least."

"Nothing wrong with that."

"No, but maybe next year you could scale back the garden a little."

Laurel squinted at her daughter. "What are you saying?"

"Just that maybe you and Dad could cut back a little."

"I am perfectly healthy, Elizabeth Ann Shepard," her mother said.

Elizabeth chuckled and gave her mother a hug. "I know, Momma. I just worry about you."

"Oh, posh. You don't need to worry about me." She held her daughter at arm's length. "You, on the other hand..."

Elizabeth frowned. "What do you mean, me?"

"Well, you spent your whole summer here instead of having a life of your own."

Elizabeth raised an eyebrow. "Well, if you'd cut back that garden a little, maybe I wouldn't have to."

"Very funny," Laurel said. Then they laughed and hugged again.

Elizabeth had learned one very important principle over the summer which she carried with her into her second year of teaching. And that was to work when it was time to work and to sleep when it was time to sleep. The year before she'd worked until the work was done and nearly killed herself in the process. This year, she pledged to be well-rested.

She did, however, find that she was still quite busy in the evenings with school work during the first quarter. It took some time to get the new system with the graders worked out. She had to figure out what she wanted and how to adapt to not reading everything her students were producing.

She told Tracy all about it over lunch at school one day a couple weeks in.

"Thank goodness for the graders, though," Tracy said. "Now maybe you'll have time for a social life."

Elizabeth just shrugged.

Tracy squinted at her. "All right, what aren't you telling me?"

"Hey, you want to be gone all summer, you're going to miss out," Elizabeth teased.

Tracy scoffed. "You were gone all summer too."

"Not by choice."

"Same difference. Come on, E. Spill it."

Elizabeth let out an exaggerated sigh. "Fine." Then she whispered, "I went out with Thomas. Two dates. It was a disaster."

Tracy's eyes widened. "Oh, my gosh! Wait, why was it a disaster? And wait, I still see you guys walking back from Sunday School together!"

"I know." Elizabeth poked at her salad. "No, I don't really. I have no idea. All I do know is that how things went can't be how things go."

Tracy raised an eyebrow. "I thought you were an English teacher."

"Oh, shut up." Tracy laughed and Elizabeth couldn't help but join in. The truth was, what she had said really just about summed it up. Crazy, twisted syntax and all. She liked walking back from Sunday School with Thomas. What that meant, she didn't want to speculate, because she also knew that she could not knowingly enter into a relationship with a man who thought every single detail of life was supposed to go his way.

The thing is, she had never suspected Thomas would be like that. It left her confused. And more than a little sad.

And so she did after that lunch with Tracy what she did every Monday morning that fall. She pushed it out of her mind, worked hard all week—and then scratched the wound open again on Sunday.

Part Three

Living Out Our Christian Faith Publishing LLC

1

By November, Elizabeth was finally settling into a nice routine, at least as far as her job was concerned. Her personal life was still non-existent—unless you counted the two-minute walk from Sunday School to church each week. She was praying about it, though, and regularly. It's just that it was hard to know what she should actually be praying for.

And so that's how it was when the holidays came around once again. On Thanksgiving morning she loaded up her car with the groceries she had insisted on buying herself and left the house at a quarter to eight. She headed north out of town and was humming along with the radio as she drove.

A few minutes down the road, her car quit. It just stopped running. The power steering went out, and she gripped the wheel hard to wrestle the car to the side of the road.

Once stopped, her heart started pounding. *What just happened?* She looked down at the fuel gauge. *Three quarters of a tank. That's not it.*

She put the car in park and turned off the ignition. Then she tentatively turned the key again. All she got was a rapid clicking noise.

Great. Couldn't this have happened any other day?

She knew full well how dumb that question was. There was no good day to have a breakdown. Out on the farm a certain amount of downtime was inevitable, but Elizabeth unreasonably thought it should never be a thing with her car.

Then her thoughts fired in rapid succession. *Farm. Combine. Schaefer's. That's it!* She remembered that Schaefer's offered tow service and with no more thought than that, pulled out her phone and dialed.

On the other end a man cleared his throat and then said, "Schaefer's," in a husky morning voice.

Elizabeth froze.

After a moment, the voice spoke again. "Hello?" It was a little more awake this time.

Elizabeth startled to attention and blurted out, "Thomas?"

A pause. "Elizabeth?"

"Hi!"

"Hello."

Silence.

"What's going on?" Thomas finally asked.

"Oh!" Elizabeth frowned. "My car died."

"While you were driving?"

"Yeah. Now it clicks when I turn the key."

Thomas grunted. "Where are you?"

"Just north of town, about three miles."

Thomas yawned. "Okay. I'll be right out."

"I'm sorry."

"For what?"

"For—well, for calling on Thanksgiving." Her brain clicked back into gear. "And for waking you up. I did wake you up, didn't I?" Suddenly she was feeling mischievous.

She could have sworn she heard him chuckle, but he ignored her question. "You don't need to be sorry. This is exactly why we offer the service. I'll see you soon." And he hung up.

Elizabeth pursed her lips and stared at the phone in her hand. Despite her broken car, the day had just taken on a new shine. "Hmph," she said, slightly annoyed with herself for feeling twelve years old again—but enjoying it neverthe-less.

She sent a text to her folks to let them know she was running late, but she didn't tell them why.

Thomas's dad had assigned him the emergency shift on hol-idays a long time ago. At first he thought it unfair that he had to take them all himself, but before long he realized there were benefits. Such as getting out of the house for a while during long, grueling holiday gatherings.

This particular call had an added benefit. It was from Elizabeth. Thomas couldn't help grinning as he threw on some clothes, doused his head under the bathroom faucet, and then headed out the door.

He parked his truck at the shop and fired up the tow. He donned his coveralls and then headed out of town. Before long saw Elizabeth's little compact pulled off to the side.

He turned on his flashers and pulled in front of the vehicle. Then he checked for traffic and stepped out of the cab. Elizabeth did the same, and they met at the hood of her car.

"Hi there," she said.

"Hello." They stood in awkward silence for a moment. Then Thomas said, "I'll take a look." He popped the hood. "Go ahead and turn the key, would you?"

"Sure." Elizabeth got in the car and did as he asked.

When it produced nothing more than the rapid clicking noise, Thomas closed it back up again.

"Figured. It's the timing belt. We'll have to order one tomorrow."

"I was afraid of that."

Thomas got busy connecting the tow cable to her car. Elizabeth checked her grocery bags to make sure they were secure and then watched Thomas work as she had a few months ago when he fixed the combine out at the farm. Now, as then, he worked steadily and confidently.

Once he had the car loaded, he said, "You can go ahead and get in the cab."

Elizabeth nodded and turned to comply. Thomas soon followed, and they headed off down the road—the wrong way—until he found a place to turn around and head back to Sutton.

"Were you going to your folks?"

"Yeah. I've got a bunch of groceries in the back. We're cooking together this morning."

Thomas nodded and then without even thinking it through, said, "I'll drive you out, if you want, after we drop off your car."

Elizabeth looked over at him. "Really?"

"Sure."

"Because, I'm guessing you've got plans with your own family, and I don't want to mess those up."

Thomas shrugged. "It's early."

"Oh, right," Elizabeth said. "You were still asleep when I called."

He gave her a sideways glance. "I was awake."

"Mm hmm."

Before long they pulled into the shop, and Thomas maneuvered the vehicle into place. When he finished, he ditched the coveralls and said, "Let's drop your keys inside."

"I need to get the bags out first."

"Right."

Together they retrieved the groceries and stowed them in the back seat of Thomas's truck. Then they climbed in the cab. Thomas put the truck in gear and headed out of town. Elizabeth stared out the window at fields of cut corn, harvested beans, and newly planted wheat. Other fields had big round bales stored end to end beside the fence rows running alongside the road.

She was startled from her reverie when Thomas asked, "Everything going okay with your job?"

"Yeah! It's going great." After a moment she added, "How about yours?"

"Pretty good. Normal."

Elizabeth nodded, then said, "How was summer Sunday School? I never heard. Did you like it?"

"Yeah, I did." He glanced across at her. "I'm sorry you didn't get to be there."

"Me too."

Before long they pulled into her parents' driveway. Thomas parked by the walk and turned off the engine. They got out and pulled the bags of groceries out of the back seat. "I'll help you carry these up and then get out of your way," he said.

"But you're coming in first, right?" Elizabeth asked.

Thomas looked up in surprise. "Uh—"

"Of course you are. Mom and Dad will want to say hello. And they'll want to say thank you." There was a sparkle in her eye, and Thomas grew just a tad breathless.

"Ok," he said. "Sure." Secretly he was very happy with the invitation. He just hadn't expected to receive it.

"Good," Elizabeth said and turned to walk toward the house.

The door opened before they got there. "Elizabeth!" her mother exclaimed and then raised her eyebrows. "And Thomas, welcome! Come on in."

"Hello, Mrs. Shepard," Thomas said. "Mr. Shepard," he added when he saw her father. He set the bags down on the island just inside the door.

Elizabeth did the same. "My car broke down, and Thomas was on call with the tow truck. Then he offered to drive me here."

Elizabeth's dad got up from the table where he'd been peeling potatoes and extended his hand. "Well, thank you, son. I'm grateful to you." He turned and pointed at Elizabeth. "Although, young lady, I would have been happy to come get you myself."

"Oh, posh!" Elizabeth's mother said. "I'm glad you did offer, Thomas, because I needed Papa right here to work on that mountain of potatoes!"

"And I'd better get back to it before the boss gets on my case!" He chuckled and sat down at the table with his potato peeler. "Although," he said, clicking his tongue, "it sure is a lot of work for one man to do alone. I could use some help, if you don't have to run off," he said to Thomas.

"Oh—" Thomas glanced at Elizabeth, who was helping her mom unload the bags. She grabbed a couple of cans and turned toward the counter, but he could swear he saw a grin on her face before she did.

"We'd love to have you stay," her mother chimed in. "When does your family eat Thanksgiving dinner?"

"Um, late afternoon."

"Well, there you go," Laurel said. "We'll put you to work, feed you at noon, and then send you off to get fed a second time!"

Thomas grinned. "Sounds good to me." Then he looked at Elizabeth again, who was back at the island. "If it's all right with you, that is."

She looked up at him. "It is." Then she looked away, her cheeks coloring slightly.

Thomas sent a text to his mom to let her know he'd be late, but he didn't tell her why. Then he washed his hands at the sink.

Elizabeth came up beside him. "I'll take your coat."

Thomas slipped his arms out of the sleeves and handed it to her. She carried it away, and he sat down at the table next to Bob and the mountain of potatoes. Laurel handed him a peeler, and he got to work.

In the back room, Elizabeth closed the door behind herself and laid Thomas's jacket over a chair. Her hands were shaking. "Stop it," she scolded, but they didn't listen. All she could focus on was this one thought: *Thomas is having Thanksgiving dinner with my family!*

She alternated between grinning and frowning. She couldn't deny she liked that he was there, but was it right that he was there? Nothing had been resolved between them.

Elizabeth slapped her hand to her forehead. *Pull yourself together, girl. Just enjoy the day.*

With that admonition firmly in place, Elizabeth opened the door and strode purposefully to the kitchen. She stopped short in the doorway. Her dad was telling some funny story, and he had Thomas—wait. Was he laughing?

Elizabeth tried to remember a time she'd seen him full out laugh before, and she couldn't do it. She floated over to the counter where her mother was rolling out pie crust and mindlessly opened the can of pumpkin. The turkey had been in the oven since well before sunrise, and its aroma filled the house. Elizabeth shook her head to clear it and then got busy preparing the filling so the pie could go in as soon as the turkey came out.

Laurel glanced over her shoulder at the table.

"Be quiet," Elizabeth whispered.

"I didn't say a word." But she cast a glance toward her daughter and stifled a grin. Elizabeth hip-bumped her mother—gently. "What was that for?" Laurel asked.

"Stop grinning," she whispered through clenched teeth.

But Laurel couldn't.

The four of them worked together all morning with a lot of conversation and laughter. By the time the Thanksgiving feast was arranged, Thomas had laughed more than he had in the entirety of his life. He had also peeled, chopped, and mashed potatoes and helped Bob debone the turkey and set it to warm in the roaster oven. He couldn't even begin to list all the tasks that Elizabeth and her mother had accomplished. But the evidence was on the island, which was filled with an overwhelming array of holiday food: turkey, mashed potatoes and gravy, candied yams, corn casserole, green bean casserole, sage dressing, homemade pumpernickel bread, cranberry sauce, and pumpkin pie with homemade whipped cream. Thomas's mouth watered.

He thought of his own mother in her kitchen. She put on a pretty good Thanksgiving spread too, but she did it all by herself.

Mom. A wave of guilt washed over him. She hadn't replied to his text, and he knew she was probably sulking. A small sigh escaped his lips.

Elizabeth looked up. "You okay?"

He quirked his mouth to the side. "Yeah."

By early afternoon the kitchen was spotless, the four of them working together again to make it so. The refrigerator was crammed full of leftovers, and Thomas had a bag of his own to take home with him. He had no idea how he'd have room to eat another entire meal at his folks' house in a few hours, but he'd give it his best shot.

Elizabeth retrieved his coat and handed it to him.

"Thomas," Elizabeth's dad said, extending his hand once again, "It was a pleasure having you with us today. Come back anytime."

"Thank you, sir."

Laurel reached out and gave him a hug. "And thank you for taking care of our girl."

He blinked in surprise. "It's my pleasure."

Elizabeth said, "I'll walk out with you."

They traversed the length of the sidewalk in silence. They walked around to the other side of the truck, and Thomas put the bag of food in the back seat. He closed the door and turned to her. "Thank you for letting me stay."

She leaned against the driver's door. "Thank you for staying. It was fun." She looked up at him shyly.

Thomas studied her for a moment. *She really means it,* he thought.

Finally he said, "I should go."

Elizabeth pushed off the truck and moved away so he could open the door. "I hope you have a good time with your family."

Thomas was touched by her sentiment, even though it was unlikely to happen. "Thanks. See you on Sunday?"

Her smile was warm. "Absolutely."

2

Thomas was feeling so good about his day with Elizabeth and her parents that not even his mother's hurt silence or his father's stern disapproval could dampen his spirits. He felt good and he didn't care if they knew it. His sister, who usually rolled her eyes at anything to do with Thomas, just looked at him curiously. Thomas didn't care to speculate why.

The feeling held beyond the day, even at work. JB, who had partied the holiday away, was hungover and grouchy. Thomas's father was as he always was. But neither of those things bothered Thomas, not that day and not the whole next week.

In fact, he was in such a good mood that when a high school thespian walked through the doors of the shop after school on Thursday, just to see if anybody would like to buy tickets for the Christmas musical that weekend, he bought two.

When Elizabeth answered her doorbell that evening, she was startled to find Thomas standing on the stoop. "Hi!" she said.

"Hello."

Her heart rate increased, and it felt like it was fluttering around in her throat. She swallowed hard. "Do you want to come in?"

Instead of answering, Thomas silently held out two slips of printed card stock.

"What's this?" she asked, taking them in her hand. Then she gasped. *Tickets to the musical?* She looked up at him in surprise.

"Will you go with me?" His eyes were serious and intense.

"Really?" she whispered. He nodded. Her eyes grew moist, and she blinked hard. "I'd love to."

A smile spread across his face. For a moment they just stared at each other, and then he added, "And we'll go out to eat too?"

"That sounds perfect."

"I'll pick you up Saturday—" he paused and thought for a moment, "—quarter to six."

She handed the tickets back to him. "I'll be ready."

Saturday at five forty-five on the dot, her doorbell rang. She took one last look in the mirror and twirled all the way around to see the skirt of her dress billow and then settle back into place. Taking a deep breath, she blew it out slowly and willed herself to be calm.

When she opened the door, there stood Thomas in slacks and a button down shirt, freshly shaven, wavy blonde hair combed neatly into place. A whiff of aftershave reached her nose. The calm she'd brought with her to the door deserted her.

"Wow," they both said at the same time.

Thomas grinned and Elizabeth chuckled. "Thank you," she said. She plucked her coat from off the back of a chair, and Thomas stepped inside to help her into it. Then they walked to his truck where he held the passenger door for her and she got in.

The truck had been detailed. Elizabeth rubbed her fingers over the edge of the seat cushion. There was not a speck of dust anywhere. "Wow," she said again. Thomas got in on the driver's side. "Your truck looks really nice," she told him.

"Thanks," he said. "I thought maybe it should." He put the key in the ignition. "Is Italian okay with you?"

"That sounds lovely."

In the silence that followed, Elizabeth remembered the first time she was in Thomas's truck, when they were going to get pizza at the spur of the moment. *So much has happened since then,* she thought.

That made her think of the last time she was in his truck just over a week ago, and so she asked, "How was Thanksgiving with your family?"

Thomas bobbed his head. "It was pretty much like it always is."

Elizabeth turned to study his profile. "Does that mean good or bad? I can never quite tell when you're talking about your family." Thomas opened his mouth and then closed it again.

Elizabeth thought better of her question. "I'm sorry. That was rude."

"No, it's okay. I just never really talk about it."

"You don't have to."

"No, but I mean, I would like to. With you." He glanced sideways at her.

"Oh." A tingle ran through her body. "I'd like that."

"Maybe just not tonight, though, okay?"

"Okay."

By the time they got to the restaurant and placed their orders, Elizabeth had relaxed a little bit. It was Thomas, after all, and she was comfortable with him. Then he said, "Elizabeth, there's something I need to say to you."

"Oh." Her jitters came right back.

"It's about what happened last summer. I'm sorry. I—" He stopped. Elizabeth watched him struggle for a moment and then reached for his hand. They locked eyes and he took a deep breath. "I wasn't trying to be selfish. I don't think." Worry clouded his eyes. "I just had it in my head that things would be a certain way...and then the whole theater thing—and then we took the break—" He exhaled in frustration and shook his head.

Her jitters went away completely this time. Even from those few words, broken as they may have been, Elizabeth knew the truth. He was who she'd thought him to be. He might struggle, just like anybody, but he never meant to be hurtful. And here he was, trying to make it right. She gave his hand a squeeze. "It's okay, Thomas. Just let the words come out however they will. We'll figure it out together."

Thomas trembled. What she said gave him courage, and he knew, in a way he'd never realized before, that he could trust her. Had he ever truly trusted anyone?

He took another deep breath. "I thought taking the break and praying about it would make it all work out. I—" He stopped again. "The thing is, I've never dated before, so I'm probably terrible at it." He withdrew his hand and looked down, feeling miserable at the confession.

"Oh, Thomas. I can tell you—from experience—you're not terrible at it." He looked up from underneath his eyebrows to see if she was being serious. She was. "Dating a lot doesn't make anybody better at it." She looked away toward the window. "It just gives you a lot of baggage," she added softly.

Thomas blinked. He'd never thought about Elizabeth having baggage. She turned back to him, and he was surprised to see something in her eyes that he'd never seen there before. What was it?

He'd seen joy—lots of joy. Worry, about her parents; exhaustion all last school year. He'd even seen a flash of anger last summer, but he didn't like to think about that since he was the one who put it there. This looked like—pain. *Who in their right mind would ever hurt Elizabeth?*

She spoke again. "I guess you could say that's what was working on me last summer, my baggage, and I'm sorry it was. Honestly, you're lucky not to have all that."

The pieces began to fall into place for Thomas. The mess from the summer had to do with both of them and the things they'd gone through in life. Not just him. How could he not have realized that?

But the idea that anything in life had ever hurt Elizabeth seeded a small dot of blackness within him. He wished he could make it all go away for her. *Please God,* he prayed silently, without even thinking. *Please heal whatever hurts she's had.*

"If I had it to do over again," Thomas said slowly, "I'd be more willing to compromise."

Elizabeth smiled. "Like tonight?"

"Yeah, exactly."

She leaned forward in her seat. "I will go with you to the track. Just not—"

"—every week?"

She scrunched up her nose. "Yeah."

"I can live with that. And I will go with you to the theater," Thomas said. "Just not—"

"—every week?"

He grinned. "Yeah."

"Deal." Elizabeth held out her hand. Thomas looked into her eyes. The joy was back, and he'd put it there. He took hold of her hand and shook.

The waiter delivered salad and breadsticks to their table. When he left, Thomas and Elizabeth looked at each other. "Shall we pray?" he asked and reached for her hand. She grabbed hold, and they bowed their heads. "Thank you, God, for this food. And thank you for...for do-overs. Amen."

Elizabeth looked up at him and her eyes sparkled. "Amen!" she said, and picked up her fork.

The musical was a typical high school affair. The participants were excited to be putting on such an event, and the auditorium was packed with family and friends. Afterward, the foyer was impossible to navigate as people moved in all directions. When the crowd threatened to separate them, Thomas reached out and grabbed Elizabeth's hand.

Finally they exited the building into the cold December air. As the doors closed behind them, shutting away the chaos and the noise, they started walking toward his truck. Thomas didn't let go of Elizabeth's hand, and she didn't let go of his.

He drove slowly and somewhat circuitously back to Elizabeth's house as she recounted her favorite moments from the show. He enjoyed listening to her and even found one or two moments of his own to throw in the mix. When he pulled up in front of her house, he put the truck in park. Before he turned it off, he looked across at her and said, "You really do love it, don't you?"

"What?"

"Theater."

"I do." She turned to open the door.

"Hold on," Thomas said. He turned off the ignition, got out, and came around to her side. When he opened the door, he offered his hand and helped her out of the truck.

They walked up the sidewalk and onto her porch. Elizabeth turned to him and said, "Thank you for taking me to the show tonight."

He looked down at her. "Thank you for going with me."

She began to retrieve her key.

"Elizabeth," Thomas said softly. He reached out and touched her arm. She looked up. He lowered his hand to her waist, drew her to him—and kissed her.

The bag slipped from her hand.

The first kiss was brief but tender. When it ended, they looked at one another, and each saw an ember smoldering in the other's eyes. Elizabeth's hands found his arms and traveled up over his biceps, across his shoulders, and behind his neck. She entwined her fingers in his hair, and he kissed her again.

Elizabeth was breathless when this one ended. She stepped back, and Thomas grasped her fingers as she did so. She blinked slowly and squeezed his hand. Then she pulled away. "Goodnight, Thomas," she said.

Thomas inhaled slowly and let it out. Then he stepped back and reached down to retrieve her bag. Straightening up, he handed it to her and said, "Goodnight, Elizabeth."

Her hand trembled as she tried to unlock the door. Finally she pressed her arm into her side and found success. She stepped inside and flipped the light switch. Then she turned around. Thomas nodded to her and turned to walk down the path. She watched him get in his truck and drive away.

Elizabeth closed and locked the door and then turned around to lean against it. She touched her still trembling fingers to her lips. They were tingling.

"Oh, my," she whispered.

3

T homas rounded the corner on his way to Sunday School and almost ran into Elizabeth.

"Oh—" she said. Then realizing who it was, she said. "Hello."

His eyes sparkled. "Hi."

They walked into Sunday School together. They sat together. And for the very first time, they left together—on purpose.

When they walked through the doors into the sanctuary, Elizabeth turned to Thomas and said, "Would you like to sit with me?"

He studied her face for a moment and then said, "How about we find a place of our own to sit?"

Elizabeth blinked. "I like that idea." She looked around the sanctuary and saw Tracy watching them. Her friend grinned and waggled her eyebrows. Elizabeth chuckled and shook her head. Then she turned back to Thomas. "Where do you want to go?"

Thomas looked across the room and inclined his head toward the far section. "How about over there?"

"Lead the way."

And so he did.

Over the next few weeks, Thomas and Elizabeth learned how to navigate their lives now that they were spending time together. *Now that we're dating,* Thomas thought. He loved to say it out loud to himself. "Elizabeth Shepard and I are dating." He could help but add the word, *finally!* quietly, to himself. He also couldn't help but smile when he did. Now, after more than a decade, Thomas finally had a new best week of his life.

As the next holiday drew near, he found himself wanting to spend the time with Elizabeth. When they shared supper at her house one Sunday evening, he brought it up. "What do you do for Christmas?"

"Well," Elizabeth said. "Always in the past I've been at home with Mom and Dad the whole time. Church on Christmas Eve, gifts on Christmas morning." She looked up at him. "I'm guessing this year might be a little different."

"I was thinking about that," he said. "I'd be okay spending it with you and your parents."

Elizabeth set down her fork. "Maybe now's the time for you to tell me about your family."

Thomas blew his breath out between his lips. "I suppose. You know my dad." He looked at her. "He's gruff and hard to please." Thomas felt guilty even saying it, but it was true. "My mom, she's always hurt if I'm not there when she wants me to be. And then Karen…" *How do I explain Karen?* he thought.

Elizabeth tipped her head to the side. "Is that the most difficult one?"

Thomas looked up at her, thoughtful. *It shouldn't be. We're only brother and sister, and we have nothing in common. And yet—*

"I don't know. Maybe it is," he said. "I have no idea why she hates me. She says I'm like Dad, which—I hope she's not right." He stopped for a moment. "But she's also still mad because I told her friend to—to leave me alone."

The question formed on Elizabeth's lips. Thomas groaned. "Her friend, Dee Dee. You know JB, right?" Elizabeth raised an eyebrow and nodded. "He and Karen go out, and he's my friend, so the four of us always ended up together. But I was never interested in…" He stopped. He couldn't even bring himself to say it.

"I think I get it," Elizabeth said. "Dee Dee liked you but you didn't like her—to put it in junior high terms." She chuckled. "Is that right?"

"Pretty much."

Elizabeth raised her eyebrows. "I'll say this much for her. She's got good taste." Then she picked up her fork and took a bite, her eyes sparkling as she did so.

Thomas just stared at her, speechless. He felt his cheeks grow warm, but he also felt a hum of satisfaction spreading throughout his chest

"Okay, how about this," Elizabeth said when they touched base by phone later that week. "You and I could go to Christmas Eve service together. Then we could hang out with my mom and dad on Christmas morning and yours on Christmas afternoon. You said they eat late, right?"

"Yeah, that's right." Thomas knew he had to introduce Elizabeth to his family eventually. Not that they didn't already know each other, but in the sense of spending time together. He just wished he didn't have to.

He brought it up to his folks the next Sunday when he was there for dinner. "So we thought we'd come here in the afternoon. Does that sound okay?"

From the end of the table, his father growled. "I don't see what's wrong with you spending the day with your family like you've always done. It's not like you're married."

Thomas opened his mouth to speak, but his mother jumped in. "That will be lovely, dear. We'd love to have Elizabeth here with us for Christmas."

Thomas turned, stared at her, uncertain he'd heard correctly. Had she just defied his father?

Across the table, Karen's mouth fell open in surprise. As Thomas turned back, their eyes met. Then his father slammed his hands down on the table, and they both jumped. "What did you say?" he thundered.

"That it will be lovely to have Elizabeth here with us," his mother replied mildly. "And it will be." Then she got up from the table and carried her plate and her utensils into the kitchen.

Thomas stared after her, again, as his father muttered unintelligibly. He stole another glance at Karen, who raised her eyebrows and gave a nearly imperceptible shrug. Then she did something that was equally as surprising as his mother speaking out. She picked up her plate and her utensils, and she carried them into the kitchen.

Thomas wasn't sure he should share that story with Elizabeth, but at the same time, he didn't want her to be unprepared. A few days before Christmas, when they were spending an evening at his apartment, he told her what happened. She listened and then said, "It'll be okay. I've dealt with worse."

Thomas looked at her doubtfully. She placed a hand on his knee. "I'm serious. There've been a lot of..." She paused.

"Bullies?" Thomas asked, half-joking.

"Actually, yes."

"Really?" he said. *This is new. Who in their right mind would ever bully Elizabeth Shepard?*

"Oh, yeah. You'd be amazed at how many people in the world think it's necessary to make fun of you because your parents are the age of their grandparents."

"You're kidding."

She shook her head. "It started the very first day of kindergarten. Mom and Dad were pretty cool about it, though. They taught me to use my words—along with humor—to defuse the situations. Most of the time that's all it took. Anyway, I've dealt with it a lot over the years."

"I didn't know," Thomas said. Again he wished he could make all the hurt go away for her.

She quirked her mouth to the side. "I think we both have a lot to learn about each other."

Thomas put his arm around her and drew her close. He knew she was right. It's just that some things were harder to learn about than others.

Christmas went as planned—and as expected. But true to her word, Elizabeth didn't let Jack Schaefer's sulky attitude bother her at all.

"Hi, Mr. Schaefer," she said, as they came into the house in the early afternoon on Christmas Day. "Merry Christmas! Hi, Karen." She raised a hand in greeting and then slipped off her coat. Thomas took it and hung it on a peg by the door.

The scene was as it always was. Mr. Schaefer was reading the paper in his chair, which was mostly pointed toward the kitchen. He never watched television and refused to have his chair facing that way. Karen was sprawled out on the loveseat across the room, flipping through the channels. She kept the sound low because of her dad. If she tried to turn it up, he growled and sent her to help her mother.

Mrs. Schaefer was in the kitchen, clattering and banging. At least she wasn't muttering, but Thomas cringed anyway. It was so different from the Shepard household. Elizabeth didn't seem to care, though. "Let's go say hi to your mom," she said and took him by the hand.

"Hi, Mrs. Schaefer," she called out. The older woman turned from the stove. Thomas went to her and gave her a hug. "Merry Christmas, Mom," he said, and dropped a kiss at her temple.

"Merry Christmas, honey," she said and smiled up at him. Then she turned to Elizabeth. "And to you! I'm glad you could be here." She held out her arms, and Elizabeth hugged her.

"Me too!" Then she looked around the room. "What can I do to help? Put me to work."

Thomas got to stay in the kitchen for a while before his dad called him out. But even after he left the room, he could hear the chatter of his mom and Elizabeth, punctuated at times by her laughter. *Maybe this will be okay after all,* he thought.

His father was his usual silent self during the meal. Karen was too, but she was keeping a close eye on her brother and his girlfriend. Thomas realized, with some surprise, that she was less antagonistic lately. Less eye-rolling, less sneering, no snarky comments to try to get him in trouble. While it was nice, it didn't mean he trusted her, so he did as always with Karen and kept his distance.

But Elizabeth was amazing. She made conversation with him and his mom and even managed to include Karen and his father, all without really requiring a reply from either of them. *How does she do that?* he wondered. *I could never.*

All in all, Thomas thought the day was one of the best Christmases he'd ever had. Having Elizabeth there with him made it better in every way.

As he took her home that evening, he kept pressing his lips together to keep the questions from popping out. He so badly wanted to know what she thought, but he was equally afraid to know.

About halfway there, Elizabeth leaned her head back against the seat and blew out her breath. Thomas looked over at her. "You okay?" he asked.

"Yep. Just tired. Christmas is always a lot."

Thomas thought that over. "I guess it was even more this year."

"It was," she agreed. "But that doesn't mean it was bad, because it wasn't."

"Even with..." he stopped.

"Even with," she said and touched him on the shoulder.

The only sorrow that whole month came in the prayer concerns on the last Sunday of the year. Jane Johnson passed away. When their son died back in August, she gave up hope. The cancer returned and in just a few short months, she was gone.

$$4$$

When school went back in session after the first of the year, Thomas and Elizabeth had some adjusting to do. She had a bit of grading work most evenings, although it was way less than it used to be. Even so, she was far busier than Thomas. Except for Bible study, he was at loose ends. There was heavy snow on the ground and no way he could work on his car. He wanted to spend more evening time with Elizabeth than she had free to spend with him.

"How about this," he said as they were cleaning up from supper at her house one Sunday evening. "I come over and just be here with you while you're grading?"

"We could try it," she said. "But I can't guarantee I won't put you to work." Her grin was mischievous.

He pulled her to him, wet soapy hands and all. "I don't think so."

She laughed and dipped her hand in the water and then swiped it against the side of his face. "Well, then you better bring

something to do, because I can't concentrate with the TV on."
She raised up on her toes to kiss him.

"I can do that," he said, leaning in for more.

One such evening, Elizabeth finished early and after putting away her work, came back to the couch to sit by Thomas. He was reading through a car magazine. She snuggled against his arm.

"That right there," he said, tapping the page. "1965 Ford Mustang Convertible." He glanced up at her. "That's what I'm working toward."

"Nice!" Elizabeth said. "That one's beautiful."

"Yeah. This guy put a lot of time and money into it."

Elizabeth thought for a moment. "I remember last summer you talked about wanting to have your own shop. Have you found a place you like?"

"No." Thomas set the magazine down and turned toward her. "Even if I did, I don't have the money to buy anything yet. I mean, I'm making progress, but it's slow."

"Hmm." Elizabeth propped her arm on the back of the couch and leaned her head against her hand. After a few moments of thoughtful silence, she said, "I wonder what Mr. Johnson does with his building."

Thomas squinted. "Ted Johnson, from church?"

"Mm hmm. He lives in that pretty white house with the blue roof just north of town. His garage has like three bays in it." She gestured with her free hand. "It sits perpendicular to the house. You know which one I mean?"

Thomas's eyes widened. "That's his? I didn't realize."

Elizabeth nodded. "I took a meal out to them when Jane was sick and again when..." Her voice trailed off. The whole story was just so sad.

It was one of those times when prayers had gone unanswered, at least the way people wanted them answered. Thomas didn't understand it, but he figured God knew what He was doing.

It is a nice building.

Thomas was startled by the thought. It was wrong to covet the man's property when he was grieving the loss of his wife and son. Thomas scoffed at himself. It was wrong to covet his property, period.

"What?" Elizabeth asked.

"Oh, nothing." He dipped his head to the side. "I just, uh—mmm. It feels wrong to wonder right now. You know?"

"I do." Elizabeth twirled her ponytail around her finger as she thought.

"Plus, I don't have the money to rent a place, either."

"Right," she said absently. Then she threw out her hand and let it drop to her lap. "Can't hurt to pray about it though, right?" she asked.

Thomas looked at her in wonder. *No, it can't,* he thought. Then he took her hands in his, they bowed their heads together, and they prayed.

A couple of weeks later as Thomas and Elizabeth made their way out of the church, they passed by Roger, who was talking with Ted Johnson.

"It's hard to be there without her," Ted was saying.

"I'm so sorry." Roger placed his hand on Ted's shoulder.

"I've got an opportunity to travel for work. It'd be something different; I think I'm going to take it."

As they passed out of hearing, Roger and Ted were bowing their heads together in prayer. Thomas and Elizabeth looked at each other, but neither of them said a word. In fact, they were back at her house after Sunday dinner before Thomas ventured to say, "Do you think—"

And Elizabeth replied, "—I do." They stared at each other for a second and then as if by mutual unspoken agreement, scrambled for shoes and coats. Thomas reached for the doorknob, and then stopped.

"Hold on," he said and looked at Elizabeth. "What exactly are we doing?"

She studied his face for a moment and then deflated slightly. "I'm not sure, but I think what we need to be doing is simply going to visit Mr. Johnson. I don't know if it's right to ask him a question like that right now."

"No, me either." Thomas chewed on his lip for a moment. Then without another word, they joined hands and prayed.

Prayers complete, they calmly climbed in Thomas's truck and drove out of town. Less than a mile from the city limits, off to the right was the beautiful two-story farmhouse with blue roof and shutters. Elizabeth could see evidence of flower beds all around the house. She wondered if they would be maintained this year now that Jane was gone.

Across the driveway was a huge building, also well-maintained, with three garage doors and what looked to be an extra bay on either end. Thomas whistled as they pulled in the driveway then looked guiltily across at Elizabeth. "Sorry."

"No, I get it," she said. "I'm having a hard time not thinking about it too."

Thomas drew in a deep breath and blew it out. Then he got out of the truck and came around to open Elizabeth's door. They walked up the path hand in hand and rang the bell.

Mr. Johnson opened the door part way, and seeing Elizabeth first, said, "Why, Elizabeth, hello!" He opened the door wider. "And Thomas! Welcome! Please come in."

"Hi, Mr. Johnson," Elizabeth said. "Thank you." Thomas shook his hand, and the three of them went into the living room.

"Please, sit down." Mr. Johnson gestured toward the couch. "To what do I owe the pleasure?"

"We just wanted to say hello, see how you're doing," Thomas said. Then he added, "We've been praying for you."

"I appreciate that," Mr. Johnson said.

Elizabeth furrowed her brow. "Sometimes you wish there was more you could do, though."

Mr. Johnson nodded. "And sometimes you wish you could change things." He sighed deeply. "But you can't."

The three of them sat in silence for a few moments, and Elizabeth began to wonder if they'd made a mistake in coming. Then Mr. Johnson stood up and said, "Would you like some tea? I'm going to have some tea."

"Sure," Thomas said.

"Can we help?" Elizabeth asked.

"Come on in." He waved them toward the kitchen.

After the tea was made, they sat at the table and talked as they sipped. Mostly Thomas and Elizabeth listened as Mr. Johnson shared memories of his wife and son. Some of them brought tears to his eyes, but there were a few that brought smiles and eventually even a laugh or two. Elizabeth remembered how her parents had reminisced when each of her grandparents died. They shared so many stories with her that even though she didn't have them around for very many years of her life, they were still firmly rooted in her mind.

"You have so many wonderful memories," she said.

"I do," he agreed and wiped his eyes. "I would've liked to make lots more, but God had other plans." He pulled a handkerchief from his pocket and blew his nose. "Speaking of plans, I've decided to do something different—I'm going to travel for work." He looked around the room. "I love this place and the memories it holds, but sometimes they're a little overwhelming."

"What will you be doing?" Elizabeth asked.

"Training. I've got the opportunity to visit other offices around the country and help bring the new people up to speed. I'm looking forward to it, actually. I like to teach."

"Your class last year was really good," Thomas said.

"I'm glad to hear it." Then he tipped his head to the side. "Say, you wouldn't be interested in keeping an eye on things around here for me while I'm traveling, would you?"

Elizabeth blinked in surprise, and she and Thomas exchanged glances. At that, Mr. Johnson back-pedaled. "I'm sorry. That was kind of abrupt. It occurred to me while we were talking that I can't just leave my house completely unattended."

"No, you're right. It makes sense," Thomas said. "What did you have in mind?"

"Well, let's see." He looked around as if envisioning his property. "Mail, making sure nothing freezes or breaks. Snow—or grass—depending on the season. I think I'll be home most weekends." He looked back at the two of them. "I could pay you."

"Oh—!" That's all that came out of Elizabeth's mouth. Otherwise, she was struck dumb. She stole a glance at Thomas and saw that he was stunned as well. *If only we could have a moment to talk,* she thought. *I don't know what to do!*

As it turned out, she didn't have to do anything. Thomas did.

"It's interesting that you mentioned it, Mr. Johnson," he said. "I'd be more than happy to help take care of your place. But you don't need to pay me."

Mr. Johnson squinted at Thomas. "You have something else in mind."

Thomas chuckled. "Well. Yes, sir. I do." He looked Mr. Johnson straight in the eye.

The older man had a hint of a smile playing about his lips. "All right. Let's hear it."

Thomas cleared his throat and began. "I'm not sure if you know, but I restore cars—outside of my job at the shop."

"I didn't know."

"Nothing special—yet—but I have a goal I'm working toward." He paused. "Actually, your class helped me learn how to get there. Thank you for that."

"You're welcome. You're the one doing the hard work, though."

Thomas dipped his head in acknowledgement and then continued. "The space I work in is a carport at my parents' house. I work when the weather's good, but I can't when it's bad."

Mr. Johnson sucked in his breath, then got up from the table. For a moment, Elizabeth thought he was going to throw them out. But then he said, "Grab your coats. Let's go out to my shed."

Thomas and Elizabeth looked at one another and then got up to follow.

Mr. Johnson unlocked the people door and they stepped inside. The building was well kept. The end nearest the road was a workshop space. It contained a few automotive tools and some for woodworking. The bay closest to it was empty. Next were two cars and on the far end, a space that held lawn care and gardening equipment.

As Thomas took it all in, Mr. Johnson said, "I imagine a space like this would let you work no matter what the weather, hmm?"

"Yes, sir, it sure would."

Mr. Johnson continued. "I only sold off Evan's car a couple of weeks ago. Jane didn't want to let it go—" His voice broke and he walked over to the middle bay to run his hand along the vehicle. Elizabeth could hear an occasional sniffle. "I suppose I should do the same with hers. Just haven't, uh…" He turned toward them. "Haven't faced it yet."

"There's no rush to do that stuff," Elizabeth said gently.

"No, I suppose not." He looked around the building. "But if this space could be put to good use, it'd be worth it." He looked at Thomas. "I used to take care of my cars, just minor stuff. And I'd do a little woodworking out here sometimes too." He pressed his lips together. "That all changed when Jane got sick. We wanted to spend every moment we could together." A small smile formed. "Sometimes she'd come out here with me, but more and more we spent our time in the house…" He shook his head. "I'm sorry."

"Oh, Mr. Johnson," Elizabeth said, going to him and placing her hand on his arm. "You don't need to apologize."

"I appreciate that," he said. "It's been good to talk about them both today. Thank you for letting me."

"It's been our pleasure," Thomas replied.

Mr. Johnson took a deep breath and blew it out. "So, what do you think? Would this work for your shop?"

Thomas looked at him cautiously. "How much would you want for rent?"

Mr. Johnson raised his eyebrows. "Consider it payment for looking after my house."

Thomas shook his head. "That's not an even trade."

"Well, now I realize we didn't cover the concept of bartering in my class last spring." He tipped his head toward Thomas.

"But the beauty of the thing is that I get what I need, and you get what you want, and we're both happy. Yes?"

Thomas looked over at Elizabeth. She bit her bottom lip and nodded. Then he stretched out his hand, and Mr. Johnson took it. "I think this will work just fine. Thank you, sir."

Later that evening Thomas and Elizabeth returned to her house with a handwritten agreement and a set of keys. They collapsed onto the couch and stared at the items on her coffee table.

"I can't believe it," she said.

"I know."

She turned on the couch to face him. "I've never seen anything happen quite like that."

Thomas turned to face her. He frowned but he didn't speak right away. Elizabeth waited, enjoying the opportunity to study his face. Whatever he was wrestling with in his head, it would be worth hearing. Finally he spoke. "Why would God answer that prayer but not the one for his wife?"

"I don't know."

"It makes me feel guilty."

"Why?"

He pointed to the paper. "That agreement only happened because of his loss."

Elizabeth thought for a moment. "That's true, but it didn't cause the loss." Thomas furrowed his brow and she continued. "I don't think God causes bad things in order to bring good things. I think when bad things happen, God brings good out of them."

Recognition dawned in Thomas's mind. Roger had said the same thing. "Romans 8:28," he said. "All things work together for good for those who love God."

"Yes, exactly. This might sound terrible. I don't know. But it's true even for Mr. Johnson. He's going to do something new in his work, something he loves. And that's a good thing, even though it came about because of a bad one."

Thomas reached out and caressed her cheek. "You're very smart, you know that?"

"Pfft." She rolled her eyes.

"You are," he whispered. Then he leaned forward and kissed her.

5

Thomas was no longer at loose ends. He dug the carport and his trailer out from under the snow so he could transport his winter-stalled project to his new shop. He didn't think he'd ever get tired of saying it. *My shop.* Every morning when he woke up and the memory returned, it was like closing the deal all over again. It was the best waking up memory Thomas had ever had.

Well, almost. Waking up the morning after kissing Elizabeth for the very first time? Near perfection.

The day Thomas loaded the car, his father came out to watch him work. "Where you taking that thing?" he asked.

Thomas was hesitant to answer. It's not that he wanted to hide what he was doing. He just didn't want his dad to ruin it with any negative comments. "I found a shop."

His father raised his eyebrows. "Huh. You get a good deal?"

Thomas nodded. "Yup."

His father watched for a few more minutes and then, without a word, turned and walked back to the house. Thomas watched him go. When it came to his dad, that was about as good as it got.

Elizabeth wasn't surprised she hadn't seen Thomas all week; it made sense that he'd be setting up his new shop and spending his time there. She just hoped it wouldn't always be that way. She'd grown quite fond of having him around in the evenings. A happy medium would do.

When her day ended on Friday with no word about spending any time together, she sent him a text.

Hey, stranger.

Lol, hey.

Am I going to see you tonight?

Yep. I have a really cool place to show you.

Elizabeth chuckled to herself. That was fine. After all, she hadn't seen his setup yet.

She met him there just after five, and Thomas led her into the building. They skirted the project car and went straight to the workshop. While the space had been far from dirty when Mr. Johnson showed it to them, now it was spotless.

"Wow," Elizabeth whispered. She turned to Thomas and then stopped. His face was shining with a joy she had seldom seen in him before. "This is amazing."

Thomas bit his lip to stifle a grin. "Thanks."

Mr. Johnson had packed all his tools from the workshop and stowed them at the back of the building. He'd also removed the car from the middle bay. Elizabeth recalled that it had been his wife's car sitting there. She wondered what he'd done with it on such short notice.

Thomas ran his hand along the hood of his project car. "Shouldn't take me long to finish this one up," he said. "I can do more of them now." He furrowed his brow. "The only thing is…"

"What?" Elizabeth asked.

"You can only sell so many in a year without a license. It wouldn't be hard to reach that limit with this place."

Elizabeth thought again about that happy medium, but before she could reply, Thomas spoke again.

"If I could find my Mustang, I wouldn't have to worry about it."

"Are you looking?"

"Some. They're expensive, though, and I'm still saving up."

Elizabeth nodded. She had no idea how much he was talking about and didn't feel right about asking the question. Instead she said, "It'll happen, when the time is right."

"I guess so."

She took hold of his hand. "It will. I mean, look at this place. It happened at the right time too."

Thomas looked all around the shop and then back at Elizabeth. "I guess it did, didn't it?"

"Absolutely! Now let's go back to my house for supper this evening. You've worked hard all week." Thomas glanced over at the car, and Elizabeth knew he wanted to stay and work. She peered up into his face. "You have to eat, you know."

"I know. I usually just grab a sandwich."

"Eh, sandwiches are for weeknights."

Thomas looked down at her, his eyes sparkling, and then took her in his arms. "And weekend nights?"

Elizabeth sucked in her breath. "Supper together," she whispered.

"I can live with that," he said and kissed her.

At his invitation, Elizabeth tried spending an evening out at the shop with him that next week. The problem was it was winter, and it was cold—even inside.

"I think I'm going to go," she finally said.

Thomas looked up. "Why?"

"Well, it's cold."

He looked her over. "We should get you some coveralls."

"I don't know."

"They really help."

"I know. It's just—"

Thomas set down his tool and came around the side of the car to lean against it. "Tell me."

Elizabeth threw out her hands. "I don't know what to do with myself here. And there's no place for me to be, really. You know what I mean?"

Thomas looked around. He could see how it wouldn't be as comfortable for her out here as it was at home.

Over lunch at work the next day, Thomas looked online to see if anybody had a used armchair that he could put in the shop. Then he found a little table and a floor lamp to go with it. He set them up in the additional space at the back of the building near his work area. It was as far from the cold blowing in through the doors as he could get, yet it was still close by. Then he asked Elizabeth to come out again.

When she saw the space, she gasped.

"Now you have someplace to be," he said.

"I love it," she whispered.

"I thought maybe you could even, you know, grade papers out here."

She turned to him. "I totally could." She wrapped her arms around his neck. "Thank you," she said, and pulled him down to meet her lips.

Thomas was reminded of the day he bought the theater tickets and asked her to go with him. Two little slips of paper. Such a tiny thing, but it made all the difference in the world. So did a single chair, one small table, and a floor lamp.

Elizabeth loved her shop-style sitting room, most especially because Thomas had created it for her. He might be single-minded about his project and his workspace, but he wasn't unresponsive. That made all the difference.

She added a comforter and a heater to her space, and now it really was quite perfect. A couple times a week, she joined him in the shop. When she did, she helped look after the property too, and on the days when Mr. Johnson was on his way home, she left a meal in the fridge for him.

One evening she finished her last grading task and put her papers away. She stretched and yawned and then said, "You know why this works?"

"Why?" Thomas said without looking up.

"Because I need it quiet and you like it quiet." He looked over his shoulder at her and grinned.

She folded up the comforter and placed it on the chair. Then she turned off the space heater. "But it's time for me to go."

"Already?"

"Yep. It's almost my bedtime."

Thomas looked at his watch. "Wow. I didn't realize."

Elizabeth raised an eyebrow. "I know. Anyway, I'm going." She stepped over to him. "Kiss me goodnight."

"I'm dirty."

"I don't care." Thomas dropped his tool and wrapped his arms around her. When they broke apart, Elizabeth ran her fingers through his hair. "Thank you."

"Mm hmm. You've probably got grease stains on your clothes now."

"They'll come out." She planted another kiss on his lips.

Thomas ran his hands lightly up and down her back. "What if you were wearing church clothes, though?"

Elizabeth tipped her head. "Then I might mind." Thomas pulled her tight against his body and kissed her again.

"Or not," she whispered when they finally came up for air, both of them breathing hard. She rested her forehead against his shoulder for a moment and then pulled away. "I need to go home." Thomas released his hold but stood staring at her. She pointed toward the car. "You need to focus." She turned, picked up her bag, and walked to the door.

"Goodnight, Thomas." She glanced back at him before disappearing into the dark.

Thomas stood there for a long time, not at all focused, at least not on his work. In fact, he gave up and left shortly after Elizabeth did. As he drove home, all he could think about was how much he didn't like saying goodnight to her at the door.

And how much he'd like to never have to do it again.

Elizabeth wasn't brave enough to go out to the shop again for several days. She wasn't sure she'd be able to concentrate well enough to grade papers out there, not after—

Goodness.

She fanned herself. Even the thought of it heated her up.

Instead she texted Thomas at the end of each day, just to say hi, and then did her grading at home.

Her system was working well. It was hard to fathom how many hours she had put in the year before. Maybe it had been a good thing to experience that, but Elizabeth had no desire ever to do it again.

What she did do with her extra time was pick up her pen. She'd only dabbled with her manuscript since last summer, but thoughts about it were always hovering on the edge of her mind. By Thursday night she had already invested several hours in it and was deep in thought when the doorbell rang. She flinched, dashed off a couple of notes so she wouldn't forget them, and set down her pen.

When she opened the door, it was Thomas standing there.

"Hi," she said. Her heart started pounding.

"Hey there."

He grinned and she felt herself flush. How was it he could do that to her with just one look? She cleared her throat—and then looked more closely at him. His eyes were sparkling and filled with joy once again. Just as they'd been when he first showed her the shop.

She stepped aside to let him come in. "What's going on?"

He said nothing but instead slipped out of his coat. Elizabeth laid it over a chair and turned back to him.

"I found it," he said.

"You found—what?"

"My car."

It took Elizabeth a moment, and then she gasped. "You mean your Mustang?"

He nodded. "Today at lunch I was scrolling through listings, just to see what's out there, and it showed up." They went over to the couch and sat down. "I called the number, and he just called me back before I came here. I can pick it up tomorrow night."

"Wait, you've already bought it?"

"Most likely. It's rough; I already know that. That's why it's in my price range."

"Wow." She wrinkled her nose. "This is amazing. We were just talking about it happening when the time was right."

"I know," he said seriously. "I figured it was years away, just because of the cost, but…" He shook his head. "This way I can get started and work on it as much as I can afford to for however long it takes."

Elizabeth looked at him thoughtfully. "First the space, then the car."

Thomas tipped his head to the side. "First the girl." Then he looked at Elizabeth shyly.

She placed her hand on his cheek. "First the girl." She then leaned in to kiss him.

When they parted, Thomas grabbed her hand. "Will you go with me?"

"To pick it up? I'd love to! Where is it?"

"Louisville."

"Kentucky?" When Thomas nodded, Elizabeth thought for a moment. "Down and back? Or are you planning to stay over?" She could feel her cheeks warming again.

"Down and back."

Relieved, Elizabeth nodded. "That'll be a late night."

"I don't mind."

She could see the excitement in his eyes. She loved—absolutely loved—that he was realizing a lifelong dream. And that he wanted her there beside him.

"No, me either," she said. "I'll pack some food."

Thomas blinked in surprise, and then a smile spread across his face. "Okay!" He got up. "I'll be over after work tomorrow. Right now I'm gonna go make sure the trailer's ready."

When Thomas pulled up to Elizabeth's house at a quarter after five on Friday, she came out carrying a small cooler. He helped her stow it in the back seat. Once it was settled, he closed the door.

"Hi," she said, brushing his arm.

"Hello." He leaned down to kiss her. She'd missed that all week.

Once they were settled in the cab, they drove south out of town and got on the highway. Elizabeth fiddled with the radio and adjusted the heat, and when the time came, got out sandwiches for each of them. They talked, and she was glad for these hours to spend with him; she'd missed that too.

When they arrived at the seller's house, Elizabeth exited the truck to stretch her legs. Thomas was already talking with the owner and inspecting the car—such as it was. To Elizabeth it looked to be little more than a frame, and not even much of that. On her own, she never would have been able to see the potential in such a hunk of metal, but because of Thomas, she knew it was there anyway. With his skill and his patience, plus a whole lot of time and money, the once proud car could live again.

Thomas shook hands with the man, apparently satisfied with the deal, and handed over a pile of cash. Then they worked together to get the car loaded onto his trailer.

Elizabeth leaned against the truck and enjoyed watching him work, as she had so many times over the years. It occurred to her just how much she had enjoyed it. Then she wondered, if he'd ever made one move toward her when they were in school, what would have happened? It was hard to imagine. They were who they were back then. Maybe it wouldn't have worked.

Just like it didn't last summer. Elizabeth shivered as she realized how easily they might have missed out on what they were now sharing. Either one of them could have been stubborn or angry or unforgiving.

Her eyes grew moist at the thought and she quickly blinked it away. *Don't ever take it for granted,* she told herself. *Please, God, help me never to take him for granted.*

She emerged from her thoughts just in time to see them finish. The two men shook hands again, and that was the moment Thomas took ownership of his dream car. Elizabeth smiled.

The girl, the space, the car.

6

As Thomas's life transformed into something beautiful and desirable, his father's life disintegrated. Always gruff, he graduated to rude. No longer grumpy but instead, bad-tempered. No customer at the shop, no fellow worshipper at church would ever know this. In those spaces, he was simply a man of few words.

At home it was a different story. Sunday dinners had grown almost unbearable. As much as Thomas would have liked to stay away, he couldn't deny his mother that one small pleasure. He was embarrassed to have Elizabeth see it and wished she could have known his dad before. It shocked him to imagine longing for his father as he had been before, to think that the way he'd been was in any way desirable.

But Elizabeth handled it like a champ, just as she had at Christmas. She chatted and laughed and helped his mom in the kitchen from beginning to end. She talked to everyone, whether they responded or not. Everything seemed to roll off her without a trace.

Until the Sunday after the show in Cleveland, that is. True to his word, Thomas had been going with her to the theater on occasion. True to hers, she asked judiciously. But that particular production impressed them both, and so it was a topic of conversation over dinner. Thomas's mother asked lots of questions. Karen listened but with a look of derision on her face. Thomas's father punctuated the conversation with snorts and the occasional interruption to demand that some dish be passed his way.

When the meal ended, four out of the five people stood. Karen, to slink away to the living room and the remote control, Mrs. Schaefer and Elizabeth to clear the table, and Thomas to help. Elizabeth moved around the far end, stacking plates as she went. She handed them off to Mrs. Schaefer and then reached for the chicken platter.

"Here, I'll take that," Thomas said.

"Oh, thanks," she replied and reached for the bowl of mashed potatoes instead. She turned toward the kitchen and then heard Mr. Schaefer.

"You set that down, boy."

Elizabeth stopped, stunned, and turned on her heel. Mrs. Schaefer sank silently back into her chair. In the living room, the sound of the television diminished to nothing. Thomas stood motionless with the platter in his hand, his face drained of color. Mr. Schaefer glowered at him from his seat, elbows on the table, one hand socked into the other as if it were a baseball glove. "I'll not be having you doing women's work." Then he turned on

Elizabeth. "And you," he growled. "Dragging my son off to the theater." He spat the word from his mouth as though it were a piece of bad meat. "You're turning him into a sissy."

Elizabeth sucked in her breath and then stole a glance at Thomas. He was still frozen. His eyes were empty—hollow even. He hadn't responded to his father's words at all, not even the words he'd spoken to her.

She'd never seen Thomas like this before. He was always quick to reach out a hand to help her when he thought she was in distress. But not this time.

She looked back at his father. Him she'd seen. He was every bully she'd ever encountered. Something clicked in her mind, and she acted. "Gosh," she said, "here I was thinking how considerate it was of Thomas to help. I know I appreciate it."

Mr. Schaefer snorted and said nothing.

"And I know his mom appreciates it too. It's a lot of work to do all by yourself." She turned to smile at Mrs. Schaefer, but the woman had disappeared somewhere deep inside herself.

"It's women's work," Mr. Schaefer muttered.

"Really?" Elizabeth said as she turned back to him, warming to the task. "I never got that memo."

Mr. Schaefer threw out his arm and pointed toward the living room. "It's right there in the Holy Bible! The home is the woman's responsibility, and it's a sin for a man to do a woman's job."

"A sin? Wow." Elizabeth chuckled in spite of herself. "You must have a different translation than I do. I've never seen that passage."

Mr. Schaefer shot out of his chair, upsetting it, his face flushing to deep purple. "Don't you dare laugh at me!"

Elizabeth blinked. "I'm not laughing at you. I just don't think that's what the Bible says."

"Are you telling me I don't know God's Word?"

I have no idea if you do or not, but I'd need you to show me that passage."

"I'll do no such thing." He jammed his finger against the table. "I'm the head of this household, and what I say goes!"

Elizabeth frowned and set the bowl of mashed potatoes back on the table. "Mr. Schaefer, with all due respect, Thomas is a grown man and as such, is responsible for making his own decisions. Nobody told him to help clear the table. He chose to do so out of the kindness of his heart, and if I'm not mistaken, out of love and concern for his mom. You should be proud of him for those qualities, not trying to squelch them."

Mr. Schaefer slammed his hands down on the table. "Get out!" he shouted. "You get out of my house right now!"

Elizabeth flinched. The anger rippled from his words, threatening to overwhelm them all. This was different from anything she'd experienced before. More. He was an adult, a grown man—old enough to be her father. Nothing more than a bully, to be sure, but with decades of success at it.

In the adult world, his kind carried a different label.

But Elizabeth stood her ground. She stayed calm, at least on the outside. She was deep in this, and a lifetime of righteous indignation at such treatment carried her through. She looked him straight in the eye, took a deep breath, and said, "Mr. Schaefer, I am here with Thomas, and when he says it's time to go, that's when I'll go. Not a moment sooner." She turned and carefully picked up the bowl of mashed potatoes then disappeared into the kitchen.

Mr. Schaefer didn't move. His chest heaved as his jaw—and his fists—clenched and unclenched. In the living room, Karen was perched on the edge of the loveseat, remote outstretched toward the TV. Mrs. Schaefer continued to stare at a spot just to the side of the pile of empty plates.

Thomas's eyelids fluttered, as though to make up for the time spent staring into space. He sucked in a deep breath, as though to make up for the time spent not breathing. Then he turned, platter still in hand, and walked out of the dining room.

At that motion, Mrs. Schaefer stirred, cleared her throat quietly, and pushed back from the table. She re-gathered up the stack of plates and silverware and carried them away. In the living room, Karen sank back into the couch cushions and cautiously turned up the TV. Mr. Schaefer stomped away from the table, threw himself into his chair, and snapped open the newspaper.

It was quieter in the kitchen that day, but there were three of them working side by side, cleaning up from Sunday dinner. Elizabeth washed dishes, and she was glad for the job because her hands were shaking, and she could hide that fact in the water. Now that it was over, she felt the magnitude of what she had done.

Thomas dried, and every so often Elizabeth stole a glance at him. His face was drawn, and he hadn't spoken a word. She had no idea what he was thinking and was desperate to find out.

When the last pot was scoured and polished and hanging on its hook, Elizabeth let out the water and cleaned the sink. Thomas hung up the dish towel and finally spoke. "I suppose we should go."

"Okay." She turned to his mom. "Thank you for dinner, Mrs. Schaefer. It was amazing, as always."

She could feel the older woman trembling as she embraced her. Elizabeth was afraid she'd made things worse.

Thomas dropped a kiss at his mother's temple. "Bye, Mom," he said quietly.

Together they retrieved their coats. "Goodbye, Mr. Schaefer," Elizabeth said. She expected no response and got none. "Bye, Karen."

"See ya," she called cheerily from her spot across the room. Elizabeth blinked and frowned and tried to catch her eye, but she was engrossed in whatever show was flashing across the screen.

They walked to Thomas's truck in silence. He opened and closed her door for her. Once inside the driver's seat, he glanced at her but said nothing. Elizabeth trembled. She needed to know what he was thinking. *Is he angry? Did I embarrass him?* But she couldn't speak. Not yet. She needed to wait.

The five minute drive across town felt like eternity. *Maybe he feels ashamed. His father called him out in front of me, and then called him a sissy for—*

Elizabeth gasped. The truth crashed in upon her like a tidal wave. In the barrage of emotions and thoughts and decisions that had followed Mr. Schaefer's vitriol, Elizabeth had missed the significance of the accusation against her. Until now.

You're turning him into a sissy, Mr. Schaefer had said.

Thomas's refusal to go to the theater last summer wasn't because he hated theater—not exactly. It was because his father would cut him down for going. Her efforts to negotiate terms for their date had backed him right into the wall of his emotionally abusive father.

Now Elizabeth was frozen. Since she'd been dating Thomas, she'd seen the gruff man his father was, but never this. If this was how he reacted to something as simple as carrying a dish to the kitchen or going to a show...her heart shattered as she contemplated the life of quiet despair that Thomas—and his sister, and even his mother—must have lived.

Thomas glanced at Elizabeth again when he heard her gasp, desperate to know what it meant. They were almost to her house; he quickly made the last turn and pulled to a stop. Then he cut the engine and undid his seatbelt.

"Hey," he said, reaching for her and unbuckling hers as well.

She turned to him, her face pale and drawn. "I'm so sorry," she whispered.

Thomas frowned. "You don't have anything to be sorry for."

"Last summer. I never understood about the theater." She shook her head. "It makes sense now."

The words were like a punch to the gut. He didn't want it to make sense. He'd wanted to protect her from all of it, and he'd failed. "I don't care about that anymore."

"But you did last summer."

"We worked it out." He hesitated and then said, "I actually don't mind going." Elizabeth smiled and squeezed his hands.

Thomas continued. "I never should have let him talk to you like that."

Serious once again, Elizabeth studied his face. "I think you had a lot of emotions going on."

He didn't accept that answer. "You shouldn't have to deal with that."

"It's part of your life, Thomas. If—" She exhaled and then continued. "If we're going to be together, then we both have to deal with it." Thomas pressed his lips together. Elizabeth peered into his face. "Team effort. Sometimes you'll be the strong one. Sometimes I will. And that's okay."

For nearly twenty-five years, Thomas had been coping alone. There was no commiseration with his mom or his sister. The idea of having someone beside him—of having Elizabeth—

"I love you," he said simply.

Elizabeth sucked in her breath. "I was afraid you were mad at me!" Her face crumpled, and he couldn't tell if she was laughing or crying.

"Why would I be mad at you?" He couldn't imagine.

"For making things worse. I was afraid I made everything worse."

Thomas shook his head slowly. "I don't think that's possible." They locked eyes as they each contemplated the thought. "You were amazing, actually. Fearless."

Elizabeth raised her eyebrows. "Only in the moment. Afterward I was freaking out. And you were so quiet I couldn't tell what you were thinking. That's when I started worrying."

Thomas looked at her bleakly. "I'm sorry. I've never been able to stand up to him."

Elizabeth thought for a moment. "But you do, though—in some ways."

Thomas furrowed his brow. "How?"

"You said it yourself. We worked it out about going to shows, and we even talked about it at dinner today. Plus, you help your mom anyway, every chance you get."

He was still filled with uncertainty, but Elizabeth held his gaze. She nodded. "You do." Little by little his doubt gave way.

She placed her hand against his cheek. "And you know what else?"

"What?" he said, covering her hand with his own.

"I love you too."

7

One might have thought it would've ranked among the worst days of Thomas's life, but it did not. Quite the contrary. Nothing had changed in his family dynamic, but he was no longer alone. And he no longer had to try to shield Elizabeth from it; she'd made that clear. Every time he thought about it, he wondered why he'd thought he had to.

And so Thomas was at peace all day Monday at work. Any other word to describe his mood escaped him, but he felt that one was enough.

JB was oblivious to all but what concerned him. Thomas's father was present, but that was all. His mood did not hang heavy in the air, and for this Thomas was grateful.

At five on the dot, JB clocked out and went home. Thomas worked late to finish the project he was in the middle of. His father moved back and forth between shop and office. Doing what, Thomas had no idea, and he didn't care to speculate.

Karen hadn't shown up for work yet, but that was not unusual. She seldom appeared until everyone else was gone, even when they worked late.

The sun had set and all the other lights in the building were out by the time Thomas finished the repair and started putting things back together under the hood.

Jack Schaefer walked into the shop again and stood off to the side, arms crossed, feet spread wide. He watched Thomas work for the space of a single heartbeat. "You better get control of your woman," he said. "Or you're gonna have a world of hurt."

Thomas froze, mentally kicking himself for letting his guard down. He sighed and kept on working.

"You hear me?"

"I hear you."

Jack snorted. "She must be rubbing off on you already, if you're so disrespectful you can't even answer."

Thomas straightened from under the hood. "Dad—"

"Don't you Dad me! I been around longer'n you have! I know what I'm talking about." He looked Thomas up and down. "Finally get yourself a girl and what, fifteen minutes later you're an expert?" He scoffed.

"I didn't say—"

"You didn't have to say nothing! I can see it in your attitude." Jack stepped forward and pointed at Thomas. "You wouldn't even be here if it wasn't for—" He stopped cold, and then backed up and recrossed his arms.

Thomas frowned. "Wouldn't be where? What are you talking about?"

His father just shook his head. A chill went down Thomas's spine. "What do you mean, I wouldn't be here?"

"Just forget it."

But Thomas couldn't. A sense of unease had permeated his soul, and his usual caution when dealing with his father deserted him. "I want to know what you mean."

"Drop it, Thomas," his father said in a low, menacing voice. He turned toward the door, but Thomas moved faster and stepped in front of him. Jack's eyes narrowed into slits. "You sure you want to do that?"

Thomas swallowed hard but held his father's gaze. "I'd rather not have to."

Jack scoffed and sidestepped him. Thomas grabbed his arm, and Jack flung him off. Thomas grabbed him at the waist, threw his other forearm across his chest, and backed him into the side of the truck.

Jack was stunned. Thomas was too, but he was also determined. Before the shock wore off and the older man fought back, Thomas looked him in the eye and said, "One way or another, we're gonna have this conversation."

The steel in Jack Schaefer's eyes faded, and his hands fell away to his sides. For the first time ever, Thomas saw a tired, broken, old man. He relaxed his grip and took a step backward. His father didn't move. He also didn't speak.

"I've got nowhere I need to be, Dad." Thomas stood with arms crossed, feet spread wide.

Jack stared at his son, a haunted and disbelieving look in his eyes. He exhaled deeply, his shoulders collapsing. He hung his head and stared at his boots. "You wouldn't be here if your brother hadn't died."

Thomas reeled, the words like a gunshot to his chest. He stared at his father, certain he could not have heard him correctly. "My br—" he stammered.

"Your brother, Andrew." Jack continued to stare at his boots. "The drunken joyride that killed your grandparents also killed my son." Something like a sob tried to escape his father's throat, but he pushed it down with a growl.

The words ping-ponged in Thomas' brain. *Your brother, your brother, your brother.* Then, through the fog of shock that had enveloped him, his father's last words registered: *my son.* Not one of my sons, or my eldest son. Just, *my son.*

Thomas backed toward the wall and sat heavily on a barstool, staring at nothing. Jack looked up at him from beneath his heavy eyebrows. Then he pushed off the truck and moved around to the front where he closed the hood. He leaned against it, palms down, head low.

The shop was silent but for the ticking of the large wall clock that hung between the bay doors. Each click was like a puff of air, swirling the dark, murky clouds of Thomas's entire existence. Decades of confusion began to unravel, one strand at a time. His father's silence. His anger and cold distance. His mother's desperate need to have her family nearby. These things began to take on meaning for the first time in his life.

But why for the first time? Why had he not known about this before?

Restless, Jack wandered to the back of the shop and grabbed another stool. He placed it in front of the truck and sat down.

"Andrew was two. You know your grandfather was an alcoholic." He looked at Thomas. "I was a fool for letting them watch him. I never thought he'd load him up in the car when he'd been drinking. I never thought my mom would let him. But he was a mean damned drunk—" His voice broke and he hung his head.

Thomas stared at his father.

"Your mother was never the same after that." Jack sniffed. He pulled a handkerchief out of his pocket and blew his nose. "She was wild with grief and wanted to have another baby right away. But I didn't. She almost died having Andrew, and I couldn't bear the thought of losing her too."

Thomas raised his eyebrows. The thought that his father actually loved his mother surprised him.

Jack looked away across the room. "She wouldn't stop badgering me, though, and I finally gave in. When she had you I told her, 'You've got your son, now. Don't ever mention Andrew again.'" Jack looked over at Thomas with dead eyes. "You almost killed her too."

Another shot to the chest.

"But you had Karen," he blurted out.

"Karen was a mistake."

Thomas flinched. "She was not!"

"Your mother tricked me. Told me she was on birth control. I never touched her again after that." He got off the stool and wandered over to the tool cart sitting in between the bays where he mindlessly pushed sockets around in the drawer.

"That doesn't make Karen a mistake."

His father scoffed. "Doesn't mean I wanted her, either."

"Dad." Thomas didn't know what else to say. In the silence that followed, he was surprised at himself for defending a sister who was so vicious and hateful toward him. But then he wondered if she was coping with the brokenness in their family the only way she knew how.

His entire perspective about Karen changed in a moment.

"Why didn't you ever tell us?"

"What good would that have done?" Jack slammed the drawer shut and opened another.

Thomas couldn't say that it would have done any good. It just seemed like it should have been done. "I don't understand how nobody's ever mentioned it."

"Didn't happen here. Happened in Kentucky."

Kentucky! What other things didn't Thomas know about his own family?

Jack stared off into the distance, as if seeing the state from afar. "I settled my folks' affairs and then got the hell out of town. Your mother was near about term with you when we landed here. For all they knew, you were our firstborn." He slammed the second drawer shut and turned to glare at Thomas. "You got what you wanted. Now get out." He grabbed a broom and started sweeping the floor.

Thomas watched him for a moment, but the older man ignored him completely. Then he got up from the stool. He walked away from the project, and the tools which were still scattered on his workbench, and made his way toward the door. He might know more than he did thirty minutes ago, but he was hard-pressed to think one single thing was better for it.

On the other side of the door, in the hallway between office and breakroom, a shadow slipped out the back and darted across the alley, unseen, unheard, and apparently, unwanted.

8

Thomas went home after that, only when he pulled in, he was in Elizabeth's driveway. He nodded to himself. *Yes. Here,* he thought. *This is where I want to be.* He went up to the door and rang the bell.

Elizabeth cracked it open slightly. When she saw Thomas, delight replaced caution. "Hey!" she said, opening the door further. Then she saw his face. "Oh no," she whispered. She took his hand and drew him inside. He just stood, unmoving, as she closed and locked the door behind him. "Let's sit down," she said.

Thomas automatically unzipped his coveralls. Then he looked at his boots and reached down to unlace them. Elizabeth watched in silence. He left it all in a pile by the door and then let her lead him over to the couch.

They sat down and she turned toward him. She placed her hand on his leg and studied his face intently. *Whatever hap-*

pened surely had to do with yesterday. I made things worse after all, she thought.

Thomas took a deep shuddering breath and looked at her for the first time.

Steeling herself, she asked, "What happened?"

For a moment he still didn't speak; he just stared at her. His eyes were haunted and filled with sorrow. She didn't see regret or anger. At least that was something. He raised his hands and gestured around his head. "It's all swirling around."

"It's okay," she said gently. "Just grab hold of something. We'll figure it out together."

"I have a brother."

Elizabeth gasped.

"Had—a brother."

As the meaning of those words took hold, her shoulders slumped, and she closed her eyes. Her head shook slightly, her lips moving but making no sound. Thomas was quiet once again as she processed the news.

When her eyes fluttered open, he said, "I was working late. Dad was still there. All of a sudden he started in on me about—" He stopped.

"It's okay," she whispered. "You can say it."

He deflated slightly. "About you."

She touched his arm, her eyes filling with tears. "I'm sorry."

But at that, Thomas came alive. "No!" He shook his head. "No, you won't be sorry about that—I won't let you. It needed to happen."

"But—"

"It gave me courage to do what I've never been able to before." He turned and took hold of her arms. "Elizabeth, I stood up to him."

Her jaw dropped, but the floodgate had opened for Thomas, and he told her the whole story.

"Oh, my," Elizabeth whispered when he finished.

"Yeah." He absentmindedly ran his fingers over the surface of the couch cushion. "I guess for a minute I thought maybe things would change." He huffed. "But then just like that, he was back to his usual self. Told me to get out."

Elizabeth thought this over. "It was a lot for him to confess."

"It was a lot for me to hear."

"Yeah."

"That your own dad doesn't want you."

Elizabeth opened her mouth to speak, but Thomas continued. "He said they wouldn't have had any more kids."

"Well—"

"And he's right; we wouldn't even be here if it wasn't for—"

"Thomas!" She placed her hand against his cheek and turned him to face her. He blinked in surprise. "You listen to me," she said, looking him straight in the eye. "You are here because God wants you here. Both you and your sister. Do you understand?" She held his gaze until he finally nodded.

"Good. Don't ever forget that." She grabbed his hand and squeezed.

"What about Andrew?" he asked in a small voice.

"Andrew got to go to heaven early. It sucks for us here, but it's a pretty good deal for him, I think." Elizabeth regretted the words as soon as they were out. They were too flippant; she wished she could take them back.

She needn't have worried, though, because Thomas pulled her into his arms and held her tight. "Thank you," he said. She looked up at him but before she could say anything, he kissed her.

Only this time, the kiss didn't end. It deepened, intensified. Elizabeth's entire body trembled. Thomas's hand traveled down her back, over her hip, and along her thigh. He leaned into her, and she melted into the couch cushions. He pulled her leg over his own. She tightened it around him as her body screamed for more.

Then her brain screamed in a completely different way.

She broke off the kiss and pushed against his shoulder. He pulled back, breathing heavily. Elizabeth disentangled herself and stood up. She bolted toward the kitchen, her breath coming in gasps. She stopped in the doorway and wrapped her hands around her elbows, desperate to regain control.

Back at the couch, Thomas tried to calm his own breathing, desperate to undo the effects she'd had on his body. *It happened so fast. So naturally.* He looked up at her, but she was still turned away.

He rose from the couch and crossed the room. Coming up behind her, he placed his hands on her arms. "Hey," he said softly. She leaned back into him, and he wrapped his arms around her. She put her hands over top of his. "I'm sorry," he whispered into her ear.

She turned around inside his embrace and put her hands on his chest. She looked into his eyes, searching.

He crumbled. "Not really," he admitted.

The tension broke, and Elizabeth giggled. She wrapped her arms around his neck and rested her forehead against his shoulder. "I get it," she whispered.

Neither of them wanted to let go, but they had to. "Have you eaten?" she asked.

Thomas shook his head. They held hands to walk the short distance into the kitchen. Elizabeth broke away and pulled leftovers from the refrigerator. Thomas leaned against the counter and watched her work. She got out a plate and loaded it up. Then she stuck it in the microwave. Turning to him, she said, "So what's next, do you think?"

Thomas nodded decisively. "I wanna know more about my brother."

9

Wanting to know more about his brother and being able to find it out were two very different things, as Thomas —and Elizabeth—soon learned. Not all obituaries—or even newspaper articles for that matter—were online from that far back.

Complicating matters was the lack of Andrew's full name, birthdate, birthplace, and even when and where he had died.

"Even just a couple of those pieces of information would give us what we need to find out everything else," the city librarian told them.

They walked away, trying to figure out what to do next. "I hate to say it," Elizabeth said as they pulled into her drive, "but I can't think of any other options. You might have to talk to one of your parents."

Thomas shook his head. "I can't, Elizabeth. Dad wouldn't, I just know it, and I'm afraid it would blow things up for Mom."

At a loss for what step to take next, they bowed their heads and prayed for guidance.

Thomas didn't do anything different at work that week; he always kept his head down and worked hard. But now he also kept his senses heightened, knowing full well that it was impossible to gauge his father's next move. JB was an open book; you could read his mood with a glance. But Thomas's father was more like a darkened window, and Thomas had no idea what was going on behind it.

On Wednesday morning, each of them was in their bays as usual. JB was under the hood of a car on the driver's side, leaning in as he worked. Suddenly Jack appeared from around the tool cart. "Where's Karen?"

JB jumped and smacked his head on the edge of the hood. "Ow! Shit!" he yelled and ducked away. He rubbed his head and then pulled his hand back to check it for blood. He glared at Jack. "What'd you gotta do that for?"

"Answer the question."

"Damned if I know. She hasn't come around for a couple days." JB checked his head again and then stalked out of the shop, muttering as he went.

Jack raised his eyebrows at Thomas, who'd watched the exchange. Thomas shook his head slightly, never looking away from his father's face. For one brief, surprising moment,

Thomas saw his dad's eyes falter. Then without another word, the older man returned to his bay.

What was that? Thomas wondered. *And why was he asking about Karen?* As much as Thomas wanted to know the answer to the first question, it was the second that consumed his thoughts. It wasn't unusual for Karen to skip a day of work, but his dad never said anything about that. Had she missed more than one day? And if so, why?

He asked JB about it at lunch, but his friend was still spitting mad about what had happened earlier. "I swear, if there was any other mechanic job around here, I'd be gone!" He rubbed his head where a lump had formed.

"Sorry. Don't give up, though." Thomas looked over his shoulder and then leaned across the table. "Someday when he retires, it'll be you and me here."

JB scoffed. "Your old man's gonna work forever, just to spite you." Thomas couldn't argue with that; he probably would. And honestly, he didn't wish his father away from the shop; he just didn't want to lose JB. For all their quirks as father and friend, they were both good mechanics.

"So you really haven't seen Karen."

"Nope," he said, apparently annoyed by the fact. "All she said was, 'I'm busy,'" JB snorted. "Busy doing what I'd like to know."

Thomas thought about this for a moment. "If she's not at your house and she's not at home, then where would she be?"

JB looked up, concern registering for the first time. "She really hasn't been home?"

"Doesn't sound like it," Thomas said. "I don't think Dad would have asked if he'd seen her there."

"Maybe she's at Dee Dee's." JB grabbed his phone and sent a text. A few seconds later, a reply came back. He groaned. "She's such a—" He looked up at Thomas. "No wonder you didn't want her."

"Don't." Thomas glared at him. "Has she seen her?"

"No."

An uneasy feeling crept into Thomas's gut. He'd been working late on Monday, past the time she usually clocked in. Was it possible she'd heard them? A shiver ran up his spine.

Thomas went straight home from work that night to shower and eat. He was meeting Elizabeth at the library again. They were going to keep searching the digital archives in the hopes they could find what they were looking for. He was just headed to the kitchen when his doorbell rang. He frowned, not expecting anyone, and went to answer.

"Karen!" His shock was complete. Not only because no one had seen her for the past couple of days, but also because Thomas hadn't seen her at the door to his apartment in well over a year.

Her eyes were bleak. She said nothing but slipped past him to come inside. He closed the door and stood rooted to the spot.

She looked around the room as if taking it all in for the first time. She ran her hand along the back of his worn chair and passed behind the couch. She crossed in front of the television and then looked toward the kitchen. Thomas just watched her, at a complete loss for what to say or do.

Her hair was stringy and dull, her clothes wrinkled as though she'd slept in them. When she looked back at him, he saw the hollows under her eyes, and how thin and pale her face looked.

"You got anything to eat?" she asked.

Thomas startled to attention. "Yeah, sure. Sandwich okay?"

She nodded and sank down onto the couch.

Thomas went into the kitchen and pulled stuff out of the refrigerator: bologna and cheese, mayo, lettuce. He grabbed the bread and put together a sandwich. He placed it on a napkin and then opened the fridge and grabbed a pop. He carried it out to the couch and handed it to her.

"Thanks," she said and started to eat.

Thomas sat down on the opposite end of the couch from her and only then realized he needed to eat too. But he didn't move.

She made short work of the sandwich and gulped down the pop.

"You want another?" he asked.

She shook her head and took another look around the room. Then she cast a sideways glance at him. "Thanks, Tommy," she said softly.

Thomas blinked. The achingly simple phrase pulled at him. "You're the only one I was ever okay with calling me that," he said. Their eyes locked, and then Karen jumped to her feet.

"I gotta go."

"Wait—" Thomas stood and followed her to the door. She pulled it open, and he said, "Karen, are you—"

She turned and launched herself at him, wrapping her arms around his waist in a fierce hug. Thomas was stunned. He barely had time to return the gesture when she pulled away again. "I'll be at Dee Dee's," she said, and then she was gone.

Thomas called Elizabeth right away. The first words out of his mouth were, "I think Karen was there Monday night. I think she heard what dad said."

"Oh, no!"

They abandoned their plan for the library, and Elizabeth went over to Thomas's apartment instead. Over bologna sandwiches of their own, he told her everything that had happened.

"She hugged you? That's amazing! Right?"

"Yeah, but I don't know what it means."

Elizabeth thought about it as she munched on a baby carrot. "Well, if she was there and heard the conversation, then she also heard you defend her." She raised her eyebrows at him.

"I hadn't thought about that."

They sat in silence for a few moments. Then Thomas took a bite of his sandwich, chewed, and swallowed. "I'd like to talk to her."

"I think you should."

"She ran off, though."

Elizabeth bobbed her head. "This was just your first contact. It's been a long time since you guys have talked, right? Maybe give her a day and then reach out." She sipped her pop. "You said she's at Dee Dee's?" Thomas nodded. "We could stop by there tomorrow." When he looked up in surprise, she backpedaled. "I don't have to go in, or even go with you, if you don't want me to."

"No, I want you to. It's just—you're okay with that?"

"Of course." She studied his face for a moment. "It's okay, Thomas. There's always going to be stuff. We just have to figure it out together."

Thomas inhaled deeply and then nodded. "I like that."

Elizabeth smiled. "Me too."

After their meal, before she returned home, Elizabeth said, "Maybe we should pray about all this before I go?"

"That's a good idea." Thomas looked down, embarrassed. "I'm glad you remembered; I didn't."

"This time," Elizabeth said. "You do other times."

"I guess."

As they stood by his door, they joined hands. Elizabeth looked up at him and said, "Do you want me to pray?" He nodded, and they bowed their heads. "Father," she said. "We just want to lift this situation up to You. Help Thomas as he reaches out to his sister. And be with Karen. We think she's dealing with a lot right now, and we want to be there for her. Please God, help her to be willing to talk with her brother. They need each other." Elizabeth hesitated as her throat constricted and tears formed. She swallowed hard. "And Father, please help this family to know Your healing touch. Amen."

Thomas kept his eyes closed a moment longer, his own throat tight. Then he squeezed Elizabeth's hands. "Amen." He looked up. "Thank you."

10

The next morning at work Thomas clocked in and then poked his head in the office. His father was leaning over the desk where his mother was seated. They were discussing some document.

The conversation stopped when he opened the door. Jack looked around and said, "What do you need, son?"

"Talk to you, when you get a minute."

"I'll be out," he said and then turned back to the desk.

Thomas continued on to the shop and pulled his first appointment into the bay. Just an oil change; nothing major. Which Thomas felt was a good thing, because he had a lot of other stuff on his mind.

He was putting in fresh oil by the time his father came out and stopped next to the vehicle. "What'd you need?"

Thomas kept working. "Karen stopped by last night. She's staying at Dee Dee's. Thought you'd want to know."

Jack didn't say anything, didn't move. Thomas finally ventured a glance at his father and saw him staring off into the distance, his brow furrowed.

"She didn't say anything else."

Jack inhaled deeply and looked down at the engine block. He glanced at Thomas and nodded. "Thank you."

"Yep."

Jack walked away, and Thomas looked over at JB, who'd gone quiet in an effort to listen to the exchange. Neither of them spoke. Thomas hadn't made a conscious decision to share that information with his father. It had seemed like the right thing to do, and he just did it. He hoped he wasn't wrong.

At lunch Thomas asked JB if he'd heard from Karen. "Late last night—finally." He leaned across the table. "Dude, that is messed up."

"So she told you." JB nodded. *Which means she heard,* Thomas thought. *Oh man.*

Right after work, Thomas picked up Elizabeth and as they drove over to Dee Dee's apartment, he filled her in.

"I guess that confirms it," Elizabeth said.

"Yeah."

"Do you know what you're going to say?"

"No."

He pulled into the parking lot, turned off the engine, and drew in a deep breath. Elizabeth looked at him. "What do you want me to do?" she asked.

He turned sharply. "Come with me."

She gave a low chuckle. "Okay. Just checking."

Dee Dee lived in the apartment at the far end of the hallway on the second floor of an old brick construction building not far from the main intersection of town. It was shabby but not dilapidated. Thomas had managed never to spend any time inside the place, but he'd had to take her home more than once. He shuddered, not wishing to relive those memories.

Together Thomas and Elizabeth climbed the stairs and stood in front of the door. They looked at each other, and then Thomas knocked.

A few seconds later the apartment door flew open. When Dee Dee saw who it was, her face contorted with ugly hatred. "Aw, hell no!" She stepped back to slam it, but Thomas was faster. He stuck his boot in the way.

"I just want to talk to Karen."

"Well, maybe she don't wanna talk to you!"

"She can tell me that herself."

Dee Dee opened her mouth to argue, but Karen appeared behind her. "It's okay, Dee. Thanks." She nudged her friend aside and reopened the door. She looked from one of them to the other, but said nothing.

"Hi," Thomas said. He scrutinized her face. "Are you okay?"

Karen shrugged like it didn't matter to her whether she was okay or not. Then she glanced behind her and stepped out of the apartment, pulling the door shut after her. She looked sideways at Elizabeth.

"I can go wait in the truck," Elizabeth said.

"No," Thomas said, grabbing her hand. "I want you here."

Elizabeth looked from Thomas to his sister. A wistful smile tugged at one corner of Karen's lips. "That's fine." Then she looked down at her bare feet and scuffed her toes against the low pile carpet that covered the hallway.

After a few moments of awkward silence, Elizabeth said, "If you guys want, we could go to my house. I've got food, and you guys can—talk."

Karen looked up from beneath her eyebrows. "Yeah, sure. Why not. Lemme grab my shoes." She disappeared back into the apartment and returned soon after with shoes and her bag.

Dee Dee yelled from behind her. "The hell you going?"

"Out!" Karen slammed the door. "Jeez," she muttered. "Let's get outta here."

The three of them walked silently to Thomas's truck. Elizabeth hesitated, uncertain of the seating arrangements, but Karen climbed in the back.

When they got to her house, Elizabeth unlocked the door and led them inside. "Do you want to eat?"

"Yeah, sure," Karen said.

Elizabeth busied herself in the kitchen. Thomas and Karen sat down on the couch. Karen crossed her arms tightly against her chest.

Thomas didn't know what to say. He didn't want this to blow up, but there were things they had to talk about. He offered a silent prayer and then spoke. "What have you been up to?"

"Nothing much. Gonna start working at the grocery store."

"So, you're done at the shop?"

Karen snorted. "Yeah, I'm done."

Thomas opened his mouth but no words came out.

"Tommy, I know. I heard you and Dad talking that night."

He closed his eyes. "Did you hear—everything?"

"You mean did I hear the part where Dad said I was a mistake? Yeah, I heard that."

"He never should've said that."

Karen raised her eyebrows and bounced her leg. "It explains a lot."

"What do you mean?"

"He looks at me like I'm a bug he wants to squash!" Then she added, under her breath, "If he looks at me at all."

For years Thomas had heard the barked commands for Karen to get to the kitchen, Karen to show up to work. He'd always assumed it was because she was slacking. He'd never stopped to think that maybe she was slacking because the only thing her dad ever did was bark at her.

"I'm sorry," he said.

Karen huffed. "It's not your fault." She looked at him guiltily. "I know that now. I didn't before." They locked eyes for a moment, and then Thomas nodded.

Elizabeth poked her head in. "I've got stuff ready if you guys want." The three of them silently filled plates and filed back into the living room. Elizabeth sat in the overstuffed chair; Thomas and Karen returned to the couch. He offered a brief prayer of thanks, and they ate.

At some point, Thomas finally said, "I'm trying to find out more about our—brother." It still felt weird to say it.

Karen stopped mid-chew and glanced sideways at him. "Why?"

"I don't know. I just feel like I need to know."

Karen didn't reply.

"Elizabeth's been helping me, but we don't have much to go on. Do you know our grandparents' names?"

Karen shook her head.

They continued eating in silence. Then Thomas continued. "You'd think they would have kept something from him." He looked up at his sister. "Don't you?"

Karen scoffed. "I've never seen any keepsakes in that house." Now that Thomas thought about it, he realized he hadn't either. Karen continued, "The only junk I've ever seen is in that bay at the shop."

Everybody froze. Then she slowly turned her head and looked at her brother. "We can't," he said.

Karen shrugged. "You can't."

"Neither can you!"

But Karen wasn't listening. She wolfed down the last bite of her meal, then jumped up and carried her plate to the kitchen. Returning, she said to Elizabeth, "Thanks for the food."

"You're welcome."

"Karen—"

She snatched her bag from the couch and darted toward the door, a wicked grin on her face. "I'll text you if I find anything."

"No, wait!" Thomas called after her. But it was too late. She was gone.

Thomas jumped up and ran to the door, but Karen had vanished. He turned around. "This is a really bad idea."

Elizabeth didn't disagree, but at the same time...

"I think it's her way of trying to help," she said, her voice gentle.

Thomas threw his head back. "If he finds out, it'll be my fault."

"Then let's pray he doesn't find out."

Thomas offered a plea on the spot for that very thing. Then, at a loss for what else to do, they cleaned up after the meal.

An hour later, Thomas received a text. "Oh wow," he said. "She found it." He showed his phone to Elizabeth. It was the image of a twenty-eight year old newspaper article from the *Louisville News,* dated September 23, 19—.

Three Dead in Drunk Driving Accident

A Jefferson County resident is dead after getting behind the wheel while intoxicated on Friday evening. Walter Schaefer, age 48, failed to negotiate a curve on Tottenhower Lane just outside the city limits. According to eyewitnesses, the vehicle exited the road and flipped multiple times before coming to rest in a field. The accident also claimed the lives of his wife, Emma Schaefer, age 46, and their grandson, Andrew Schaefer, age 2. Andrew is survived by his parents, Jack and Doreen Schaefer, also of Jefferson County.

"It really is true," Elizabeth whispered after reading over his shoulder.

"Yeah." Thomas realized that some part of him hadn't quite accepted that fact before now.

After a moment of silence, Elizabeth looked up at him and said, "We've got more to go on now. If you still want to."

"I do."

It didn't take them long after that to fill in the blanks. Within several days, they had Andrew's birth date and burial location.

Thomas was quiet, taking it all in. A thought was forming in his mind; he wondered if it was crazy. He hadn't spoken of it yet when Elizabeth said, "Do you want to go see it? His grave, I mean."

He looked at her, astonished. "That's what I was thinking about."

"I thought you might be."

"Is that crazy?"

"Not at all. Plus, we already know the way to Louisville."

Thomas's heart warmed. "Yes, we do." He wrapped her in his arms and held her close.

Elizabeth rested her head against his shoulder for a moment and then looked up. "You should ask Karen to come along."

Thomas said nothing. There had been just the one text between them. Karen hadn't responded when he wrote back—or when he tried to call. She had, however, apparently done a good job of covering her tracks. When Thomas went to work the next day, everything looked the same as always, and his father said nothing. The last communication he'd sent to her was after they'd completed their research. *"Thank you,"* was all it said. Still though, Elizabeth was right. Karen should have the opportunity to go along. Thomas pulled out his phone and dialed.

He was surprised when she picked up.

"Hey," she said by way of greeting.

"Come with us to visit the grave." Thomas figured it was best to get right to the point.

She was silent for so long that Thomas thought maybe they'd lost connection. He checked his screen. All good, so he just waited.

"When?" she finally asked.

"Saturday."

"Okay," she said. "Text me details," and hung up.

On Saturday, Thomas picked up his sister and then drove to Elizabeth's house. She came out, once again, carrying a cooler.

Karen rolled her eyes as they loaded it in the back next to her, but she also couldn't resist peeking inside.

They were all quiet on the drive down. Elizabeth didn't feel that she and Thomas could have their usual conversation; she didn't want to exclude Karen. But she also didn't think Karen would join in. That left silence as their only option.

She did speak up once, however, as they neared the metro area. "Isn't this where we turned off last time?"

Thomas nodded.

Karen perked up. "Whaddya mean, last time?"

"We drove down a couple months ago," Thomas said. "I bought my Mustang."

A small gasp came from the back seat. Elizabeth glanced at Thomas out of the corner of her eye, but he kept his on the road. After a minute, there came from the back seat a small, satisfied, "Cool."

When they arrived at the cemetery, Elizabeth read out the directions she'd been given for how to get to the gravesite. They found the section and parked the truck. Elizabeth got out to stretch her legs but held back.

"Come with us," Thomas said.

"I'll come later. I want you guys to have time." She glanced at Karen who was watching her closely. Elizabeth climbed back in the truck and sat with her door open.

Thomas and Karen walked across the grounds until they arrived at their brother's grave. It was located along the right-hand side of the expanse, not too far from the woods that wrapped all the way around to the back. A mausoleum was visible in the distance and from where Elizabeth sat, she could hear, but not see, a fountain.

She watched them as they stood side by side, staring silently down at the stone. *Despite their quarrels,* she thought, *they are so much alike.*

Elizabeth contemplated that. *Only in some ways,* she corrected herself. Karen didn't put much stock in church attendance; that much was evident. It probably meant she wasn't actually living a life of faith.

And therein lay the difference between them. Thomas was seeking God. Karen was not.

Elizabeth realized Thomas was motioning to her. She got out of the truck and walked through the grass. She stood off to the right of Karen and looked down at the simple gravestone. The cemetery itself was well-kept, but the grave was littered with the debris of winter. She knelt down and started brushing away leaves and twigs. After a bit Thomas pulled out his handkerchief and started wiping the headstone. Then he went back to his truck and returned with a small brush. Together they worked to clean up Andrew's resting place.

Karen watched all this silently and then finally walked away. When she returned, she had a fistful of dandelions. Elizabeth glanced up at her. "I like dandelions," Karen said fiercely.

Elizabeth grinned. "So do I. And those tiny wild violets too." She looked around, saw some just beyond her, and reached out to pluck a few. She handed them to Karen and then stood. She brushed the dirt from her jeans and backed away.

Karen arranged the flowers in her hand and after a moment, knelt down to place them on the grave. Then she too backed away and stood once again between Thomas and Elizabeth. No one spoke. After a few moments, they turned as one and walked back to the truck.

Once they were outside the city limits, Karen handed out sandwiches, and they ate in silence. It had been a solemn day, and Elizabeth still could not see how to bring conversation into it.

It was Karen who finally spoke, though, at a point about halfway to home. "I thought he was going to kill you," she said quietly. Elizabeth blinked, looked at Thomas, and then turned to look at Karen. "Our father," Karen said, her voice dripping with scorn on the word. "At dinner."

In a low voice, Thomas said, "I'd have taken him out if he tried."

Elizabeth trembled as she locked eyes with Karen. Then she turned back and reached for Thomas's hand. She didn't let go the rest of the way home.

Back in Sutton, Thomas dropped Karen off at Dee Dee's. "Hey," Elizabeth called to her from the window. Karen turned back. "Would you come eat supper with us again sometime?" Karen regarded her for a moment and then shrugged. "Yeah, sure. Why not." Then she turned and disappeared into the building.

The silence lingered on the short drive to Elizabeth's, but when Thomas pulled in her driveway and turned off the motor, she could wait no longer. She unbuckled her belt and turned toward him. "It didn't feel right to ask on the way home, but I have to know. How are you doing?"

Thomas chewed on his lip as he thought this over. "I'm okay, I'm just not...I don't know. Satisfied, maybe?" Elizabeth nodded. "It made it more real, seeing his grave, but I still wish we could talk with Mom and Dad—or Mom, anyway."

Elizabeth took both of his hands in hers. "I think that's something to pray for—the opportunity to share that part of your life with your family." She looked at him questioningly.

"I think you're right. Let's do it now, okay?"

Together they bowed their heads.

11

As prayer became a more natural part of his life, Thomas found himself doing it more, remembering it more easily. In fact when he got home after the trip to Kentucky, he added his family, with all their mess, to his list.

It wasn't that prayer fixed everything or that God answered the way he wanted Him to every time. It was more about knowing that he wasn't alone in dealing with all the stuff of life. God was always with him, even when Elizabeth or his church family wasn't. God never changed, never got tired of hearing from him. He wasn't fickle or broken or limited like people were. Thomas liked knowing he could lean on God no matter what.

Another thing he found himself doing was keeping his father up-to-date about Karen. Briefly. Just enough so his father knew she was okay. He couldn't have said exactly why he was doing it except that it still felt like the right thing to do. For all his father's growing anger and hatred over the last few months, ever since that night in the shop, Thomas thought he'd seen hints of remorse in his father's eyes, in the way he carried himself at work.

When he let him know that Karen was taking a different job, it showed up in his voice too. "Not surprised by that," his father said.

"Maybe it'll be good for her to be independent."

Jack worked his jaw for a long time but when he finally spoke, all he said was, "Maybe."

When Thomas prayed for his dad, he tried to lift him up as a broken human being, albeit one who had never done anything to try to get better. It didn't excuse the hurt he'd put on his family, but it was better than railing against him as a monster, as though he felt nothing for his wife and his children. Thomas knew that wasn't true, even if it wasn't visible. Over time, his heart softened toward compassion for his dad, even through the hurt.

It helped that he and Elizabeth were also praying for these things together. They often talked about whatever they were praying for, over a meal or on a drive, trying to work out their own actions and reactions to whatever was going on in their lives. It was a form of intimacy that Thomas had never even known existed. How could he? He'd never seen it in his parents.

It made him long for more.

Not too long after their trip, Elizabeth said, "I'd like to invite Karen to join us for supper. Do you think she'll come?"

"All we can do is ask."

And so Elizabeth did. Karen accepted, and once they got through their initial awkwardness, they each began to relax.

Thomas and Karen even talked a little bit. Elizabeth made a quiet pledge to extend the invitation on a regular basis.

One day not long after that, when his father was staying late at the shop, Thomas decided it was time to bring up Andrew again. It was one of the things he and Elizabeth were praying about. He knew the risks, but he felt like he had to try. After he clocked out, he walked over to lean against the tool bench in his father's bay. He watched and waited, choosing not to speak until his father did. This time, it didn't take so long.

"What do you need, son?"

"I've always loved watching you work." Thomas blinked in surprise at his own words.

The older man's hands stilled for a moment, and Thomas decided to plunge on in this unexpected direction. "Thank you for teaching me."

Jack went back to work then, but his fingers were restless and unproductive. "Not a great teacher," he said, "but you were a good learner."

Over the years his father had said many things that knocked the wind out of him. These words did that too, but in a completely different way. Thomas's throat constricted, which was just as well, because he had no idea how to respond.

Before he could figure it out, Jack wiped his hands on a grease rag and turned to lean against the vehicle. "What can I do for you?"

Thomas noted the change in words and wondered about it. Pushing the thought aside, he swallowed hard and said, "I want to be able to talk with you about Andrew."

Jack sighed deeply, seeming to collapse in on himself, and Thomas rushed on. "That one conversation explained so much—about everything. About our lives. But I want to know more." He stopped and studied his father's face. He was listening, so Thomas continued. "And I want things to be better—for all of us."

Jack looked away across the shop. It was silent all around them except for the ticking of the clock which hung between the bay doors. Thomas just waited. He'd said his piece; now it was up to his father.

Finally Jack reached into his pocket and pulled out a ring of keys. He found the one he wanted and held it out to Thomas. "Guess you should start there," he said, tipping his head toward the back bay.

12

E arly that summer, Elizabeth and Thomas joined her parents for supper. When all the food was put away and dishes washed, Thomas said to Elizabeth, "You want to go for a walk?"

"Sure."

They walked along the field behind the house. This was the only one her dad kept for himself this year; all the others he had rented out. Bob Shepard had actively farmed for nearly sixty years; it was okay to pass the baton.

They wandered through the trees which formed a small bit of woods on her parents' property. The dog joined them, running ahead to sniff out any potential threats. When they strolled by the garden, Elizabeth couldn't help but smile. Her mother had reduced its size by more than half—but she'd never said a word about it.

Eventually they ended up in the machine shed, where her dad's shop was. Thomas stopped just inside the door, in the first bay by the tractor. Elizabeth went a couple steps further and looked around at the familiar space.

"I haven't been in here for awhile," she said, taking note of what had changed—and what hadn't. Memories washed over her. "You know, this is where we first met."

"I remember," Thomas said.

Something in his voice caused her to turn. That's when it struck her. He was standing in almost exactly the same spot he had been when she saw him for the very first time.

He was taller now. More confident. He was still quiet, but he was no longer silent. Elizabeth looked at him, and she loved him. Loved every new thing she learned about him—the kindness and care that came so naturally. She cheered with him over the goals and dreams he was finally beginning to realize. Grieved alongside him for all the sorrow and heartache he'd been carrying alone for so long.

All these things she loved. And she loved the way he looked at her. Just as he was looking at her now.

He held out his hand, and she stepped forward to take it. They locked eyes. Thomas brushed an invisible strand of hair from her face. "From the first moment I met you," he said softly.

Elizabeth smiled.

"But it wasn't until these past two years that I finally began to *know* you. How much you care for your parents. How dedicated you are to your students. How important your faith is." He stopped and caressed her cheek with his thumb. "How you won't let anybody walk all over you."

She pressed her lips together, willing the tears not to fall. She wondered if she'd always cry when they spoke of it.

"How you wouldn't just let me ignore you last summer."

Elizabeth swiped at her cheek.

"How you gave me another chance."

A sob rose up in her throat. He had given her another chance too. *Thank you, God, that he gave me another chance.*

"And every single one of those things makes me love you more."

"Oh, Thomas," she whispered.

"Elizabeth, will you marry me?"

She didn't know how he'd done it; she hadn't seen it happen, but in his hands he held a box. And in that box was a ring. The most beautiful, perfect ring she'd ever seen.

She looked up at him again, the tears in her eyes finally spilling over freely. "Yes," she whispered, placing her hand against his cheek. "Thomas Schaefer, I will marry you."

At those words, Thomas wrapped her in his arms and kissed her.

Epilogue

Late that summer, Mr. and Mrs. Thomas Schaefer embraced in a hotel room. There would be no more goodnights at the door. Thomas had waited for this day for so very long.

She was beautiful. Radiant. He unbuttoned her blouse and let it drop to the floor. Elizabeth did the same with his shirt, and then placed her hands on his bare chest for the very first time. Thomas's blood stirred. He touched her skin. Her waist, the small of her back. His hands traveled up and over her shoulders and eased the straps of her undergarment out of his way.

Elizabeth quivered, exhaled. She looked up at him and they locked eyes. There was anticipation in hers. And something else; what was it?

"Tell me," he said softly.

"I just—" She leaned her forehead against his jawline. "Nervous," she whispered. "I haven't done this before."

He hadn't thought he could feel more for this woman, his wife, than he already did, but this answer to the question he had never dared ask exploded into every cell of his being. He needed her. Now.

He took her face in his hands. "Neither have I." Then he kissed her.

The kiss deepened, intensified. When their hearts were racing and their breathing had turned ragged, Thomas broke off. Elizabeth whimpered and reached for him. As she drew him back to her, he whispered, "You know what this means." He brushed his lips against her face, her neck.

"What?" She entangled her fingers in his hair, her breath soft against his skin.

Thomas pulled back and looked her in the eye. "That we get to figure this out together." Then he scooped her up and carried her off to bed.

About Me

I t's funny how quickly you become something.

When I wrote ***Right Where They Belong: Sutton Series Book 1***, suddenly I was an author. In the past I've been a homeschool mom, the egg lady, a church pianist, the goat lady, a bookkeeper, and even on occasion, the cat lady.

I am most especially enjoying being an author lady—writing stories of faith, hope, and love. Stories about relationship and navigating through whatever life throws your way.

These days Christopher's painting, and I'm writing. (Bookkeeping too; still have to earn a living, you know.) While our two sons are off conquering the world, we're hanging out in rural Ohio with lots of animals—and plenty of small towns nearby.

Acknowledgements

It has been SO MUCH FUN being on the journey for book two with my friends and family! You guys rock. Thank you so much for your support and encouragement (and even occasional nagging; you know who you are...).

Christopher, I love my cover art! Thank you for being willing to paint it for me. I hope you'll do book three as well.

To my editor Caryn and my cover designer Lynn, thank you. Jenny, thank you for your marketing support. I appreciate you all!

Leave Feedback for *Not What They Expected*

Books by Chantal DeYoe

Right Where They Belong: Sutton Series Book 1

Not What They Expected: Sutton Series Book 2

Coming Soon!

Sutton Series Book 3
(not yet titled but very much taking over my brain...)
www.chantaldeyoe.com